P E T R A

Also by Shaena Lambert

Radiance
Oh, My Darling
The Falling Woman

PETRA

SHAENA LAMBERT

RANDOM HOUSE CANADA

PUBLISHED BY RANDOM HOUSE CANADA

Copyright © 2020 Shaena Lambert

www.penguinrandomhouse.ca

LIBRARY AND ARCHIVES CANADA CATALOGUING IN PUBLICATION

Title: Petra / Shaena Lambert.
Names: Lambert, Shaena, author.
Identifiers: Canadiana (print) 20200191942 | Canadiana (ebook) 20200191950 |
ISBN 9780735279575 (softcover) | ISBN 9780735279582 (EPUB)
Subjects: LCSH: Kelly, Petra Karin, 1947-1992—Fiction.
Classification: LCC PS8573.A3885 P48 2020 | DDC C813/.6—dc23

Text design: Lisa Jager
Cover design: Lisa Jager
Image credits: (woman) © Carmen Jimnez / EyeEm;
(Berlin Gendarmenmarkt square) © bluejayphoto / iStock; both Getty Images

Printed and bound in Canada

2 4 6 8 9 7 5 3 1

Penguin
Random House
RANDOM HOUSE CANADA

For Bob

You will hear thunder and remember me,
And think: she wanted storms.

—ANNA AKHMATOVA

THE MISSILES

Night

Petra was soaking in the bath, reading the newspaper, when she called out from the bathroom: "Manfred! You simply won't believe it!"

This was at the farmhouse, our hub for political organizing, thirty kilometres southwest of Bonn. The house was just outside a village whose name was never important to us. Picture a few desultory cows. A pile of tires in the field next door, unmoved for the five years we occupied the space. We were here for the cheap rent and the large kitchen under heavy blackened beams. The thick walls smelled of yeast and were cool even in the height of summer. We organized, talked, yelled sometimes; the bedrooms were often covered in mattresses for the itinerant activists who came and went as we built our movement.

I was bent over my cast-iron skillet like an old grandmother in a fairy tale, cooking a lamb stew. I'd browned the cubes of meat, adding wine, then stock and vegetables, scraping the good bits from the bottom. A piece of mushroom had found its way into my beard. When Petra called, I glanced up to see frost on the window. It looked like a towered city capped by blazing stars.

That city of frost has stayed with me long after other memories have died. Ice is important to this story. Petra, when she finally decided to flee, would flee to a land of ice. But in my memory it is mixed with another image: that night I wore an apron that Katrina (ex-girlfriend) had left behind when she stormed from the house, banging the walls, kicking the door with her big black boots. It showed a jovial chef brandishing a barbeque fork on which was affixed a beaded bratwurst sausage. He himself wore an apron with another chef also brandishing a bratwurst, and so on and so on, the chefs and their sausages becoming tinier and tinier, to infinity.

January 1980. Exactly two months after the announcement that rocked Europe. NATO planned to station intermediate-range nuclear missiles in West Germany. An ultimatum to the East, to Russia and its satellite states: remove your own nuclear missiles, the SS-20s, from East Germany, or in less than three years we roll ours in. A faceoff across the Iron Curtain; the United States spoke of fighting a "limited nuclear war" in Europe; everyone was afraid for the state of the world. As now, it was hard to think about the future without feeling a profound sense of Total Despair. These nuclear weapons were like sick boxes of death, each one full of a firepower that could destroy the world a hundred times over. The esteemed *Bulletin of the Atomic Scientists* set its nuclear clock two minutes closer to midnight.

But at the centre of this dangerous world, our little band of sisters and brothers—led by the charismatic Petra Kelly—had a counterplan. It focused on the new political party we were building.

The stew was bubbling. I stirred in a bit more broth, and then picked my way through the many shoes in the hallway to the bathroom.

I should say that Petra and I hadn't been lovers for over a year. This wasn't my choice, and I still had hopes. In the last year, the Irish trade unionist had fallen away (too possessive), and the Hamburg artist had been tasted and dismissed (his art was

minimalist, but he was a cluttered mess of needs and recriminations), and it was me, Manfred Schwartz, pushing open the
bathroom door. Petra shook the newspaper at me. The pads of
her fingers had softened from the water. Her short, wet hair lay
flat against her face.

"Just listen to what this NATO general has done!"

Gone from her face was what I thought of as her scissors
look—pinched and pale, stripped of humour. She started to hand
me the newspaper, then grabbed it back and read out loud:
"*Commander of the 12th Panzer Division of the Bundeswehr!*"

The gist was this: at a much-publicized Rifle Club banquet
in Marbach the night before, a NATO general had made a scene.
"A black-tie event! You can imagine! The women must have all
been in long gloves, gowns covered in sequins. But here—listen.
There's a tradition in the club of bringing a massive roasted pig
into the hall, a *Spanferkel* on a platter, with an apple in its mouth,
while the military band strikes up a ceremonial march. Well, the
military band chose to play the 'Badenweiler Marsch.'"

She looked at me pointedly, and yes, I understood. This was
Hitler's march, played whenever he entered a public rally. This
fact was well known to us, and it underlined, without further
words, how fused the present Bonn elite was to the old system—
ancient Nazis recycled and turned into judges and politicians.
For non-Germans it might have been possible to listen to the
"Badenweiler Marsch," with its whistles of flutes and piccolos
followed by the three distinctive horns, and not hear the darker
resonance of Nazism, but not for people of my age, children of
the Nazi generation.

Petra shook the paper straight and continued to read: "*No
sooner had the band struck up the tune, then General Emil Gerhardt,
Commander,* etcetera, etcetera, *pushed back his chair, crossed the
room and tapped the conductor on the shoulder. 'I would prefer it,' said*

the general, 'if that particular march was not played. Neither here nor on any occasion.'"

I could picture it: the banqueting generals surrounded by their jewelled wives, the room fat with satisfaction; two men holding aloft the pig, basted in dark beer and with an apple in its mouth, a display of headcheese, pomegranates and roasted peaches around its haunches and cloven feet. A yelp of appreciation bursting from the grey beards in the room, and then this general requesting the conductor's attention, while he glares in surprise and keeps waving his baton, and the tuba and the bassoonist begin, with mounting discord, to lose control of the music, until at last the whole thing founders with a final bleat of the trumpets. "I say," says the general, "would it be possible for you to play another song?"

Petra dropped the paper on the floor and stood, sloshing water. "Pass me a towel, Manfred. I'm going to write him a letter." She was dripping; little breasts so pretty, hip bones framing the dark patch of hair.

"No, you are not! That's ridiculous."

"I am."

I handed her the towel and she began to dry herself vigorously. "He could be an important ally."

"Unlikely."

"Yes, is that so? You know the mind of this general already?"

"I know he can't help us, if that's what you mean."

I went back to the kitchen, where the stew had cooked down too much. Bits of potato and lamb were stuck to the frying pan. I poured in some wine, but the whole thing now had a slight burnt flavour.

Petra came in towelling her hair and wearing her customary loose pink sweatpants and a T-shirt—SWORDS INTO PLOUGH-SHARES. She tossed the towel onto the back of a chair, went to her room and came back with a couple of postcards, one of Rosa

Luxemburg, the other an innocuous vision of the Rhine in springtime. She chose the latter, sat down and scribbled quickly, then read aloud: *"Dear General Gerhardt, I heard of your act of conscientious objection to call attention to Hitler's odious march. Well done! If you have other values of this sort, come! Be part of our movement! Join the Green Party of West Germany!* What do you think?"

I placed a bowl of stew in front of her. "It got burnt," I said.

"It smells good."

As I handed her a spoon, she took hold of my hand and kissed the back of it. "We need everyone," she said.

I sat.

"We must believe in human goodness—isn't that our job, as people on this earth?"

"I don't think so."

"You're angry with me," she said.

"Why would I be?"

She was silent, chewing a piece of meat. "We need more allies from the centre."

"A NATO general? Is that the centre?"

She shrugged.

"And what? You will write him a postcard and tame him? Gentle the general?"

Watch out, I wanted to say. *He's old enough to be your father.* She had a father thing; it was well known. She and I even occasionally laughed about it: her proclivity for older men. Her father had disappeared when she was five, without a word or note. He left her with a father-shaped gap in her chest, a place where the wind blew in, and a Pez container he'd bargained for in the American sector, shaped like Mickey Mouse.

Watch out for fathers, I wanted to say. But I didn't.

2

Strangers from Another Time

This was West Germany, 1980. In other words, you couldn't throw a stone on any university campus without hitting students who felt like they were carrying the ghosts of Auschwitz on their backs. And the silence of our parents' generation, up on our backs, alongside the ghosts. They handed us their abominations without a word, in homes soaked with the good smells of apple pie cooling on the windowsills, happy times in front of the fire. They just forgot to mention the piles of bones, the whitened corpses buried in the backyard behind the trees, and we, detectives and prosecutors, had to dig them up ourselves.

What's this, Daddy? Holding out a collarbone, a breastbone. *I found it behind the shed.*

A metaphor. But it felt like this, just under the skin of our daily lives.

At the Freie Universität Berlin in the late sixties, my friends and I had spent hours in mental agony: Who were these people, our parents? We knew them intimately and yet we feared them, and we distrusted ourselves, because we were their offspring.

But for Petra Kelly it was different. She'd moved to the States when she was twelve, after her mother married Commander Kelly, a US soldier, and stayed there until her mid-twenties. This long sojourn away protected her from the self-disgust. She was from the land of Coca-Cola, had campaigned for Robert Kennedy and Hubert Humphrey and had marched on Washington for civil rights.

These things made her clean, made her attractive to our movement.

She didn't have a Marxist bone in her body, and the politics of the sixty-eighters—the ardent politicized students of Germany, with our fury at the duplicity of our parents—was quite foreign to her.

We are all interconnected. This was what she loved to say, loved to think. And she'd quote from Gregory Bateson: "What pattern connects the crab to the lobster and the orchid to the primrose and all four of them to me?"

As for the use of force, she opposed it utterly, because (I hear her voice speaking) *we all have a core of goodness in us.* This is what she thought. Even the most unhallowed criminals. Even the man who sits in the pit of the missile silo with his finger flexed on the button. My Marxist self would take umbrage at her belief in human goodness. *But him?* Petra would say. *Why, he's just a child following orders!*

And what about the man who gives the orders? I would ask her. *And the man who gives the orders to the man who gives the orders?* There they were, lined up like the chefs on my apron, one inside the other, and yes, according to Petra, they were all interconnected, and all redeemable.

The only real evil in this world came from reducing a person to the status of evil. That was what Petra Kelly thought.

A memory. Petra shared this with me after we rode my motorcycle to Günzburg together, to see the place where she'd grown up. Later, in bed, she told me this story.

She was five years old, crossing a barley field, brushing the palms of her hands against the feathery heads. Her father walked beside her. Tall, brown-eyed. He kept warning her to watch for snakes. Then, for some reason she couldn't recall, he began to tell her about how one day the sun would burn out. He was probably the sort of man who enjoyed his bits of knowledge, but Petra was horrified. She absolutely couldn't believe it. Such absence of light, such monstrous blackness! She ran from him and hid behind a millstone beside the Danube.

"I was sobbing and sobbing, but I also kept thinking, 'Will he find me? Will he know how to find me?' I suppose I had doubts even then about his commitment. Anyway, I didn't move an inch. And as I sat there, I began to make an elaborate plan. *I* would save the sun! With a large lasso, or some such thing. A rope and pulley. It would be up to me."

"And did he find you? Down by the river?"

She smiled. "Oh yes. He did."

But not long after, he was gone for good, disappearing one night or early morning, a vagabond father running for the train—that was how she pictured him, with a kerchief sack tied to a stick, like the hobos in American comic strips.

"Sometimes I really do believe he left me a note." She turned to me in the half-dark. "I can imagine what it said. *I'm leaving her*—my mother, that is—*but I'm not leaving you.* Maybe he was just going for a little while, maybe he wanted to make good—isn't that what people do? They strike off because they can't bear to be poor, to be nothing, but they want to return to their loved ones, their little girls, with gold in their pockets. I think he meant to do that with me. But then something terrible happened."

I waited, and she said, "I used to imagine he got struck by lightning. I know—an unlikely scenario."

"Poor Petra," I murmured. She had her head on my arm.

I leaned over and kissed her hair. "And stopping the sun from burning out. Did this continue to be your job?"

"From the earliest age. Yes." She met my eyes, and I could see the child inside her, ardent and fierce, already committed to an impossible task.

As for me, I had issues with my father as well. Mine, Konrad Schwartz, had been a POW, shot down over Britain and then transported to Canada. He had, in other words, missed the worst of the war. He never wanted to speak about it, except to say that his family, a conservative Catholic one, had feared and distrusted Hitler.

He ran an oculist's shop in Freiburg, and we—my father, my mother and I—lived in the apartment upstairs. There was a stairwell to the second floor with thick walls, and once, at around age six, I flicked my jacket against the whitewashed wall and coal dust rose to the surface like a black blush. I came into the kitchen and showed my father my stained jacket. *Look*, I said, *there's coal inside the walls*, and he said, *How did this happen?* and I said (afraid now), *I hit my coat against it, Father*, and he said, *You shouldn't have done that*, and something in the way he spoke, the shiver of compression that touched his mouth, made me realize that he had only barely suppressed the urge to hit me.

I remember one truly terrible beating. The rest were harsh, but this one was awful. One afternoon, I took off my clothes at the urging of the next-door girl, Gabriele, and so did she. Then we adorned ourselves in my mother's scarves, pretending we were gypsy slaves. Such fun we were having! I tied Gabi to the wooden post that held up the ceiling in my bedroom, and I was delighting in the sensations of dominant pleasure brought on by her captive self, and so was she. However, Father happened to close the shop early and come upstairs, appearing suddenly at the door. We must have been a picture of terror as we tried to flee out the window and across the roof. Gabi made it (she was a year older and faster), but Father caught me and laid me across his lap and whipped me with his belt, leaving streaks and welts on my buttocks and legs, which Mother later treated with butter.

He hardly ever spoke of the war, but I knew he'd been shot down over northern England. I've always pictured a slow falling out of the sky, plenty of time to realize he was going to be captured, and perhaps shot in the head. But the British didn't shoot him. They shipped him off to Canada, to a POW work camp in the Alberta prairies. There he met my mother, Esther Blodgett, who delivered milk from her family's dairy.

One day, so she told me, he was standing by the wire fence and he asked her for a cup of milk. She blushed and stammered, and then poured him some in a metal cup. He drank it back, a lonely figure of great handsomeness caught behind the wire.

After awhile, the POWs were dispatched to work on nearby farms. He ended up on my grandfather's dairy and beet farm. I imagine the scar on his cheek caught the light as he ate dinners with the family, making my mother's heart catch too, as though the scar were the mark of a Heidelberg sword and he a silent hero chained by a system that had left him meek and imprisoned. Like their large horse, Fred, who could kick you dead, but who instead was yoked each morning to the truck to deliver the steel cans of milk and cream.

Poor Mother! She expected to feel this complex mix of pity and love forever. She didn't realize how quickly everything would change once she had married him and he had brought her back to Germany to set up a new life in Freiburg.

One day when I was ten, on a field trip to a neighbouring town, I saw my father in the square, eating lunch with a woman I'd never seen. I saw him take a forkful of omelette and hold it out for her, and I realized that he was different. He seemed light. I didn't approach. But later I thought a great deal about seeing him like that, and I began to wonder if the man I'd seen had even *been* my father.

This memory has a strange emulsive sheen, like the scar on my father's face.

By twelve I'd figured things out. I heard my parents arguing in the bedroom, his voice hard and loud, and hers so sad, patiently lapping at the spaces in between, like a tide against rocks. *Lap, lap, lap.* You see, her job had been to liberate him—to witness him step from behind the prison fence. But now here was the consequence of freedom: endless affairs.

If I was going to draw a picture of loneliness, it would be my mother reading Shakespeare in the armchair by the window, in that town she didn't like, with its language she couldn't master. I believe that reading quietly in that upstairs room, listening to the ticking clock, she felt like a prisoner.

At fifteen I crossed the courtyard behind the shop, near the cages where my father kept his hawks. Glancing down, I felt my father imprinted in the face of the stones. Not his personality or self, but something akin to his essence—his juice. I felt it in the cobbles: his way of seeing things, his absolute prosaic silent darkness, his lies to my mother, his going downstairs to work Monday to Friday, his profession of helping people to see, fixing their glasses, his precise instruments and his blindness to her suffering. I felt that he had leached into the cobbles, and that he was capable of seeping into the geraniums in their pots, stopping their growth—tethering every piece of vegetation to himself, as he had tethered the spindly apple tree to the wall, espaliered its slender limbs in the one spot of backyard sun.

As he had captured everything.

3

My Dog Shits on the Neutron Bomb

I woke in the farmhouse next morning to an onslaught of pinging on the tile roof. Hail! Fabulous. This afternoon was our first demonstration against the missiles. In this weather people would stay away, and the aloof Hofgarten, the open park in front of Bonn University, would look barren and lonely—a few scattered protestors near the stage and dozens of journalists to record our defeat.

I got up and dressed, then went into the kitchen. Petra came in as I was trying to fix the toaster. She gave me her scissors look, and asked me to please stop. I kept jiggling at the toaster with a knife while she watched and seethed, taking in my beard and Birkenstocks, my fuzzy socks. Then she shook her head, as though she had water in her ear, and asked if I'd seen her comb. It wasn't in the bathroom.

"Why would I have your comb?"

But she went into my bedroom and found it on the windowsill, among the dying plants.

It was still sleeting as we drove. Petra kept her eyes closed, practising her speech. She was anxious, always was before any public appearance.

"Why the Hofgarten?" I asked.

"It was Freya's idea."

Freya Fertig—head of Frauen für den Frieden, a powerful coalition of women's groups.

"She wields too much control." I said this knowing that Petra would not agree. She supported all her "sisters," especially those who had risen to positions of power.

We manoeuvred off the autobahn and entered Bonn's old town, where we were immediately stuck in a cacophonous traffic jam. Buses disgorged masses of people carrying signs. BETTER ACTIVE TODAY THAN RADIOACTIVE TOMORROW. MY DOG SHITS ON THE NEUTRON BOMB.

"Oh!" cried Petra. "Look at all these people!"

I squeezed into a parking space, and we pushed our way along the slippery sidewalk to the Hofgarten.

The crowd completely filled the lawn, from the bare trees at the park's edge to the castle-like facade of the university, while police circled the perimeter, beating their truncheons against their thighs. Petra reached for my hand, as though to reassure me: *No, it won't be like that.* We passed from group to group, pushing towards the stage. Bagpipes bleated from a cavalcade of men in kilts. Then kazoos. African drummers. We pushed past a group of Cyndi Lauper look-alikes, pigtails and ballet skirts, the violent scent of hairspray. Farmers, teachers, anti–nuclear energy citizen's groups, fathers with toddlers up on their shoulders, a bevy of nuns, their noses pink from the cold. And then the chanting started, led by Freya at the microphone: *We will resist! We will resist!*

Amazing! Petra mouthed. She looked transformed, fed by the crowd's wild heart.

Yet when we reached the base of the stage, her mood shifted back to nervousness. She felt around in her jacket pocket and thrust a note at me.

"I didn't have a chance to show you this."

"You want me to look at this now? You're about to go onstage."

"It's ugly, Manfred."

I unfolded the paper. A single line, pencil marks gouging the paper. *Hi Petra. Bet you've got a sweet green cunt.*

"You see?"

Hatred rose from the note, not just from the words, but from the juvenile block printing, the two tear holes. We'd seen a number of these anonymous notes before. They were disgusting, focused on Petra's body, her genitals in particular. Often they came with swastikas gouged in the paper, or drawings of vaginas with teeth. You could smell the pleased cruel head that had bent over the piece. The idiocy laced with malice.

"They're trying to rattle you," I said.

"Well, guess what? They are, Manfred. They are rattling me."

"We can talk about it afterwards. Now look: it's your turn."

She made her way up the steps as though about to be hanged. Onstage, Freya took her by the elbow. Freya was an ally, a peace diva in her own right, with wild, frizzy red hair, sharp blue eyes and a twitching, fox-like nose. She'd never been put off by Petra's popularity.

"You know, your friend Katrina is looking everywhere for you," Freya called down to me. "Oh—there she is."

I swivelled in time to see Katrina emerging from the crowd like a bird of prey. She wore ripped fishnets, army boots and an army coat that was large and unbecoming on her boxy frame. Her hair, last seen with feathered turquoise ends, was now standing up in tufts of shoe-polish black. Her face, with its wide cheeks and Slavic cheekbones, was coloured by fury. She fixed her grey eyes on the right side of my face. *What's more frightening?* I found myself thinking, *Nuclear missiles or Katrina?*

"I want my clothes," she began. "I want my things. I called yesterday. I called the day before. Is something wrong with your phone? I left six messages. They're not your *personal* missiles, Manfred. I've been busy fighting them too. And in the meantime, I need to come and get my bedding. And those are my good pots. And my father needs his albums back."

I glanced towards Petra, but it was hopeless to expect help from that quarter—she was preparing. And in fact, as I watched, I saw the customary spasm run up her body. I once saw a jackrabbit do this in a field after escaping a dog. It stood up on its hind legs and shook the panic right out of itself.

Just at that moment, someone pushed between Katrina and me, and I took that chance to slide away from her to a spot in front of the stage. I never got tired of seeing Petra speak. I always thought, *She can't do it again.* The crowd was cold. The drums had gone on for far too long, and there'd been the greeting from the mayor of Hiroshima, translated line by line by an interpreter, boring everyone to tears. But now Petra came towards the microphone. Boyish honey-brown hair, thin face. A police siren rose from the direction of the Rhine, then stopped. The crowd put out its ears. It was like a single body now, an animal—and that was good, because Petra Kelly spoke animal.

4.

Innere Führung

Much later—perhaps two years after that day in Bonn—Emil Gerhardt told me that the first time he heard Petra's voice was on his car radio as she delivered that speech. He was in his Peugeot with his wife, Helena, driving from Munich, where they had spent the day shopping and lunching with friends. They were on the autobahn, returning to Veitshöchheim, a little village near Würzburg, where they lived and where the 12th Panzer Division was based.

Helena was asleep, her head resting on the passenger window. Rolling hills flashed by. It began to rain, spattering drops that hit the windshield and then seemed to leap up from the roadway itself, as though the rain was being driven upwards out of the asphalt. "You know that kind of heavy rain."

Even with the wipers beating at full speed, it became difficult to see, and Emil pulled into a rest stop. A man rushed past, a newspaper covering his head. And then there was nothing but the steady drumming on the car roof.

Emil was a handsome man, with wavy salt and pepper hair and a toned upper body from his general's regimen of morning push-ups. He was an interesting mix of strong-willed and yet distant, ironic almost, in his attitudes towards the world, as though he moved through it but it didn't quite touch him. He smiled now, remembering. "There was Petra in full force." A laugh. "Oh, yes, she was in full harangue, going after NATO and all the short-sighted generals."

A single Pershing missile contains enough firepower to wipe out life on earth several times over. But will we stop loving, my friends? They can knock down our bodies, but they cannot knock down our hearts.

He'd reached out to change the channel. His fingers hovered above the dial, but something stopped him. Her whole self seemed to lean into the words:

Little animals . . .

SS-20s . . .

The sound of destruction.

She began dropping BB pellets into a tin can in front of the microphone. Each little metal ball represented the firepower of the bomb dropped on Hiroshima, the cumulative sound becoming the firepower of the Pershing II and cruise missiles slated for West Germany. The rain on the car roof mixed with the dinging pellets, and then the relentless *ping, ping* grew heavier than the downpour, a rain of darkness and destruction, filling every inch of the car with static.

It seemed to go on forever.

Emil's heart had begun to hammer. The car was too small, too close—the sound was making him sick. He was about to thrust the door open when he realized the sound was lessening. By increments, the pellets could be heard individually again, and then, at last, with a final patter, they stopped.

That's the sound of death, my friends. It is the sound of pain. The sound of fear. It's the sound of ground zero. But let me make this clear. It is also the sound of zero imagination, because the men who thought up their mega-death failed to imagine us standing in this place, willing to lay our bodies on the line.

Helena lifted her head. "Who on earth is that?"

"No one."

Emil turned the radio off.

"It didn't sound like no one."

He started the car and took the ramp onto the autobahn, picking up speed.

"It was that Green girl," Helena said. "The one who's always talking."

It was dusk as they approached Veitshöchheim, their house on its quaint street backing onto the river. They ate scrambled eggs and toast, watched the news and went to bed early. Emil rolled over and held Helena, and kissed her gently near the ear, which made a popping sound in her head.

"I forgot to tell you," she said. "There's a postcard for you downstairs. It's from that girl."

"Who?"

"The one on the radio."

As well as commanding the division at Veitshöchheim, Emil had an office at the CENTAG headquarters at Heidelberg, and for the next several weeks he kept to his routine, driving to Heidelberg mid-week, putting together a memo on procurement, finishing several other large files. Then, one morning, he took a clean sheet of paper from the drawer and inserted it into the typewriter. This memorandum was one he did not intend to dictate to his secretary.

To: *Herr Hans Apel, Minister of Defence, Federal Republic of Germany*

From: *Major General Emil Gerhardt, Divisional Commander, 12th Panzer Division.*

Regarding: *Impending Deployment of Intermediate-Range*
              Nuclear Missiles

He sat with his fingers on the keys while the principal points of the letter formed in his mind. *Regret. Only reasonable choice. Stand behind other* NATO *decisions and* NATO *and the Bundeswehr as crucial institutions for the liberty and protection of mankind.* (Humankind? Yes, humankind.) *All this goes without saying.* (Without need for reiteration? No. Without saying.) *The impending deployment of highly flexible intermediate-range missiles runs counter to national and global security.* (Yes, good words.) *In point of fact, while these missiles are intended to improve East–West stability, their first-strike capability and hair-trigger responsiveness could have a catastrophic result, to which I, in good conscience, can no longer be a party.*

He was using military language, coating his words with a varnish. But could he seriously be taking this step? He started to sweat. Heard the radio voice again—a feverish sharpness near his right temple: *Even the animals are outraged. And the ancient spirits of this earth.* And then that postcard out of nowhere, lofted to him by gods who wanted to drive things home. Fate speaking in a few scrawled words. He'd flipped the postcard to see the Rhine covered in sparkles, and remembered his mother telling him of Lorelei. White dress. Stars in her hair. A voice no man could resist. Ridiculous, of course, to let his mother into his head now, of all moments. She had no place in what was happening to him, with her blond hair and stone blue eyes, her huge (as it had seemed to him, as a child) forehead and her strong fingers, which she manicured and cleaned after working all day in other people's gardens. Rich people's gardens. How she had detested being of service to the rich when she herself, as she had told him, again and again and again, had once been rich. *Of a good family*, was what she said, sniffing loudly.

With a shake of his head he banished her, then shrugged to release the tension in his shoulders. He was a miracle of tension, a cluster of clenched muscles. What was he doing? Every now and then a secretary clipped by in the corridor, wearing what he knew were attractive shoes, though one clacked along in leather boots (less attractive). Then he heard the *shush* and *creak* of the mail cart, the squeaking wheel of the coffee trolley. He had meant to bring oil for it; he had told the coffee girl he would, and she'd laughed and said, "I'm sure you have more important duties, General." He'd liked that. Nothing beneath him. But he'd forgotten.

He ought to be thinking about the missiles, the balance of East and West, the complex game the two sides played, like chess but with volatile pieces, each of which could blow up the world. He wanted his letter to reflect this truth. *The military balance isn't balanced. We are on a precipice. I must, in full conscience, speak.* But what was making him sweat, really sweat down his sides, was the question of money. If he took this step, how would they live? He was only eight years away from retirement, and if he resigned now he'd have to settle for three-quarters of the pension he was due. He had Helena to think of. She liked to live well: it was part of her essence, her aristocratic Dresden background, which, though ripped away by the war, managed to reassert itself in an appreciation of porcelain, silk slips and fine woollens. The other day in Würzburg, as they passed a shop window displaying cashmere sweaters, Helena had made a small, pigeon-like murmur of desire in her throat. The sweaters were arranged in stacks, from moody violet to throbbing crimson, passing through all the colours of the spectrum: moss-green, gold, wheat, almond. Emil learned the names later when he returned to the store, the clerk holding up each one for him to feel the weight. *A wearable sweater,* the woman kept saying, as though she had stacks of unwearable ones in the back. In the end, Emil bought a sweater in charcoal—not quite black, not quite brown. It had a V-neck and would look pretty with Helena's knee-length leather skirt and gold jewellery. Yes, he even knew how his wife would accessorize her new sweater.

To resign would mean the end of buying cashmere on impulse. And though Helena might, with or without sweaters, applaud him for his courage, she might also (and this was far more likely) tell him that he was being high-handed. She might even guess (this he would not admit to a soul) that his resignation was in part personally strategic, as his involvement with Julia Kunst (junior secretary, blond, plush white ass) had become complicated. He wasn't sure what Helena knew about Julia. He and his wife could go long periods without discussing important issues in their marriage; in fact, non-discussion seemed to aid their particular form of coexistence.

Emil pushed back his chair and stood.

He went to the window and looked down at the parking lot, with its line of American trucks covered in canvas camouflage. Directly below, in the civilian lot, a few bare ash trees stood root-locked in concrete planters. A woman in a red beret exited his building. At first she appeared as nothing more than the red dot of her hat, but as she crossed the lot he caught a glimpse of slender legs clad in black tights. Her back was to him, but she seemed pretty. He detected a ponytail. *If she looks back*, he thought, *I will take this next step.* She strode across the lot. Emil leaned closer, misting the glass. *Look back*, he willed her. *Look back, look back.* The ash trees were splayed below him, mealy and desperate, but one tree stood by itself in the square in front of the original barracks. A beech tree. How different it was, standing by itself like a king, naked and powerful, limbs lifted to the sky, older than the parking lot, older than CENTAG. When he glanced up from it, only a second had passed, but the girl was gone.

Abruptly he crossed to his desk, pulled the sheet of paper from the typewriter, turned it over and, taking the fountain pen from his breast pocket, wrote two words.

Innere Führung.

Inner leadership.

The words stared back at him. The *I* and *F* looked alarming, as though his handwriting was someone else's. He had heard of that. Handwriting changing in a crisis, becoming heavier, more slanted. He stared down at the penned words for a full second, perhaps two, and then his mood dissolved. He shook his head, glanced at the closed door, embarrassed by this grandiose flourish, which a moment before had seemed like a spasm of necessary action. Now it seemed showy, absurd.

Innere Führung: the concept, so crucial to the West German military, had many layers, but it boiled down to the idea that those who put on the uniform of the Bundeswehr must never again shed their individual morality, never again say *I was just following orders.* The idea had spawned its own central office and thousands of pages of briefing notes and handbooks—and most recently, a lecture series by a bald-headed psychologist from Koblenz. This *innere Führung* education was dictated from above (ironically), causing some senior officers to grumble; it seemed to them a barren substitute for the grandeur of German military tradition. Not that they were *vocally* nostalgic for the Nazi years, far from it; it was the symbols of the officer corps that they missed. The Code of Honour. The autumn manoeuvres. The pageantry of the oath. The procession of banners and the torch-lit tattoo. All this had been erased, and in its place was a code that often felt quite clinical and abstract. Some had dubbed it "inner strangulation."

Emil could see their point. Why serve an army if it had no history, no sense of grandeur or manliness? It was unappealing.

Yet he could hear the words of the lecturer from Koblenz, pointer in hand, egg-like head lit from above: *We must develop our innate sense of inner guidance. Never again can we take orders without taking personal responsibility for them. We must know our actions to be just.*

Ah!

It hurt. It actually hurt. That was what the Koblenz psychologist never mentioned. What not one of the thousands of pages of briefing notes detailed. What you must find out for yourself. It hurt in the chest. A hand squeezing his heart. Perhaps he would have a heart attack. Now there was an idea. He smiled wryly at the thought: a heart attack from following his conscience. *Watch out*, he told himself. *Trying to be a better man just might kill you.*

What would have happened to him if he had acted according to his conscience his whole life? If, for instance, he had confronted his mother over that dirt she used to spew about some of the people whose gardens she tended. *High and mighty airs*, she said, *but inside they are lowly people.* She was always tired, not so much from her work as from riding home on the bus afterwards, long trips from suburban estates to their cramped rooms in Munich, the yellow and grey wallpaper with raised flowers and wheat sheaves that caught the kitchen grease with their fuzz. How he had hated that wallpaper! Supposing he had held up a hand and said no to his mother? He remembered her voice when Hitler came to power. *Now a man takes over who can set things straight.* Had he said a word, a peep? Of course not. He'd enlisted in the Hitler Youth as soon as he could. He'd marched with the rest of them, polished his shoes until they gleamed.

Or on the Eastern Front, at Krivoy Rog, that nightmare place that haunted his dreams. Suppose this sense of inner leadership had risen then. *Find another soldier to do your bidding. I refuse.* All ideas of such behaviour were, of course, ridiculous. A single bullet in the brain would have been his reward. Or he would have been strung from a tree, as they did with the partisans. The fields had been dotted with dangling black figures. No. There was no going back, only forward.

He rolled a new sheet of paper into the typewriter, placed the pads of his fingers on the keys.

Go, he said to himself. *Do it*.

Go.

5.

The Programme

I think I'm starting to get the hang of this memoir I'm writing. When I began, I was sure I would need to stick strictly to the facts. I would verify every incident from the past with a document retrieved from the copious Petra Kelly archives, housed at 35 Eldenaer Strasse, along with the Heinrich Böll Foundation papers. But I've started to realize that the facts can't be my truth. Not entirely.

On my research mornings, I arrive at the archives full of determination. I unwind dockets bound with red thread. I buttress my memory with speeches and timelines, make photocopies, underline in red and green. Then I tuck what I've gathered into a folder marked *Petra*. Only biking home after a day of this does it hit me—a sense that what I've collected is weighing me down like a fatty meal.

As I bike along the path, with the scent of spring newly in the air, sunshine opening the hard leaf buds into a haze of soft green, I imagine Petra. She's delighted with my growing recognition of the uselessness of a strictly archival truth. My Marxist materialism has somehow once again been vanquished by her belief in organic wholeness, the mystery of life's inner workings. Spirit versus matter. This is what I imagine as I ride home along the familiar streets towards Charlottenburg.

So. I can tell this story as it happened, but I have begun to realize that I must also "tell it slant," as Petra's Emily Dickinson would have had it, her stark clarity adored by the lonely, high-school-age German girl in Virginia. There is too much I can't get at if I stick blindly to the record or stay lodged in my own skull like a caveman hammering out my one point of view. When I think of sticking to *me* as the through line, I get a clogged sensation in my throat and a hood falls over my head, the way my father used to blind his hawks and falcons. Every time I imagine taking the leap into one of the others' minds—Petra's, Emil's, Helena's—I feel a lightness under my ribs. And with it comes her voice—your voice—urging me on.

That's right. At last, Manfred! Just look at you! You're getting it down. And who are we . . . here your voice rises, turning to address an invisible crowd . . . *who are we if we can't make the tiny but million-mile leap into another person's heart?*

This is what I imagine you saying.

I write at my desk in an alcove of the bedroom. It faces onto a cobbled square that fills and empties according to the time of day. From 7:30 to 8:30, students and office workers make their way to the bus stop, or whizz by on bicycles; at 10:30, the mothers and Turkish nannies come out with their strollers. There is a small privately run daycare across the street, and at 11:00 a half-dozen children descend its steps to the street, where their caregivers get them to line up and hold onto a yellow rope before they head for the park. They will feed the ducks and geese. I know this because they often clutch little plastic bags of seed importantly in their hands. I am in love with the sight of them, and I never want to miss their passage through my day. I've grown sentimental.

I am recently retired. So this writing could be seen as a retirement project. Something old men do, like fixing antique cuckoo clocks. That idea stops me short. I see myself so strongly as not that type. Yet age has taken me in its mouth. I am older than Emil was when he died. I am older than my father was in 1980. And, for reasons I am not even sure of yet, this *fact* must also find its way into the story.

But now I am back at the farmhouse. Manfred Schwartz. Thirty-two years old—a man in his prime. I've got a beer in my hand (my second) and a pile of marked-up pages on the kitchen table in front of me, out of which I must attempt to create a first draft of our federal programme for debate at our upcoming convention. It surprises me to think that, yes, there I was in my youth, and I spent every second working, planning, strategizing, though the Greens could cough up only a half-time salary. Never mind. This was my passion, our passion. This was the eighties, and I wasn't holed up in a punk bar, bashing my head against the wall to Die Toten Hosen or the Sex Pistols, or just generally fucking around as one believes one ought to have done, looking back.

Youth is wasted on the young, etcetera.

Half of me loved the party we were creating, and the other half wanted to blow it up. *Two Greens, two opinions.* That was what my fellow activists liked to say, as though it were a point of pride. So that afternoon, I kept my head down, gulping my beer, while trying to meld the mass of disparate ideas into one coherent document. In January 1980, this seemed the way forward: ecological politics. The sixties were long over, the years of my late teens and very early twenties: violence in the streets of West Berlin and Frankfurt, brick throwing and garbage cans ablaze, the murder of Benno Ohnesorg leading to confrontations with "the pig system" (as we'd excitedly called it) and beatings and mass arrests. All this had turned murky in the seventies as we'd split into factions and some activists had gone underground—manifesting far-left conversions to Eastern

Bloc communism and violent spinoffs like the Baader-Meinhof Group. Chaos and dissolution, in other words, or desperate grabbing at totalitarian straws. Yet many of us had continued to work to gain effective political power. And now, in 1980, the only sane way forward, for so many of our generation—the way to channel both our love and our fury—was the new Green Party.

All right. I took a swig of beer. *Let's go.*

It was like a potion: you had to get the mix of ingredients right or the thing would explode. First, a dose of feminism to satisfy Freya Fertig and her powerful group, Frauen für den Frieden. *Because women must be the heart, Manfred.* But wait—the non-violent pacifists, a cranky bunch if ever you saw one, wanted civil disobedience to be at the heart. Gandhi. The power of satyagraha. Many of the influential citizens' initiatives wanted the fight against nuclear power to be the focus. Four minds, four opinions. Four thousand minds; four thousand opinions. I added a small dose of anarchism for the Spontis (spontaneous leftist politicos): the basement lovers, the ex-squatters of Frankfurt and Berlin (like me). But not too much, or the mix could combust, causing infighting and narcissistic posturing. And I had to keep the Hamburg Red-Greens happy: militant anti-capitalists, they'd joined the Green Party because they saw it as the path to power. They could smell power the way worms smell rain. They often met in cadres, establishing their line and then voting as a group. Their politics was dogmatically left-wing, Marxist stuff; many supported the Eastern Bloc, though they were too savvy to make this public. Then there were the farmers, the visionaries, the conservative ecologists.

Fucking Jesus, this is difficult.

Start again.

The telephone rang. I picked it up. It was Petra, calling from West Berlin. Her conference on radiation victims had ended early.

I complained to her that the programme was close to impossible to pull together in draft form—we were such a disorderly rabble.

"So what?" she said. "We're still beautiful."

"We're a fucking mess."

"A beautiful fucking mess." Then she almost whispered, "Actually, Manfred, I just called to hear your voice. I'm sad."

"Why? Tell me."

"I went for a walk and I turned a corner and the wall was in my face," she said. "Barbed wire at the top, and two soldiers, and the watchtower. It made my heart rush. Sometimes I forget—isn't that crazy? We get so busy fighting for peace, I forget the literal reality—that the wall is so close. I started to cry, just standing there—feeling the power of so much ugliness. The SS-20 missiles on the other side set on hair triggers, and our side getting ready to match them. I started to think about the radiation, Manfred, and my whole skin got prickly with it."

"Petra."

"What are we doing to the earth?"

I heard a thickened silence, and I knew she was crying on the other end of the phone.

"It's awful, but we're fixing it," I said.

"Fixing the whole world? Are we?"

Again there was silence.

"At least we have this news about the general," I said, offering him up. Yes, that was what I did.

"You saw?" she said.

"I did. He's left NATO."

"Yes. That's good news."

"He's opposing nuclear missiles. We should be rejoicing today."

"Maybe." I heard a train whistle in the background.

"Where are you?"

"I'm at the zoo, the Tiergarten. I've been walking for an hour."

The train whistle sounded again. I could picture her in the pay-phone booth at the Tiergarten. The sad beavers in their blue cement holding cage. The panther behind glass. In the nearby playground, children were laughing and falling off a roundabout.

"Hello?" I said.

"Anyway, we'll see for ourselves," she responded. "I'm to debate him on TV tomorrow. They called into the office to arrange it. Women's role in the military."

"Why didn't you say so at once?"

"I'm not sure."

When she hung up, I cracked another beer and went back to the programme, consciously unclenching my jaw. *Easy, Manfred.*

Petra would debate this general. This dignified, amused fellow I'd seen in news photos and on TV, with his head of mostly brown hair, a little salt and pepper at his temples. This fellow with his fit body and dark eyes. A clean yet sensual face with a strong jaw. Probably needed to shave twice a day, and lathered with an old-fashioned wooden brush. He cut a dashing figure, that was undeniable. It was a piss-off.

And then there was Petra's bossy optimism about the programme. She seemed to forget it was I who had brought her into the world of protest politics only a few years earlier.

There had been a particularly large demonstration slated for one Saturday at Wyhl, not far from Freiberg, where there was a huge, ongoing protest against nuclear power. Some bigwig European Community boss was supposed to come from Brussels to give a message of support, but he couldn't make it and sent along his assistant instead. I can't even remember the boss's name. What I do remember is that the field of stubble was dry and hard to walk on, and that a little group of us, including this assistant, walked in silence towards the large concrete platform where we gave our daily speeches.

I glanced down at the thin little thing beside me, the blond-brown hair cut to her chin, the sallow face. "Are you delivering his greetings, then? He gave you something to read?"

"I could," she said. "But I have something of my own." She dug some foolscap pages out of a pocket.

"I don't think we have time," I said, but she looked at me sternly. "It will help with gender parity," she said, and she was right, the programme was mostly men. I told her to be brief then, only two minutes, and I thought, *Interesting. This no-name assistant intends to have her moment at the podium.*

When it was Petra's turn to climb onto the platform, I regretted my decision. She stood there pale as a dying plant, and I thought she might faint from stage fright. She turned to the crowd, and I witnessed the settling of her spirit that I now know always happens when she speaks publicly. She leaned close to the microphone, and as soon as the first words came out of her mouth, the crowd, which had been talking, began to listen, first in ones and twos, then all together. Then they began to clap, and then to cheer. The hair on my arms stood up, and I, too, began to clap, to yell out words from her speech. How can one describe this? She seemed to catch the fire of the crowd and pass it back, laughing, as though we were throwing a fiery ball back and forth. It was crazy. It was beautiful.

What had she said, to get inside the skin of the crowd? She wasn't fighting *against* nuclear power—she made that so clear—just as she wasn't fighting solely against the ugliness of the nuclear weapons when she took to the stage now. There was always something else woven in, something vibrant and alive—and I tried to remember the words she'd used at Wyhl that had caused such a warm vibration in my body. Yes—I had it. I could hear her voice in my head.

We have a new job to do now as humans. We must be tender towards the earth, tender towards the animals and plants. Love, not nuclear radiation, love—that is our task. That is how we'll awaken a global consciousness.

She'd made it all feel so close.

I heard a car door slam. I glanced out the kitchen window to see Katrina coming across the drive carrying a milk crate. *Great.* The safety pin in her lip glinted like a message of war. Her black hair had a purple shine to it. She passed in front of the scarecrow that wore my old motorcycle helmet and burst in the door. I said her name, but: "Look," she answered, "I don't want to talk. Okay? I don't want to say a single word. I just want my father's albums. He's asking."

She headed for the old record player, sighed in disgust at the sight of albums out of their sleeves. She carefully resleeved each one and then began to pack them into the milk crate. She did let me help her carry them to the car, where she grabbed another crate and some garbage bags and plunged back into the house. I followed her as she gathered sheets, shampoo, the soap, even.

"Katrina, let's talk, let's be rational."

"I don't want to talk. You're an asshole. That sums it up."

Then she was out the door and back in the car, turning it wildly, narrowly missing the ditch, and I was again sitting at the kitchen table, my mood foul beyond compare.

My feelings about Katrina went like this: I missed her body on top of mine. I missed her laughter. Her alarming hair. But I had only ever *liked* her. I wasn't in love. In truth, she bored me. We'd lived together at the farmhouse for six months while Petra fucked the Irish trade unionist and travelled to other countries, busy being Petra with a capital *P*. I'd taken refuge in Katrina's body, but we'd both known I was still in love with Petra (that "vulnerable piece of wreckage," Katrina had called her once).

When Petra came back, the Irish affair in tatters, I took up with her again. Katrina might have known it would happen, but she didn't forgive.

But I'd liked her. I really had. I'd really liked her father, too. I thought of the two of us drinking beer at the family's home in Lübeck one night, Hans bringing out his albums. He'd been a jazz musician when he was younger, had gone to New Orleans and played in the scene there, and then moved on to New York at the time of the folk awakening. He was a good guy—and strangely like me in body type, and with a beard, too, much more neatly trimmed than mine. Now, of course, he would despise me.

Working now was hopeless. It was either four more beers, landing face down in bed, followed by some mindless masturbation, or TV, half a dozen bratwurst sausages and mindless masturbation.

I ended up doing it all.

6.

The River Elbe

On the morning of the debate, Helena drove Emil to the television station. Morning had its usual friable edges, and the left side of her skull felt numb. She glanced at Emil, ashen-faced and preoccupied in the passenger seat, a notepad in his lap. Such a strong face, with his brown eyes, his one wayward mole beside his fine, rather fleshy nose. Such a head of hair. He was looking soft, though—irresolute and confused. As though he'd stepped from a bus and found himself in thin air.

"Who exactly is she again?"

"The leader of the Green Party."

"Ah—but they say they don't have leaders. I heard her interviewed the other day."

"Did you?"

"I did."

She'd been darning Emil's hiking socks in their back room, a crocheted afghan across her legs. A shaft of sunlight cut between the leafless birches on the other side of the river. The radio was on, and strains of Rimsky-Korsakov filled the room. *Scheherazade.* Imprisoned by a selfish emperor husband. Forced to tell stories. Yet out of that forced isolation and anger and cruelty came *One Thousand and One Nights*, genies and sea monsters, flying horses made of ebony, enchanted underground gardens rich with diamond dewdrops on amethyst plums. As she prepared to stretch the heel of the sock, sunlight made the wooden knob glow as though lit from within. Old tools were the most beautiful. This one she had inherited from her grandmother, one of the few things her mother had brought to Berlin from Dresden just before the bombing. This little thing had escaped the firestorm.

In the solemnity of the afternoon, broken by the ticking and half-hour gong of the grandfather clock, she felt the tug of her childhood, the stone house covered in ivy beside the Elbe River.

They come towards her in their familiar way, her brother, Peter, and the dogs. To Scheherazade's melody they come. First she is climbing out the window at dawn to meet Peter, who has whistled for her. He stands on the grass, looking so mature, seventeen to her fourteen. She runs across the lawn, and the borzois come running too, leaping to press their rough paws against her shoulders. You could dance with dogs that big, waltz around the garden, but this time everyone needs to be silent, so as not to wake her father or mother. Miraculously, the dogs stay quiet, falling in with their loping strides as she and Peter run barefoot to the river.

The memory was unfolding in all the right ways, but suddenly the music was over. Now the radio announcer was introducing the girl—Petra Kelly—the one who'd made such a racket as they drove back from Munich. Her voice, bright and forceful, filled the room.

Dear God. She was just like a fly in a jar, battering herself against Pershing missiles, cruise missiles—insisting, in that American-tinged voice, that it all came down to dominance of men over women, patriarchal formulas that control us whether we're conscious of them or not. Helena remembered Father with his big, hairy ears, his storms of anger, and all the work that went into his eventual appeasement. How often her mother had pushed her into her father's study. *Go. Sit on his lap.* And it would be her job as a five-year-old, as a ten-year-old even, to cross the big room towards her father in his chair, sunk in a gloom of deepest reproach. It was her job to climb into his lap, to work out the knot of gloom in his soul by resting her little girl's body against his smoky woollen one. Why was this her job? Nobody explained. It just was. She was sent by her mother again and again, an envoy of girlish love, as though her innocence had a power and purpose, which was to melt whatever was grinding in her father's gut.

"Fathers dominate little girls," Petra was saying, "and wars dominate people."

"And sexual freedom," she heard Petra say. "Sexual freedom is part of it too."

The interviewer cut in, "You really link free sex, as it's called, with the issue of Pershing missiles?"

"Compartmentalizing has blinded us to the suffering of the earth. So yes, we aren't afraid to look at the whole web. Our new party—actually an anti-party—can see the connection between sexual violence and the military outrage against men, women and children in the mountains of Tibet—"

The interviewer let out a small chuckle.

"—or pornography and dissidents behind the wall. They're all one story of humans—almost always men—wielding power unjustly. We must see around corners and not be afraid to look at what's beyond. Global equity, women, north and south, poverty, non-violence, sexual freedom—they're all linked."

The interviewer continued with his ostentatious chuckling, then said, "And you intend to win over voters with this platform?"

"Oh, yes—we need two million votes to gain access to the Bundestag."

"Well, much luck to you."

Helena stared out the window as the music began to play again. Across the river, the skin of the birches had turned blue in the dusk. She felt as though Petra's voice was unwrapping an iron hoop that circled her chest. This idea must have come from a fairy tale, something her mother had told her or read aloud, iron fingers wrapped around a woman's ribs. A prince pulls them away one by one, and the woman can breathe.

It seemed so audacious to proclaim the power of free sex on the radio. To say that the angry, sad faces behind the wall had anything to do with pornography. Or that nuclear power had anything to do with cruel, unbending kings. What might have happened to her, Helena, if she hadn't bent so often, crossing the floor at her mother's urging, climbing into her father's lap, a tool in the subtle war between them? Yes, it was true. Her mother had also relied on Helena's pliable nature later, in Berlin, during the final days of the war. Helena, so well trained to cross floors, to do as she was told. There was no need to remember, but still she did, and what she saw from above was herself and the other tenants of Uncle Rudy's Kreuzberg apartment building, hunkered against the cellar walls, shirt backs stained from the dust. They went there night after night because of the bombing, and so they were lined up like ducks when the bombing stopped and a Russian soldier shone his flashlight on them, the light settling on Helena's face. Then the fast, merciless beat of his language, not a soul understanding a word, but knowing what he wanted. And always it went the same way, this memory she hated but that came almost as often as Peter and the dogs. *You must do as he wants, or he'll shoot us all.* Nobody had said it, but still she knew. Her mother's eyes on the floor, not looking at her. Cross the floor. She had been the sacrifice.

This was the wrong memory.

Stop. Choose another.

As she darned, a last streak of sunlight reached her face, and she closed her eyes to feel it on her eyelids. Yes. Better. She saw herself climbing over her stone windowsill, holding on to the woody vines, no sense of dropping, then running across the grass, the dew cold on her bare feet. The bright shock of it running up her legs. The borzois slipping from their kennel and leaping on her, an ecstasy of greeting, yet somehow this part with the dogs is a tableau silent as a Greek vase, the dancing dogs, the girl in her nightdress, the brother holding a finger to his lips.

Helena felt him so close, the brother who loved her so and who died at Stalingrad. He knocks the dogs away, holding out his hand. And now they run towards the river, their Elbe, which flows past the glorious cathedral and the balustrades. Florence of the Elbe. The jewel box of Europe. *Quick!* Now they are in the rowboat under the cascade of the willows, moving between reeds that divide at the bow like parting hair. Peter rests the oars to light a cigarette and pass it to her, a strong French tobacco that makes her dizzy and excited. And now he takes a piece of paper from his pocket. Unfolds it on his knee. It is a poem he has written. He needs his little sister's opinion. Is it ridiculous, or is it good? He doesn't know. It must be up to her to say. This is the point. Peter is in love with the dark-eyed Magdalena, who works at the apothecary. Love is important. It takes up all the room in the boat.

Yes, the poem is good. Yes. *It's wonderful, Peter.* And satisfied but full of brooding love, Peter lies back and smokes, his feet on the seat, while they listen to the chorus of the birds.

"How was she?" Emil repeated, and Helena glanced at her husband, clutching his earnest little notepad as they drove.

"Oh—you mean the girl on the radio?" Where would she

start? Scheherazade? Unbending kings? The borzois? Her coal-stained blouse? Or the darning mushroom, lit from within? "I really can't say."

"I suppose a woman like that would seem an awful shrew to you."

In the field beyond the many lanes of the autobahn, three children were running with an enormous red kite. It shot up and then fell over the littlest one. The car flashed on. If she and Emil had been able to have children, everything would have been different. She could have offered him something so dense and beautiful: a house full of laughter. Children's toys on the stairs.

"The interviewer kept calling attention to her ideas," Helena said. "*Your platform sounds like a list of every wrong committed by humanity.*"

"I dread the Greens. They do far more harm than good. They should focus on *one single issue*—keeping the missiles off West German soil."

What did Helena think of this? She searched her mind and came up with exactly nothing. The Green girl had been more interesting. Emil's opinions felt like shrouds, covering Helena's own ideas.

She took the next exit and soon they were driving along quiet streets. At a stoplight Emil shifted to look at her directly. "I came home last night to celebrate with you."

"Is that what we're doing?"

"You know what I mean."

"I saw the roses. I just wonder at your choice of words."

He shifted back to look out the window.

"Emil. I heard about your resignation on the radio. How is that even possible? The whole of West Germany found out at the same time as I did."

"I called but you didn't answer." Then he said something she couldn't catch. She asked him to repeat it, and he said, more loudly, "I had to act alone."

"Oh! Like a hero in a Western. Or one of those detective novels you love."

He shook his head.

"I felt slain," Helena said. "Speechless." These were words she had used before about his affairs. "You say you had to act alone, but what about me, your wife of thirty-three years? What about us?"

"I'm genuinely sorry, Lena. A husband should consult his wife about such a thing, but it all happened quickly, and often, when I call home, you aren't in a state to talk."

There it was.

"Let's speak about this later." He touched her leg. "We'll have time."

"Nothing but time."

"I could take you for a long weekend of skiing. I could tell you every part of what has led me to this place. Would you like that?"

She nodded.

"Good. That's settled, then."

As Helena swung into the parking lot, she pictured snow falling around a cabin. It would fall all day, onto a balcony railing, a millimetre, a half centimetre, two centimetres. "I love you," she said, because it was true—still true—and he reached out to stroke her cheek. She pulled into a spot near a small playground, probably for the children of station employees. Emil took a breath to collect himself.

"You'll do fine," she couldn't resist saying. "Being a man of principle can't be all *that* difficult."

7

The Debate

In one, twos, and then all at once, the audience were on their feet, clapping and calling out to Emil as he walked onto the stage. *Thank you! Well done! Down with NATO and the Warsaw Pact!* An ovation. As if for a hero. He collected himself, waving as he took his seat under the lights. Applauded like a hero. Him. But perhaps he was. Wouldn't that be something? He let it sit for a moment and then dismissed it. He was, in the deepest possible way he knew how, merely doing his duty. Ah—yes. And this thought of *innere Führung* settled him. He caught sight of Helena at the back, in a row near the exit. Their eyes met, and for a second he felt that he could fall right into them.

Sometimes he thought of her as frail, but that was wrong. No, she wasn't frail; she was adaptable, like one of those butter-flies who survive by having two hues to their wings—blue under-neath, to meld with the sky, wheat-coloured on top, to disappear against wheat. He tried again to lock eyes with her; he wanted to beam the fact that, despite everything, they were in this together, but Petra Kelly walked onto the stage.

He'd seen news photographs, which, though often grainy, made her seem attractive. And hadn't she once deserted an inter-view when the newsman asked her what such a good-looking woman was doing in politics? He was expecting exceptional prettiness, but this young woman greeting the audience, heedless of her lateness, offered little to get excited about. Certainly she didn't have a shadow of Helena's beauty, the full mouth, shapely eyebrows, oval face. Petra was sallow and small, in her early thirties yet built like a child, with thin shoulders and thin hips. A skinny boy of a creature.

Emil's senses were distorted by nervousness, but still he heard something different in the applause for Petra than what had greeted him. Below the clapping was a thickened rustling. He heard a male voice call out, "Petra! Give it to him!"

She flashed a grin, then turned to Emil. He felt the energy in her body.

"So you're the famous general."

"Ex-general. At your service."

"It's a great thing you've done, quitting NATO." Her voice had the slightest tinge of an accent—he'd heard she'd spent years in America.

"I have reservations about the Euromissiles," he said. "Deployment raises crucial questions."

"Is that what it does?" She appeared to be laughing at him.

"I'm concerned about the balance of mutually assured destruction—how this new breed of nuclear weapons threatens that balance."

"Yes, you generals do put a high stake on that balance of destruction." She glanced backstage. "Do you understand the reason for this delay? I think I'm getting a cold."

"I believe," he said, "that the delay was caused by the tardiness of one of the debaters."

She raised an eyebrow but chose not to respond. "Anyway, good luck," she said, then put out a hand for him to shake. He held it for a moment, and then, quite without thinking, he clipped his heels together, raised her hand to his lips and kissed it. He heard the exhale of surprise from the crowd, from Petra, too, for this most unfeminist gesture. This courtly kiss!

And what could she do? People in the audience were watching closely, expecting her to do something—but what? Admonish him? Laugh? She smiled at him carefully, narrowing her eyes.

"Ah, I see you are off to a good start," she said, knowing that her face had turned red. "Would you kiss a man's hand before a debate?"

"I doubt if I'd want to. But there's a first time for everything."

"You treat women differently. We'll see how well that goes down today."

"I'm sure you'll make mincemeat of me."

Was he mocking her? He shrugged as though it was inevitable, and she had to laugh.

"I have never been in a debate before," he said simply. "But don't go easy on me. I insist on equal treatment."

She had the voice Helena remembered from the radio. Staccato with surety. "You obviously don't understand our sex. We are not as soft as you are suggesting. We can kill, just as men can kill, but this is not the point."

Emil kept smiling like a cat, adoring being berated, and the crowd laughed.

The Green girl flashed her grin at the audience. "General, I can imagine no graver mistake than to section off one half of the population, and say that they are, alas, gentle, compassionate and unfit for battle. Men and women are both a mix of good and bad, compassion and terror, and to say otherwise is to reveal a real misunderstanding of human nature. Not to mention incredible naivety about the nature of women."

Laughter.

"General Gerhardt," she continued (and Helena noticed how the girl seemed to like stressing the military title), "it's not women who are unfit for the military, but the military that's unfit for women. And not just for women, with our 'empathetic souls,' but for thinking and feeling men as well. The point isn't who can outdo the other in killing—with rocks, swords, bayonets or nuclear bombs—but to find a way to make violence obsolete."

"That's a dream." Emil sat back in the chair, smiling at her.

"A dream, as long as men like you smile at it."

Helena saw a yellow worm climb over her eye—a Valium worm, which she sometimes got in the mornings. This one was the exact colour of the cushion she had just purchased in Würzburg for the settee in the back room, which was where she wished she was now, listening to the ticking of the grandfather clock, the unfathomable spaces between each half hour. The worm went, but Helena stood and pushed her way past the students beside her, their bony legs a barricade of jeans, then found the exit door and pushed it open. It led to cement stairs. She hoped the click of her boot heels couldn't be heard: she didn't want to fill the auditorium with the sound of her flight. At the bottom was a foyer smelling of urine. For a moment she thought she was trapped. But she made out the sheen of a door, and next thing she was blinking in the winter sunlight, the little playground in front of her, the one she had seen as they parked.

It was bleak. A real pittance of a thing, likely built out of some contractual obligation of management's, with a see-saw and swing set, a sand pile covered by a sheet of plywood to keep out cats. It felt sad but fitting to land here, in this barren children's playground, as though life wanted to add symbolic weight to her melancholy. She could almost hear the sound of playing, the invisible ones who had never come. She sat on the bench.

In place of children, she had to keep this vigil of the self, which she could never understand how to *do* properly. So much lonely time by herself, and for what? It was as though something was expected of her, as though loneliness was a substance, real but invisible, like gas; with enough of it she would burst into flame.

She recognized the signs of what was to come.

And Petra was no Julia Kunst either, with her endless smiles and her "How are you, Frau Gerhardt? May I get you coffee?"

"Call me Helena," she had said, but Julia never did, as though their vast age difference made it impossible. Julia Kunst and her enormous ass. No. This girl had looked outraged when Emil kissed her hand, and then she had briskly talked about killing, about state-sanctioned violence, *as though she knew.* Words pouring from her in shafts and barbs, which had grazed Emil in an enlivening way, like a dry bristle brush against his skin.

Words.

She, Helena, had actually felt the weight of state-sanctioned violence.

Why think about it?

She moved to sit on the lip of the sandbox and tried not to, but it was no use. The two Russian soldiers came lurching forward, one with a red nose, hairs shooting from the nostrils. He led her from the cellar to an apartment above, told her to lie on the bed, and then squatted on her chest, pinning her arms, breathing like an ox. The rest was so brutal and disgusting she couldn't think about it, even now. Only minutes after he was done, the second soldier had come into the bedroom. Diffidently. Like he was a professor in his other life of long ago. He had sat on the bed and asked her name, then he lay beside her and stroked her arm, told her to turn from the wall, look at him. He wouldn't hurt her. He had some German. Wore glasses. *You are like Helen of Troy, you are so beautiful. Don't be afraid.* But then it was all the same; worse than with the other because she had expected some kindness, and when he was done, this one had called her a whore, as though she had caused it.

The girl didn't have a clue. Not a clue. And the first clue to her cluelessness was that she kept talking when none of this was meant to be put into words. It was for dreams, its weight and smell too much for the light of day. You didn't bandy it around. You didn't seduce a man onstage by making allusions to violence. You kept silent. That's what you did. And in that tower of silence, slowly, slowly, you let the world grow back around you, brambles and thorns encasing the stones. Birds calling to each other.

Helena sat for a long time looking at the swing set, and each time she felt a jab of anger in her body, she closed her eyes, breathed and smoothed her thoughts. She turned her face to the sun. What did it matter that the girl, Petra, didn't know a thing about what she was talking about? What did it matter that Emil might go wandering for awhile? He always came back. That was their pledge to each other, their promise: that they were each other's in an essential way, but that Emil must be allowed to experience life. Must. Or something vital in him would wither and die.

So what must Helena do?

Close her eyes, feel the sun on her eyelids and calm herself by picturing animals. It was hard sometimes to love her fellow human beings, but it wasn't hard to love animals. She pictured a rabbit hopping across a field. Finding a hole, slipping into it. Now a lynx, then a creeping vole, though she wasn't entirely sure what a vole was. Then a cluster of brooding birds high in a tree. A group of lemmings throwing themselves from a cliff. No—too dramatic. She pictured a walrus, its massive nose and blubber and squeaky flippers. Then a panther creeping through a jungle aflame with tropical scents, like a painting by Henri Rousseau. Each of the animals was in its place, in trees or on ice, or picked out by the moon, unseen by human eyes.

8.

To Franconia

General Emil Gerhardt carried his wife's bags around Bonn's market square after the debate, opening and closing doors for her, going with her to the late-afternoon movie she wanted to see. They bought a selection of jams and chutneys in glass jars, because Helena loved the way they looked stacked in the store window, glowing. In the car, as they drove home along the Rhine, Emil admired the valleys with houses in their creases, the suddenness of village steeples, hills repeating themselves yet taking on heft, until, at last, they would rise to become the Alps, smothered in gentian and edelweiss.

He knew he should censor or suppress the love he felt for his homeland, his *Heimat*, but still it came, the summer smells of the hills, cow dung in the pastures, little flowers they'd pass on hikes. And with these memories, hovering over the landscape, came the girl. As he changed lanes, as he pulled over for gas, the eyes of the girl followed him like a cat, watching him from above, and from the side of the road. He drove and saw her, drove and saw her, her sallow face, glints of blond in the brown of her hair, circles under her eyes, and that wolfish smile as she cornered him, pummelled him with her well-timed jabs.

He could hear the cheering of the audience, hear her bright, angry, Americanized vowels, though she also had a hint of a

Franconian accent. A young voice but an old one; full of America but flavoured by the older tones of the Danube and the forested hills, walled medieval towns of surpassing beauty, surrounded by moats.

He thought of the public slapping she'd given him. Of the impulse that had made him click his heels together and then bend to kiss her hand. The surprise on her face—disliking the public gesture and yet finding it amusing, even secretly liking the gallantry. Blushing. She had won the debate—wiped the floor with him, really—but he had won something else.

9.

Here I Am

Petra and the general were keynote speakers at two rallies, then guests at an anti-missile citizens' forum in West Berlin. It was after this session, as they were talking in the foyer of the building, that he invited her out for dinner. He was wearing a belted winter coat of expensive-looking wool. Shined shoes. Clothes so deeply out of place at the forum. Did he know how different he looked? Did he care? This quality in him delighted her. A man who dressed as he thought was right, even to the tie.

They went to a cellar restaurant in Kreuzberg, lit by a stone fireplace and heavy, tallow-smeared chandeliers. When their eyes met across the table, Petra felt a jitter run through her body. It wasn't fear, but it was a cousin of fear. Yes, fear's cousin, moving from the top of her tingling head, down her spine, into her clitoris, which dinged like a small bell.

As he leaned forward, she studied his eyes under thick eyebrows, his wry, almost diffident, searching smile. He seemed uncomfortable, as though not quite sure how to start in on her. As though she were a large steak and he hadn't quite found the right knife. Yet he was shy, too, or something close to it: he wanted to make a good impression. She suspected she wasn't the first woman he had attempted to seduce in a dimly lit restaurant, yet when he knocked his fork to the floor, he seemed truly nervous. He placed the heavy fork back on the table. It was good, this cutlery, and the truth was, she liked good things—the white tablecloths, the aproned waiters, the fire-lit luxury—though she reminded herself that this entire place represented another face of the status quo, another face of German conservatism. Still. Who could deny the pleasure of settling down in the firelight, feeling his eyes on her, neither of them really knowing what to say next? She sensed an adventurous spirit under the well-made suit jacket. After all, this man with his closely manicured fingernails, cuticles tended (unlike Manfred's), had upset the entire West German military. And then there was that moment at the Rifle Club—pushing back his chair, crossing the floor, stopping the bandleader in his tracks.

"That must have taken courage," she said. "I sent you a postcard after that. Did you ever get it?"

"Yes, and I'll tell you something strange." He paused, then reached into his breast pocket and pulled it out. The Rhine covered in diamond sparkles. Her scribbles on the back. Multiple exclamation marks.

"No!" she cried, completely delighted.

He shrugged. "It gives me courage."

"You seem to have that on your own."

He paused and regarded her seriously. "You'd be mistaken if you thought that."

"But stopping Hitler's march, and then resigning from NATO. Speaking about it in public. These are the actions of a courageous man, Emil."

He shrugged. "We'll see."

She took this in. His response seemed ambivalent, even slightly vacant. "I don't know what you mean—'We'll see,'" she said, as he gestured for the waiter. They paused to order, and when the waiter left, Emil gave her a bright, false smile. "You mustn't think too much of me, that's all."

But his saying this increased her esteem. He wasn't pompous or self-glorifying, that was clear.

"So tell me." She took a small sip of her wine (it sometimes upset her stomach). "Why did you stop the band from playing Hitler's march? This non-heroic gesture of yours."

He shook his head. "It just happened."

"What do you mean?"

"I suppose I think of courage as something you do—something a person ought to do—*after* thinking. But that was quite spontaneous. I couldn't bear to hear that song one more time."

"And did quitting NATO just happen too?"

This was an open wound still; he winced. "That took more thought," he said at last.

"And now," she said gently, "how is it sitting with you?"

"It felt right at the time. But . . ."

"But what?"

"We are too serious. I want to hear about you."

"Not so quickly. Tell me the rest of that thought."

He leaned forward. A copper plate above the fire reflected this movement, and for a moment it seemed there were two of him—the vision in the copper and the man in front of her. "All right, then, I'll tell you. I put my uniform in my closet. I zipped the plastic casing. That was just this morning. I tell you—it looked truly forlorn in that plastic case."

"Yes, I see."

"It was my identity, I suppose one could say."

Again she felt surprised. She had pried, yes, but did he owe her such honesty? She thought of the postcard in his pocket, over his heart.

"And now, I suppose I feel naked," he said. Then he smiled. It was that word, *naked*. He hadn't even known it would end up on his tongue.

They were silent for a moment, and she covered his hand with her own. Immediately he turned to clasp it, moving his hand up her wrist. His touch felt graceful to her, knowing and yet exploratory. They both looked down at the finger on her wrist, and then he withdrew it.

"You must join the Greens," she said. "That would be a good next step."

In his hotel bedroom, she excused herself and went into the bathroom. He stood by the window, looking towards the Berlin Wall. What was he getting himself into? The almost hostile clarity of her gaze caused a new kind of sensation, a kind of psychic spilling. And it went with everything he had experienced in the last weeks—the shock of overturning his life.

The wall wasn't visible from the window, but it gloomed in his imagination, just a quarter mile away: the dog runs and watchtowers. Beyond the graffitied concrete, the Brandenburg Gate stood isolated at the rump end of Unter den Linden. It hurt to think of this formerly lush boulevard, sidewalks built double-wide for parasols and baby carriages, with its striped awnings, its gay life, which he'd witnessed as a child and then, later, on leave, all now leading to the wall with its death strip.

A few people had breached the wall. Emil could remember a photograph of a boy of sixteen, gunned down at the base of the wall, moaning in a pool of blood. Emil shook his head. Though he had spent three decades in the service of the Bundesrepublik, and the wall had been a permanent scar for almost that entire time, he had never gotten used to it—would never be able to. And who were the people on the other side of the wall? These totalitarian enemies. Helena, growing up in Dresden, might have become one of them if she hadn't gone to live with her Uncle Rudy in Berlin. She was a Saxon, and described herself so to this day. Yes, pick up the wall, throw it with giant's hands into the ocean, and what you had were German people: Bavarians, Franconians, Saxons, Prussians. Yet . . . here he paused, self-disgust suddenly filling him. This was the new thing. *Watch yourself. Watch your thoughts. Watch, above all, the need to simplify.* This voice in his head was part of his new thinking since his resignation: to live by one's conscience (as he was trying to do, even if incompletely) was a physical act. *It was a physical act.* But what did that mean?

It required steps.

First, he had to acknowledge when his mind hit a well-worn groove. A group mindset, as the psychologist had called it.

Then he must pay attention to what was happening, as though he were looking down a hillside at a broken military manoeuvre, men and tanks out of line.

Then regroup. Cast off the military metaphor. In his mind now was a green pasture—a vivid memory he couldn't place— and he was young, running across it, towards dappled cows in the distance. Free.

Now close your eyes and say what you think.

This was, roughly speaking, what he tried to do to arrive at a moment of *innere Führung*: military disarray (he often sweated, as this part hurt), leading to regrouping (vertigo), and then the child running across the pasture towards a distant hillside. Then out came the truth. It was glorious each time he became the boy running, and saw the cows, and found the words of his heart. He wasn't sure where the cow memory came from—it almost felt like a dream; it had that intensity—yet he knew he had once run with joy towards the cows. The moment was like a stone he could hold, a stone in his pocket. It led him to his better self.

That boy, lying beside the wall in a pool of blood. The German Democratic Republic had been real to him as he ran towards the wall, as his heart pounded, as he leapt towards the end of the death strip, heard the rough *Halt!* then the crack of gunshot. He'd bled to death in a fetal position at the base of the wall, caught by a Western camera. Emil had seen the picture.

So do not tell yourself that we are all Franconians, Saxons, Germans, my friend: that boy died trying to cross the line.

Petra cleared her throat behind him.

She had taken off all her clothes and stood naked on the flowered carpet, toes tensed. It had been, he realized, a long time since he'd seen a woman completely naked. Sex with Julia Kunst often happened in his car, cursory but satisfying; Helena always chose to wear silky nightgowns. But this girl was totally exposed. Slender legs (unshaven, of course). Knobby knees. Flash of dark hair at the pubis—a crow's wing. A little beggar boy stomach. A determined, proud yet vulnerable face. *Here I am*, that face said. *You say you want me, and so here I am. Now let's see what will happen next.*

10

The Love Bomb

The atomic clock ticked ten seconds closer to midnight. The Pentagon kept talking about limited nuclear war, with Europe as the battlefield. We were the sacrifice, the nexus point for what, in seconds, would combust into total nuclear annihilation. The mass protests, gigantic from the beginning, swelled—each one louder than the one before—and to our surprise East Germans beyond the wall found ways to protest too: holding meetings in churches, gathering in candlelight vigils against the Russian SS-20 missiles, actions that often ended with the protestors rounded up and jailed in the Stasi cells of Normannenstrasse, the secret police headquarters. We heard about these acts through the work of underground journalists, samizdat bulletins and messages smuggled across the wall. The actions were often led by Clara Pohl and her husband, Ulrich. Petra spoke out vehemently in support of the Eastern peace groups, pledging the whole Green movement.

Yet what did the press want to cover?

A Farewell to Arms read one headline—a profile of Emil, mentioning his close working relationship with Petra and the Greens.

The King and Queen of German Protest, another piece called them.

Petra showed me that headline and laughed out loud. "The press are nothing if not reductive," she said. *King and Queen.* The words conjured up a Renaissance tapestry complete with a bugler and a horse tossing its head, a dog scampering to avoid high-strutting hooves. Still, I could tell she was gratified to be linked with the debonair general.

But other Greens complained. We were making real strides politically. Our new bus, the Green Caterpillar, took us to market days and rallies, disgorging tuba-playing folk in loden hats, honking the West German national anthem. One of our more popular pamphlets said: *Yes to NATO! Yes to Rearmament! We Want to Die so America Can Live!* After years of drab Bonn politics—the ruffle-no-feathers approach—people were hungry for a political party that could make them laugh and get them dancing.

"Come on," Petra said at one press conference. "Are you here to talk about Emil and me, or about the Euromissiles?"

"Both, actually."

Even the camera crews laughed.

Time, during this period, could be measured by the general's visits to the farmhouse and the number of nights I was forced to sleep with a pillow over my head, blocking the bedroom sounds. Or his dozens of attempts to tidy the shoes in the hallway. The number of times his bag of neat toiletries got knocked from the puce-coloured windowsill. Or the many mornings in which, emerging from Petra's bedroom in a sweater and trousers permanently pressed, having completed his push-ups and knee bends, he entered the kitchen and seemed to want badly to order me to do the dishes. The mess and chaos of our farmhouse tried him sorely.

But time would be far better measured by what took up most of our days: preparing for the federal election; electioneering on street corners; tramping from building to building, door-knocking with our pamphlets. Time was spent arguing with, and wheedling concessions from, the Hamburg Red-Green faction, which tried to torpedo Petra's focus on non-violence and feminism in favour of a programme that could involve trade unions and the working class. They smoked massive numbers of cigarettes (she and I joked that you could tell who belonged to the Dogmatic Left by the amount of smoke they generated), and they were a thorn in Petra's side. Even drawing up a new pamphlet required negotiations deep into the night.

"Reason with them," she appealed to me. "They're your brothers in arms." She meant from my days in West Berlin a decade before, living in a squat, reading Marcuse and Adorno, wearing a Mao jacket stained heavily beneath the armpits. "They don't want a green world," she said. "They want a Marxist paradise. They'd cut down every tree to get it."

But Petra didn't actually need my help anymore. Not like she had at the nuclear protests at Wyhl. She was by far the best known of the Greens, and the press usually wanted to speak to her. When asked about the potential for a Red-Green split, she came out with a stunner: "We're neither left nor right—we're out in front." The press loved this, and it appeared everywhere. The next day I scolded her. "It's like what the pigs say in *Animal Farm*—'Four legs good, two legs bad.' It's that simplistic."

"Never mind." She laughed at me. "It's saving our bacon."

I had to laugh too.

I remember one meeting with a cadre of Red-Greens where she listened to their reams of multisyllabic theory and then rejoined fiercely: "You've tethered yourself to a rampant-growth paradigm. Your socialism is just as damaging to the earth as capitalism."

I tended to agree with the Red-Greens, but I was moved by her courage, going at that roomful of big dogs, all of them men.

I had to leave to find a phone and okay yet another print run of T-shirts. A half hour later she found me.

"Well?" I asked.

"The wording will be as we want it."

I gave her a hug, kissed her forehead.

"What? Has something happened?" She looked worried that words of love were about to pour from me, but I shook my head. I was actually a bit choked up.

"I just realized," I said, "that we're going to stop the missiles."

"Ah. And what made you realize that?"

"You."

"Oh, give it up." She laughed lightly, but she was pleased.

I was jealous, of course. That goes without saying. Scorching sensations moved in me like dark, lively snakes. They pressed against my chest, making me want to hate the general, even as I admired him for the personal risks he had taken, coming over to us. And what rights did I have, I asked myself, hearing them in her bedroom at night? None. I was the door she had used into the nuclear movement, and now she'd passed through it into a grand hallway. She was the queen, and I was arranging for more T-shirts.

Still, if anything, since Emil had arrived on the scene, I felt Petra's sexual energy more powerfully. I kept remembering how, after I told her about my father and his beatings, she got on top of me in bed and slipped the shaft of my penis in, then rode me with her palms pressed against my chest, as though she would pluck out my grief. As though this was her most secret skill, ardent and gentle—to pluck out pain. And now this gift of physical absolution was all for the general.

The peace movement soon shifted to make room for him, and I had to admit I found myself impressed by this man. He was exactly what we needed. We used him the way a child might pause in a schoolyard fight to fetch his bulldog. He said in public that the missiles were "unacceptable," that any nuclear engagement would lead to full-scale nuclear war. Even his tendency to break into a kind of automatic grey-speak, full of abbreviations and acronyms—ICBMS, MIRVed dual-track, not to mention the accords, SALT 1 and SALT 2 (*Help me!* I wanted to cry out when he started to speak)—even this worked. Long words from an ex-general were exactly what we needed to capture middle-ground voters. And every now and then something rather magical would happen and he'd say something truly quotable. *We are searching for a new way to be German.* That was one. But what did he mean? The press crowded in, and he instantly became less articulate, while Petra erupted in a barrage of meaning: *We will do politics differently, we will move beyond politics, we will think for the earth.* But that was not what Emil had meant. I could see it on his face. He meant he wanted to erase the old Germany, with its wounds. And I felt for him, because we all wanted this, though we were of different generations, with different experiences of that past.

Hatred. Admiration.

I liked his self-deprecating smile, his way of pausing before speaking, staring at his manicured fingers for a moment too long, as though listening for a cue from within. He came from the previous generation, with its mass of sins, yet he'd been able to shake them off, to take a stand against the next wave of insane, governmentally planned mass killings. Our generation, with our "luckiness of being born too late," could be morally pure and condemnatory. But this man had lived through the Nazi era, been picked up in the great jaws of that eternally justifying yet totally lawless society, and here he was now, saying *No*.

So we arranged for Emil to appear on stage after stage. Petra enlivened the crowd and then handed things over to him to speak his general-speak, until Freya took me aside and said Petra absolutely must speak *after* him. Emil was great on facts, but he was an absolute buzzkiller.

One afternoon Petra skipped offstage quivering like a tuning fork from the power of the Thing that had moved through her body and electrified the crowd.

"How was I?"

I took her lightly by the shoulders. "You've gone and been brilliant again," I said. But she turned to Emil, wanting his praise, not mine.

"It was incredible," he said. "But you must be very tired."

Her face fell. But then she nodded. "You're right. I've never been more tired."

"Let's have a night without work."

"I have to finish my speech for the campaign meeting tomorrow."

"You'll be better able to concentrate if you take a break."

She raised her eyebrows at this.

"Rest," he repeated. "We'll all work tomorrow."

I couldn't resist. "Emil, we Greens don't dictate how women spend their time."

"He's not dictating," Petra said.

Emil turned to me. "You're tired too, Manfred."

"Ah—so it's a universal."

"We all deserve a break." Then he added, "After difficult manoeuvres, I always gave the men the night off. Surely you deserve what they had. Or is the army a softer taskmaster than the Greens?"

"He's got us," Petra said, and laughed.

That night at the farmhouse he baked a quiche, with Gruyère cheese and ham and chives, serving it with a salad (Petra was enlisted to chop the green onions) and a good Chianti. I followed his orders, putting the rolling pin in the freezer before he rolled the pastry, while he tsk-tsked at the sight of old bowls of muesli and stew stored in the fridge, their spoons still in them. I even managed to find a dusty, multicoloured candle, shaped like a mushroom, and it flamed and sputtered slowly in the centre of the table as we ate.

That night, enjoying good food at a farmhouse table, our lives suddenly felt simple and pleasant. The campaign receded. Strangely, the evening reminded me of the night Petra and I first talked about the general as she had her bath. Now, through some sort of odd magic, we had manifested him, conjuring a military commander from the other side. He was pouring us wine, serving us second helpings. *Is this how change occurs?* I remember thinking. *Does it come from goodwill? A meal shared?* If the editors of the *Bulletin of the Atomic Scientists* knew about us, would they turn the atomic clock back a quarter minute?

Honesty: Petra

"And what about his wife?"

I said this to Petra one night six months into their affair. We were at the farmhouse. It was late summer now, and we sat in the bay alcove of the living room, with the windows thrown open, a spot Petra loved.

"I don't know what you mean."

I thought of Helena, whom I'd seen at their first debate, her face calm yet ashen. She seemed like a dignified woman, and a likeable one.

"He's told Helena about you?"

"Yes, obviously." She looked out the window at the lush fields.

"You believe in free love," I continued, "but free love shouldn't be damaging to one of the parties. You don't do the dance of free love on someone's head."

She breathed in quickly, hurt by my words. But then she said evenly, "No, of course not."

"This is one of the things about you . . ." I stopped. I didn't want to launch into this, how her honesty about other lovers had caused me so much pain. It had always been such a hard dance, being free with Petra Kelly. "I think he ought to tell his wife his full intentions towards you."

"*Intentions?* What a word. You are sounding very old-fashioned and patriarchal."

"I'm talking about fair-dealing."

"Yes, I know."

"You never spared me. It was official openness every day, whether I wanted it or not. You practically telephoned me from that Irish trade unionist's bed."

She had. To read parts of a speech she was to give the next day, in Dublin. She was in bed with another man, but so what? That's what she'd said. *Everybody is a grown-up.*

I looked at her, curled in the window seat. We'd been sitting for ages, and dusk was beginning to rise out of the fields outside, out of the copse of trees. Night always seems to come from the land first, the sky being the last thing to darken. *I should leave this alone*, I told myself. *Leave it now.*

"I've seen him picking up flowers," I said. "Whenever he visits you, I think she gets a bouquet."

"So what?" She stood now, spilling her tea. "So what?"

"I just want you to be honest with yourself."

12

Honesty: Emil

Three days later, at the market in Bonn's city hall square, Petra waited for Emil. He had invited her on a picnic. A picnic! In the middle of their fight to win voters. To gain a foothold in the Bundestag.

She stood by a vendor's stall, looking down at the ripe tomatoes and cucumbers, thinking about this man, this old-fashioned, picnic-proposing man. There could be no question, anymore: she was in love with him. It didn't feel casual or transactional, as some encounters had felt—though in truth, with every affair, even the briefest, she tended towards love. And trying to understand why you fell was impossible. It came like a second skin you slipped on and walked around in. And then the things the person did took on a power that you knew, rationally, they shouldn't have.

So, for instance, she was in love with Emil but also in love with the way he polished his shoes. His attention to them, his military care, aroused her and touched her. It reminded her of what he'd sacrificed, leaving NATO, but also of how men used to care for things. (Was her father like this?) Emil belonged to a different culture, where people were responsible for their footwear, even placing them on wooden shoe holders. A kind of adult responsibility that was quite lost in the new world of running shoes.

She got an odd feeling every time she thought about his leap into the void. Her postcard. Then him quitting NATO. That such a truly conservative man would take such a leap. It made her realize that conscience, raw conscience, was alive in the world. Manfred had teased her, saying she was trying to change the world one general at a time, but that wasn't it. The point was that Emil was changing the world by living his life differently— joining her anti-party, loving her. She felt he had a plan, deep inside, to confront the person he'd been, who he was. It had a mythical quality. Like a knight's quest, to shake off the winter of a cold land, to return it to spring. And to do this required individual change, as she'd always thought: mass change was one thing, but in the end change had to come from inside. From a deep internal reckoning.

A shadow crossed the sun. All these feelings were alive in her mind, so when she turned to see Emil entering the square, she was surprised. From a distance he seemed shorter. Her eyes, cleansed by distance, saw clearly that he was smaller, more compact, more Gallic in his stance than she pictured him. With his hands in his jacket pockets, shoes gleaming even from this distance, he seemed vulnerable, but to what? To being seen without all the attendant ideas? But then he looked up, and an electric spark leapt between them.

Then he was beside her. He kissed her and took her right into his arms, the vegetable vendor smiling at this display of desire. She smelled the wool of his coat and his spicy aftershave. A hint of Morocco. And underneath that the male smell of sweat, salty and richly warm. She wanted to bury her nose in the collar of his shirt and stay there for a long time.

When they let go, he saw her concern. "What's wrong?"

"I want to speak to you. From the heart."

"I wouldn't expect anything less."

"It's about Helena," she said simply.

At that, he abandoned the idea of a picnic. Instead, they sat together on the patio of the Stern Hotel, she with a coffee, he with a beer. All at once she wasn't afraid to speak of her love openly.

"You feel as I do?" She was leaning forward, and she saw him engaging in the thing she loved about him above all, that quiet inner listening. Then he took her hand and brought it to his lips. He would be open with Helena, he said. He would be open with everyone.

13.

Honesty: Helena

And so that weekend Emil and Helena walked by the Main River in Veitshöchheim. They sat on a bench and he told her the truth. It wasn't merely sex with Petra (as it had been with Julia Kunst). It wasn't a passing fancy.

"You love her," Helena said stonily.

"I love you both."

He tried to meet her eye, but she wouldn't look at him. The river was glazed by bits of light. By the shore, willows dragged their fingers in the water. He was being honest—but why? He had never been perfectly honest with Helena before; the comfortable silence had been exactly the right milieu for their marriage. Their childless sorrows. Her anguish, and his mute care. His wartime memories wrapped in a cushion of shadow. They were children of the war. Too much light could destroy them.

When Helena spoke, her voice was steady enough. "I'm not quite sure what you want me to do."

"I don't want anything." Emil was relieved but horrified. "Do nothing."

"And what? This will burn out of your system? It doesn't sound like that is where you are headed at all."

"I don't know. I don't know what will happen. I'm sorry."

"But what am I to do, Emil? Wait for you. Wait like a fool?"

"Nobody thinks you're a fool."

"Everybody does. They think I'm a perfect fool, but they think the same of you, with your quest for youth! The Greens!"

It sounded ridiculous when she said it out loud.

"You are like a man who sets out at dawn with a bedroll, thinking he can reclaim his youth by sleeping in ditches." She stopped. "Never mind. It's useless to say a thing. You're in it now. Let's speak of other things. Who is going to take care of Felix?" The basset hound. "It doesn't matter how onerous your new political schedule turns out to be, Emil, I am not going to be solely responsible for that dog's care."

He promised to return home as necessary. To walk the dog.

"Felix will be happy with this arrangement," she said, then stood and walked on. Emil followed a few steps behind. She moved like silk beside the water, yet, for the sake of this new thing working through his bones, she had now been told to her face that she was being supplanted, at least for now, a telling that seemed, in this moment, utterly senseless and cruel. He was used to the old ways: healthy doses of duplicity, followed by healthy doses of roses, great bouquets of scented freesias.

For me? What's the occasion?

Because I love you.

A pattern they both understood, which, roughly translated, meant: *Let me make up for what you don't know about, by giving you a gift I don't explain.*

14.

Education of the General

One day I was at the kitchen table when Emil and Petra pushed through the farmhouse door, laden with several boxes. Petra set hers on the table, then went immediately to her room, while Emil placed his boxes on a chair.

"What have you got there?"

"Books," he said. "Petra's been storing them in Freya's locker."

"Everything fine?"

"Oh, well . . . the press conference was gruelling." He found a bottle of wine (he kept the cupboards stocked) and uncorked it. He seemed to want to say more, but at that moment Petra burst from the bedroom, pulled open one of the boxes and began to lay books on the table. She handed one to Emil.

"Here." Her voice was choked, and I realized she was angry.

He read the cover. "*Collected Poems of Anna . . .*"

"*Akhmatova.*" She waited for him to give an expression of recognition, but his face was fixed. "Russia's most famous dissident poet, Emil. She recorded the suffering of the people in a great poem called "Requiem." Here . . ." she opened the book, leafed to a section and began to read.

The stars of death stood over us.
And Russia, guiltless, beloved, writhed
under the crunch of bloodstained boots,
under the wheels of Black Marias.

"You see? She is the soul of Russia's anguish during the Stalin years."

Emil smiled grimly and passed her a glass of wine.

"I don't want that," she said. "It upsets my stomach. But here—listen to this."

Rising from the past, my shadow
Is running in silence to meet me.

Her face was lit up. "Isn't that beautiful? Don't you feel like that about the past?"

"I don't know," he said shortly.

"Don't know what?"

"The past is complicated."

"Of course it is, but don't you think Akhmatova has caught it? Don't you?"

He looked at her, strangely blank, and I could see a pulse beating in his temple.

"Manfred!" she turned to me. "Tell him he must read Akhmatova."

Beyond a doubt, this was a private argument, yet I couldn't resist. I closed my eyes and recited:

You will hear thunder and remember me,
And think: she wanted storms. The rim
Of the sky will be the colour of hard crimson,
And your heart, as it was then, will be on fire.

"Manfred!" Petra cried. "You know it by heart."

I nodded, not hazarding the second verse, and she turned back to the general. "So what do you think? Isn't she wonderful, this voice of dissident Russia? Don't you want to read her and *know* her? And look, here are other sisters and brothers, people to know, to love." She handed him another book. "Rosa Luxemburg. Shot dead for her beliefs, her body thrown into the Landwehr Canal. A martyr to socialism and feminism. She said, *Those who do not move do not notice their chains.*" A pause. She was willing Emil to burst into flames of appreciation, to pledge to read what had moved her so deeply. Again I saw that vein pulsing in his temple, and noticed his fingers slowly turning over the books.

"And these others?"

"Gandhi, Thoreau, Malcolm X, Martin Luther King—"

He opened one and read the title page. "*Principles of Gnosticism.*"

Petra shrugged. "It describes the growth of early Christian thought, before St. Paul seized it all and made it his. It's about the egalitarian roots of the church."

He put it down and picked up an enormous tome. His hand trembled. "Emma Goldman—*Living My Life.*" I could feel the heat of his discomfort, and I realized that I'd never seen him hold any book other than a detective novel. He went through the stack, turning them over, examining the author photographs, the first pages. I felt as though we'd cornered a bull. At last he put the final book down.

"What?" said Petra.

"I think you know."

"I don't."

"I won't be reading any of these—not even to please you, Petra."

She stared at him, hardly able to take in this defiance. "But you said you wanted to be part of our movement."

"I also have to be myself." Abruptly, he left the room. He may only have gone to change out of the clothes he'd worn to the press conference, but his exit felt dramatic. Petra followed him. I heard her voice through the open door.

"You couldn't even say you stand for non-violence. What will happen when they ask you about Ostpolitik, or dissidents behind the wall, or radiation, or feminism, or the rights of children, the rights of animals? You have to understand that these issues are interconnected."

"To me they aren't."

I imagined them staring across the bed at each other. "I don't believe you," she said. "Why would you join our movement if you don't believe in the web of interconnectivity?" Even when she was angry, she could spit out the multisyllabics. Silence. Then I heard her voice again: "I found it humiliating at the press conference. We openly contradicted each other."

"Because I don't agree with you, and I say so. I don't see the 'interconnectivity,' as you put it, between all these different issues, and I think it makes us seem foolish—linking sexual freedom and abortion, for instance, with autonomy for Tibet."

"Then why are you here at all? Why join the Greens? Why spend so much time away from Helena, and practically move in here, if you won't even look at my books? Not even Thoreau."

His voice was so soft I could barely hear his reply. "I've told you before."

"Well, tell me again."

"I have beliefs."

"I know. That's exactly it. That's why I want to feed those beliefs with these incredible writers."

Pause. Pause. Then that same flattened voice: "I'm a more simple person than you, Petra."

"What does that mean?"

"I don't think about theory."

"What do you think about, then?"

Ah, the poor general. I heard the creak of springs as he sat on the bed.

"I really want to know, Emil. I'm . . . I'm fascinated."

"I can't explain."

"Yes, you can."

He didn't speak for a long while. When he did, he seemed stripped bare. "I . . . ever since leaving NATO, I have a rule for myself. I try to keep things simple."

"I don't know what that means."

"It's . . . Sometimes I don't even think about the words. I just try to hear—hear what I feel, as it were. Because I never want . . . I don't want . . ." He stopped and began again. "I slow my thoughts down. I try to get above them, if you understand my meaning. I . . . I see certain images that help me."

Her tone was more tender now, more listening. "What images?"

"It's too strange."

"Tell me."

"It's a memory. It helps me to become calm within myself. I can't even say where it comes from—isn't that strange? But when I feel clear, I make my response."

"But what does that *mean*? What image do you see in your mind? I don't understand. Give me an example."

"Okay," he spoke evenly. "You—standing there."

"What about me?"

"I hear you. I listen. I can see that you're angry. You want me to read more. Perhaps this worries you—you think I'm unschooled."

"I never said that."

"But since . . . since breaking with my life . . . since this change, I try not to pay attention to words only, Petra, not really. What I try to do is . . ." Again he paused, and I knew he was embarrassed by this focus on his inner world. He was such a private man. "I really don't believe this is any different from what other people do, when they visit their consciences and try to do what's right."

"Go on."

"Well, I simply try to listen. And if I pay attention, really pay attention, it will come to me, as it used to when I was a child, the simplest truths just pouring into my body, often when I was running, or playing sports." There was another long pause. I heard the springs of the mattress as she sat down. "What I see here, between us, what I see, is that you are—as you always are—tremendously passionate. That's the truth that I see. Your burning passion for things, and how I—"

I heard the bed creak again. Then I heard her say, "Go on."

"How I depend on it. How it touches me as nothing ever has."

I knew I should stop listening, but they could have closed the door if they wanted privacy. He said, "I'm so attracted to the fire in you. It feels sometimes as though you will burn me alive and I'll come out new."

"Come here."

At which point one of them did swing the door shut.

Alone in the kitchen, I felt astonished. This man had spoken so simply about listening to his heart, the steps he took to consult his conscience. Most astonishing, he had refused Petra's campaign of reading, and yet, in that refusal, he had somehow won her. He had even managed to turn *not reading* into a virtue! Staying away from fat texts by Emma Goldman now seemed to be yet another sign of *innere Führung*.

15

One People

Emil returned to Helena on many weekends and walked poor Felix along the river. She made no outright recriminations. No mention of Petra. Just dinner and the slow dripping of the kitchen tap. This was their deal. She would not be solely responsible for the dog's care. Her expectation was that he would burn Petra out of his system. It had happened before. Julia Kunst's gracious, formidable ass receding—setting, at last, like a vast moon.

Helena had placed a silver box with a smoky glass lid on a side table beside a long-necked vase, and the two objects, grouped so tentatively together, told a sad little story of her life now: they'd been purchased in the Hauptstrasse in Würzburg, wrapped in tissue, brought home, placed here or there, before finding a final resting place on this table. All done with such silence and care that viewing them now, Emil was inclined to hold his breath.

Monday came. She extended her papery cheek and he kissed it like Judas and felt a lurch in his stomach. She was his wife, and look what he was doing to her. It appalled him. Where was his inner leadership now? He was being as honest as he possibly could with Helena—no sneaking around, no secrets—and was hurting her far more than he'd ever hurt her

with lies. But what could he do? He wasn't giving up Petra.
That had become unthinkable.

At the Green office, a group had gathered around Gisela Fuchs,
a skinny, energetic woman of forty with wiry brown hair, and a
strong, aristocratic nose. Her feet were clad in handmade leather
boots. Somewhere far back, there was money in her family, Emil
had heard. Gisela belonged to the feminist torch bearers.

"Make way for the general," said a tough little fellow named
Jürgen Wolff. He'd suddenly appeared among the Greens, having
cut his teeth in the Frankfurt squatter movement. According to
Manfred, he was "a radical Sponti leftist." He stunk of Gauloises,
his fingers stained yellow, and looked like a gnome from a fairy
tale. It was rumoured that Jürgen had thrown more than a few
Molotov cocktails in his time. He'd been arrested many times
fighting the Schweinesystem, such a ridiculous, embarrassing
term. Emil flinched every time he heard it.

Petra said it was proof of the growing strength of the Greens
that a man like Jürgen would join them. "He's welcome with us
as long as he adheres to the principal of non-violence. And
besides, he's no threat. He may have been a big man in Frankfurt,
but here he's a bit player."

Emil wasn't so sure. The umbrella of the Greens sometimes
seemed excessively large.

He pushed his way through the gathering to the back, to join
Petra. He could feel the Greens appreciation of him, and he
smiled and even lifted a hand to wave at those he knew personally. He felt desirable. An older man in his prime. He was of use
to these people, and as a military man, he liked to be of use. After
the quiet of the weekend with Helena, it was a relief to be in this

room full of youth (though this thought brought an ache because Helena was, as usual, alone.)

Petra squeezed his arm. "Here you are at last."

"Why aren't you at the front?" he whispered.

"I'm letting Gisela shine."

"Power to the sisterhood?"

"How well you catch on."

Gisela Fuchs raised her eyebrows for silence and continued with her briefing. The press had discovered that the Bonn government had a secret depository of important cultural possessions holed away in a cement-encased chamber under the earth. Materials set aside for future generations. And why? Because of the real likelihood of nuclear war. "They are preparing for this nightmare at the same time as their policies bring it closer! How organized, how quintessentially like them. They've preserved a plan of Cologne Cathedral, but forgotten to preserve children. And not a single word of Schiller, or Goethe, or Thomas Mann. Who wants to be part of our response? We want to do something theatrical."

Emil saw scorn on Jürgen Wolff's elfin face, but Petra immediately put her hand up, and Emil knew that the "something theatrical" now included him.

Bundestag. Noon. Drizzling cold rain. Eight women, two by two, approached the group of supporters, who huddled together to keep warm. The women wore long black skirts, faces painted white, a ghostly procession. Each carried a "significant cultural possession." Gisela's was a funeral shroud on which her own face had been painted in pale relief—to indicate that living people were the country's first cultural possessions. Next came two

women holding children by the hand. Then came Petra and
Freya, looking like sombre goths, carrying leather-bound books:
Thomas Mann and Schlegel's translations of Shakespeare.

Emil had worn a suit, as he always did to these protests. He
looked around: a few government officials were coming and going,
which caused him to feel both weightless and embarrassed.

He watched the women place their offerings on a quilt in the
centre of the circle of supporters. The children, pleased and solemn,
sat cross-legged amongst the things. Now the costumed women
joined them, and everyone held hands. The drizzle stopped and
the sun cast a pale, sharp light. He looked from face to face. There
was the lean schoolteacher, with his beaked nose, chiselled lips,
heavily lidded eyes. He caught Emil's glance and smiled. There
was the plump theology professor who so often came to the demonstrations, her greying hair pulled back severely. But now her
face, rather than seeming potato-flaccid and homely, as it usually
did, was suffused with grace and forgiveness. *She would never harm
me*, he thought, *even if she knew everything I had ever done.*

What a gift such a thought was.

He held the gloved hands of two men, one on either side of
him, and they, too, would never harm him. He had done right to
follow the strange path that led him here, hard as it had been.
He'd done right to listen to the whispers of his body, because now
he was among his fellow humans, and not one of them would
raise a hand against him. And the faces around him glowed with
human beauty. He caught the eye of first one and then another.
The human family! The lump in his throat grew. Even the old
peace grandmother, who showed up at every demonstration, and
who looked so much like the Queen of England with her iron-
grey curls under a folding plastic rain hat—even she radiated love
in the strange overcast light.

16.

The Secret to Petra

One Sunday in Veitshöchheim, Emil, marooned with Helena, thought about making love to Petra. All morning he couldn't shake the images. He held them in his mind as he sliced the toast—a thin piece for Helena, a fat piece for himself—and as he delivered the toast to his wife in bed and then crossed to his office to unfold the newspaper, finding two articles about the Greens and one about himself.

Again he felt that pulse of desire. But it wasn't just desire; it was the sense that she was inhabiting him, listening to his thoughts. A visitation. She was like a hummingbird, coming close, wings moving at invisibly quick speeds, keeping him alive. He wanted to touch her, kiss her upturned face, hold it between his hands, then kiss her again, more roughly. He wanted to kneel, put his face into the seam of her jeans, smell her crotch.

The secret to Petra.

Briefly he imagined gathering a group of Greens together. Difficult, hairy Manfred, with his Birkenstocks and history of Marxism. *Das Kapital.* And that imp, Jürgen, and the starkly handsome Gisela Fuchs, and Freya with her bright, accusing eyes, and all the other followers, including the ex-lovers, the Irish trade unionist, the Hamburg artist.

I have found the secret to your leader—and he didn't mean that the tip of his tongue had moved around the sweet, hard curve of her clit, though there was that. The secret—and of course he must disperse the imaginary people he had gathered, because to say it right he must say it only to himself—the secret was that he had desires he'd never spoken of to anyone: to make love in all its forms, to a woman who seemed like a boy, a child, a man, as well as a woman. This was highly erotic to him, and as he sat in the sunshine with the newspaper, the thought of her slender hips, her small bottom and slight breasts made him groan aloud.

He always had to push her hair out of her eyes, the better to see her response as he penetrated her. Then her shyness after—this was like a child. As she lay naked and turned away, he saw the little-boy knobs of her spine. Yet she was fully a woman too, demanding and surprising, wanting sex this way and that way, suggesting tantric breathing, occasionally getting caught up in ideas, though sex (he knew this deeply) worked better when you suspended thought. More than once he had surprised her by covering her mouth with his hands. *Enough talking.* And she'd liked that! On top of everything else, she liked the feeling of giving up control. The surprise in her eyes as she realized her roiling brain could stop. That she could lie back on the pillow. Feel his tongue.

Her hard little button was so different from Helena's. Helena's was long and furled, and reminded him of Vienna somehow, of delicate teacups. Touching her there was like touching a piece of German history. But touching Petra ... It was like feeling between the legs of a woman-man—a boy-girl—feeling that sweet, hard little button clench under his mouth. Its surprising efficiencies.

17

The Fisherman

A cup of milk can be a cup of milk. Or it can be a cup of milk with sorrow attached. A motorcycle helmet on a broomstick in the garden can be a frivolous amusement of an afternoon—*Ha ha, nice scarecrow*—or it can be a reminder of what has been lost. I couldn't look at it now without remembering how Petra and I rode all the way to Günzburg, her straddling the seat behind me, inner thighs pressing against me. We'd found the house she'd lived in near the creek, then followed the creek to where it joined the Danube. We'd walked the charming half-timbered streets and had a beer in the local Rathskeller, and all the while I kept feeling this bright, sharp sensation in me, and I even thought, *Careful, Manfred, or you'll fall in love*—not realizing that these sensations, the feel of air on my face, *were* love, and that I was already gone.

Now, when I looked at the helmeted scarecrow, I thought if you scraped away my flesh, I'd be just like it. A stick.

This was a bad feeling and I wanted to shake it, but it was getting worse, not better. And repeating to myself *I like Emil, I admire Emil* didn't cleanse me. Their daily beauty made me ugly, to paraphrase Shakespeare. "The Bard," as Mother insisted on calling him, always with reverence, as she sat in her window corner, turning the pages of the massive volume she'd brought from Canada. Fondest possession. A book to explain every passion.

I was lucky, I suppose, that she read so much Shakespeare to me, in English (not Schlegel's beautiful translation, which she tried but put aside—her German was never very good). Her suffering brown head bent over the text, she got me fixated on "the Bard" too. Now I could recognize Iago when he rose in me.

I have 't; it is engender'd: hell and night
Must bring this monstrous birth to the world's light.

But I didn't have it. I had engendered nothing. I had only the impulse to cause them pain, because I was in pain.

Coming home one night after a difficult meeting, I found Petra curled in her alcove by the living room window, reading a book. I hovered by the door. Dusk had come early, and she'd kept the lights off, just as we'd been in the habit of doing when we were lovers. We'd enjoy the fall of evening, its way of creeping into a room and changing the shapes of things—breadbox, coats in the hallway—so that the commonplace became full of shadows and mystery.

"What are you reading?"

She flashed me the cover, so quickly I couldn't catch it. When I came close, I saw that she was reading, not some analysis of MIRVed ICBMs, but a large illustrated book of poetry. The page was open to the poem "Der Fischer," by Goethe.

She pulled back her feet to allow me to sit.

"We used to do this a lot," I said.

"I know. I miss it."

"Can you read it to me?"

"Do you want to hear?"

"Yes. Very much."

She began to read, forming the words that sounded so much like water moving, water churning.

Das Wasser rauscht', das Wasser schwoll,
Ein Fischer saß daran,

You know the story. Out of the water comes a nixe, a magical woman of the river who scolds the fisherman for his cruelty. She tempts the fisherman to come with her, and he slides into the water, never to be seen again.

It made me think of my mother, tempted by my father, the watery scar on his cheek. I thought of myself, too, unable to let go of Petra. How the murky waters of love fascinate us, making life on the shore so dull.

When Petra finished, she put aside the book and beckoned to me.

"Can we sit as we used to? I'd like that."

I rested against the window frame, and she laid her head on the curve of my chest. Outside I could see the outline of the neighbour's fence, his pile of tires, which in the last light could have been anything. Stars were coming out. First one, then another. We sat like that for a long time.

"Ah, there it is," she said.

"What?"

"You still love me."

"You know I do."

"I love you too, dear Manfred," but the *dear* was a snag. It meant "like a brother." Like a friend. But friends sometimes end up as lovers again, and lovers become life partners. They look back on the rocky path that brought them to live together forever, and they laugh. They tell their children, *Oh, I was in love with your mother for ages. And then one night, as dark came on . . .*

I was on this train of thought, stroking her hair, when I realized she was shaking. She turned and put her face into my chest and wept soundlessly, crying so hard a wet spot bloomed on my shirt. I said soft things. I held her, and eventually the worst of it was over.

"Do you want to talk?"

She shook her head, sat up. I went to the bathroom and brought back toilet paper. She laughed, and took a large wad and dried her face. Blew her nose. "I'm sorry to dump this on you."

"You can, you know."

"I just feel so alone," she said. "People leave me."

"You mean your father?"

"And everybody else. They're so far away—my mother, my stepfather—and they don't give a shit about me. I send them press clippings. They don't even bother to write back." She wiped her nose again. "You know, I thought I saw my father the other day on the bus. He was sitting near the driver, on the side seat, reading a book. It's funny, I often think of my father as having a bit of a tadpole look to his face, which is because of a photo I have of him, I think. Big brown eyes and a soft mouth. Anyway, there was a man looking just like that, and for a moment I froze—I was so sure it was him. But then he met my eyes, and there was no recognition. I could see he was a complete stranger. And then it hit: with all the things I'm doing, if my father wanted to find me, he could. Always. He'd see my face in the papers. Recognize my name. But he doesn't bother."

If he's alive, I thought, but I didn't say it. Instead, I asked, "What does your mother say about him leaving?"

"What *does* my mother say?" She made a sour face. "That's such a good question. She always says he was not a man who could stay, and that she was lucky he left—yes, lucky he took off, and that my reliable stepfather, Commander Kelly, stepped in. She was saved from her folly by an American!"

"Just as we all were."

"Exactly." She looked over at me. "I really remember my father's face—not just from pictures, but as he was. He had gaunt cheekbones and really kind eyes. I remember him leaning over my bed, telling me that there was a man in the moon. Then my mother calling from the next room that it was a woman in the moon. But my father insisted it was a man. Every time I see that face in the moon, I think of him." She paused. "What a pair we are, you and I. I feel for you, too, you know—those awful stories of your father hitting you with the belt."

I nodded. She knew all about this, knew it was part of who I was.

"I just think, with these fathers, these fathers of ours, that they must have been terribly wounded," she said, "or they would never have done what they did. Your father's beatings. My father *vanishing*." She winced. "Would you vanish on me?"

"Never."

"Yes, well, you're special."

We were silent for awhile, and when she spoke again it seemed natural that she was now speaking of Emil. "He says I open doors for him," she said.

"Which is funny, because he is always throwing open doors for the ladies. I saw him do it for Gisela, and she practically bit his head off."

"I don't mean literal doors. Doors to life."

"I know that's what you mean, Petra."

"But he's a man of his word, and so he will not desert Helena. It's not in his code of honour. A wife is . . ." She stopped, and I knew she had been about to say *forever*. She straightened. "Imagine me of all people crying because I can't have a man to myself. It's ridiculous. Yet I hate how he goes to her almost every weekend. And he has secrets with her, and all the stuff about wanting children, which he has confided in me. They wanted to have babies, but they couldn't. She couldn't. Because of . . . well, I suppose I can tell you. Because of things that happened to her in the war. She got an infection that makes it impossible to carry a child to term."

"I'm so sorry. That's terrible."

"I know. He wants to be with me, but he feels so obligated. He can't just walk away. And on top of all that . . ." Here she closed her eyes. "He has a sort of pact with her. An agreement. They made it years ago, when he had taken another lover. Oh, yes, I'm not the first! He said no matter what, he'd always come back to Helena, and be with her when they got old."

"That's a pretty shitty pact. Where's the honour in that?"

"It has a constancy to it, at least."

"You're a feminist—you don't need me to spell it out. That's terrible for both women, and totally self-serving. He can fool around, but his wife gets his old age. He should patent that."

"Look. He feels a deep concern for the well-being of his wife. I'm not going to fault him for that. Even if it seems hard to understand, politically. He's actually trying to be open with both of us."

"Ha ha. He learned that from the professor of openness herself."

"I know."

"It's fate coming full circle." I couldn't resist. "When we were together, openness was like a stick you kept hitting me with."

"Stop it!"

"It was." But I kissed her hair, to show—to show what? To show I could weather it.

"But you know what it also means—this pact with Helena?" She breathed in deeply, and I could feel her wanting to cry again, then stopping herself. "It means he is hers. Ultimately. I may be just an interim *thing*." She hit the word *thing* like it was disgusting.

Perhaps I ought to have taken heart. After all, this story meant that at some point in the future he would give Petra up. But instead I simply felt a kind of hollow amazement.

She wanted it to be forever.

Petra of the free sex, the multiple lovers, the we-must-learn-to-share, that's-how-we'll-change-the-world blah, blah, blah.

She was hooked.

18.

Meanwhile, Helena

Helena telephoned her friend Stephanie, but Stephanie didn't return the call. This meant that Helena's earnest, quivering voice would sit forever on Stephanie's answering machine. Or that it had been erased immediately. Actually, Helena didn't know what had happened to her message, and didn't want to.

She had always found it difficult to make friends. In many ways, the formalities and orchestrated events of being a general's wife had suited her perfectly. When she'd gone into the shops and galleries of Würzburg, she'd been known, and this respect had greased the wheels of her life. Now the shopkeepers kept her waiting.

Or they were kind to her.

The dressmaker, Trudy, said that Helena had the most elegant figure, and that she made the clothes hang perfectly, as a model would. But Helena knew that Trudy was one of the kind ones, because Helena was a ghost. Yes, she was a ghost. She could visit every street in Dresden in her mind. She could smell the lilac bushes beside the stone walls of Loschwitz, the nearby village.

Every morning she emptied the remainder of the bottle of gin down the drain. But then, at night, she rooted around and found the other hidden bottle at the back of her bedroom closet, and with an almost sacred relish she opened it and fixed herself a gin and tonic, and let the other ghosts come as they would. They rose out of the birches on the far side of the river, they swam and danced, and she wanted to cry at the beauty of them.

After the first drink, she saw friends from her girlhood putting wreaths of flowers in each other's hair, daisies and sweet peas they'd collected in the Loschwitz graveyard. She remembered floating down the Elbe in the rowboat, dressed as Ophelia, her maiden aunt taking photographs.

The ghosts were friendly after the first drink. Less so after the second. Then they came as something terrible. Magdalena's family gone in the night, the apothecary taken over by Herr Franz, who had worked for Magdalena's father for years. Helena remembered seeing Magdalena from the bus window one day, after Peter went to fight in the war. She was walking through the streets of Loschwitz with a yellow star on her jacket, hair covered with a scarf, head down. How different she seemed from the proud girl of Peter's infatuation, and Helena had looked away. Now she wished she'd gotten off and run back, but everything was different, and she couldn't, because Magdalena was a pariah, just as Helena was now, and should be, because she never, never ran back, only saw Magdalena's covered head through the bus window.

One night while lying on the living room floor, she looked up and saw her brother, Peter, at the front window, looking in. But when he uncupped his hand from his eyes, it was Emil. He came through the door and picked her up and carried her into the bedroom and placed her on the bed. He didn't even bother to take off her clothes, just laid her there like a sack, and she said, "How is your lady friend?"

He gave no answer, though she noticed his jaw tense. She thought she could smell Petra on his fingers, which were now tenderly pushing the hair from her eyes. There was love between Emil and Petra, and Emil had love for her. Love enough for everyone. And yet she was completely lost.

He wiped her mouth with his handkerchief. She ought to have felt humiliated, but his soft ministrations moved her. And again she felt the sharp, smart girl in his hands, little Petra hands, so like a monkey's. She wished she could warn him. *You can't go back—you can't erase time. The ghosts don't let you move around like that.* He was so shallow, with his manly resolve; he didn't know the rules at all. And yet this shallowness of his moved her too. It was almost like innocence.

"You look thin," he said. "We'll go for lunch tomorrow. Would you like to?"

"No. Not in Würzburg. People stare."

"They don't."

He had no idea.

"I saw you two on the television yesterday."

"About the missiles."

She nodded. "That woman can talk."

Emil laughed. "I think she could explain the world, then turn it inside out and explain it again." He bent over, unlacing his shoes, and then he was in bed beside her, holding her gently from behind.

She closed her eyes, let his familiar body rock hers.

Thirty-three years of marriage left such an imprint on the body, the molecules. And Helena almost felt sorry for the girl, with her fierce voice and monkey hands, that she didn't know this basic fact about marriage.

19.

Yad Vashem

As that year, 1982, moved into a long, hot summer, we prepared for our big election push—to try to get Petra, myself, Emil and other Greens into the Bundestag. We had six short months to pull this off. "And if we succeed, we'll be well placed to stop the insanity of the nuclear missile deployment." Petra told this to two young men on a Bonn street corner. She and I were passing out leaflets. They didn't seem convinced and walked on.

Petra turned to me. "I wanted to speak to you about something. After the election, whether it's successful or not, Emil and I have decided to move in together."

I watched a child cross the road, holding his mother's hand. Her grip was too tight, and you could see he wanted to pull away, but she wouldn't let his hand go. As soon as they were across, he pulled it free. "Goodness," I said. "A house of your own. That sounds like the pinnacle of domesticity. Does Helena have any say in this? Or will she live with you?"

A car honked. We gave a wave.

"Don't," she said.

"Don't what?"

"Don't be bitter."

"I was simply enquiring after Helena."

"She drinks a great deal," Petra said, slowly. "And this

predated me. Emil says there are pills involved as well. It's not easy."

"Which? The drinking? The sharing?"

She laid a hand on my arm.

"What?"

"We need to draw on our best selves for this. It is, for me at least, a lesson in expansiveness."

I saw that she meant it. She was trying to conquer her own jealousy. And for a moment I was impressed, but then I couldn't resist: "But you're the one he's expanding with. Helena may see it differently."

She cocked her head, considering. "I really don't wish her anything but good. If anything, I try to think of her as a sister. She suffered a great deal in the war. She and Emil are bound in that way. I know that."

Ahead of us, in a small café, a waiter was going after leaves with a broom. A cyclist whizzed past. I'd thought I was used to Petra and the general. The sex. The way she softened when his name was spoken. But this. Living together in a little place of their own, with what? Cats? A child? It took me by surprise. I felt tugged by something dark. Imagine a Renaissance devil, one of those skinny creatures at the top edge of a fresco, riding the air in a bowl steered by a wooden spoon. "The war," I heard myself say. "Yes, it binds everyone of that generation."

She had turned away. I couldn't judge her expression. "Our gentle general was once a Nazi soldier," I said. "We forget that."

Now I got her scissors look. "I don't like how you say that."

"I'll try to say it more gently. Because all at once we're being gentle, aren't we?" I waited a moment and then relaunched: "Do you ask him about the war? I'm curious."

She let a series of cars go by. Then she said, "No, Manfred."

"No, you never ask him?"

"No to all of this."

"Come on, Petra."

"I won't be party to it."

"Really?"

She reached up to my beard. Pulled away a bit of fluff. "There," she said, "that's been bothering me for ages. Now let's end this conversation. We can't be standing on the corner arguing when we need to be talking to people and winning votes."

I nodded.

"What?"

"You have never asked him. I'm realizing this."

"Stop it!" She actually reached up, childishly, to cover her ears. "It feels vile, Manfred. He's been through so much. He's trying so hard."

"What does that even mean, 'He's trying so hard'? Don't we have an obligation to the past?"

She smiled at a stranger in a duffle coat, pulling him towards her with her radiance. It seemed to come off her in licks of flame.

"Where did he fight in the war?" I persisted.

The duffle-coated man took a pamphlet and went on his way. Petra turned to me again. "Emil is an *extraordinary man*, Manfred, hard as it may be for you to believe that. He's not like so many in his generation."

"Yet he was also a Nazi soldier in a Nazi war."

"Is that what you see when you look at him? I pity you, then, and all your sixty-eighter brothers and sisters who lock yourselves in the past, condemning everyone. What I see is a man desperate to move forward, to create good in a complex world." She paused. "And as for the situation with Helena, we are all doing the very best that we can."

———

There is a well-known word in German that means coming to terms with the past. *Vergangenheitsbewältigung.* One of those mouthful words that our beautiful language excels at producing. I'd explored this phrase at university in West Berlin a decade earlier, poring over my Adorno and my Marcuse and the Mitscherlichs' *The Inability to Mourn,* which I carried everywhere in my backpack. It detailed all the sins of our fathers (and mothers): their failure to face their Nazi collusion; all the dodging, excusing, forgetting; the use of defence mechanisms to ward off the intensity of guilt; a dance of forgetfulness, excuses, quick grabs at absolution, blaming others.

I thought of this as I lay in bed that night, wondering about Petra's surprising blankness on the subject of Emil's war. Really, she had surprised me. I had assumed that in bed, coiled in the sweat- and semen-soaked sheets, they had traced each other's pasts, as she had with me, calling out the hurts and old pains, the secrets.

I didn't *try* to do a single thing. Yet, looking back, I think my pointed questions to Petra released a sort of pheromone of distrust into the air. That's the best way I can describe it. An invisible substance, like a gas leak in a house.

Several days later, we called a press conference to announce data from an omnibus poll showing that individual Green candidates were polling neck and neck with many in the SPD, with Petra in the lead! We couriered out a press advisory, and after some argument about who should break the news, we put Emil and Petra at the table, with Jürgen and Gisela available for interviews.

At the packed conference, the questions were flying. All at once we were being taken seriously. If elected, would we form a coalition with the Social Democrats? How would we work with other like-minded parties? If cooperation was out of the question, were we even trying to acquire political power?

I was at the back, as usual, press releases clutched to my chest. From this vantage point, I saw Rainer Beckman from the *Frankfurter Allgemeine Zeitung* raise his hand.

"Herr Gerhardt," he said. "Coming close to political power in this way calls for additional scrutiny, one feels."

Emil gave him an open smile. Such a winning man. Really, one could feel our poll numbers increase every time he smiled.

Rainer continued, "The war crimes tribunals have, with justification, focused on the crimes of Hitler's inner circle, and the SS, and those who committed the worst depredations in the death camps. Yet more and more evidence shows that the regular German soldiers of the Wehrmacht had much to be responsible for. Can you tell us about your experiences during the Nazi period?"

A pause. People turned to look at Rainer, and someone at the back of the room hissed, though it may have been a tense outbreath. Everybody seemed to feel that this question simply wasn't fair play, especially when it was addressed to our Green general. Even Jürgen, the bad boy of the Greens, looked concerned.

Emil cleared his throat, leaned forward and spoke into the array of media microphones. "I was in the Hitler Youth. That is a well-known fact."

"Do you look back at those experiences with regret?"

Emil glanced at Petra. I felt the flutter of her returning glance.

"The words 'Hitler Youth' can inspire nothing but regret. This goes without saying."

"Tell us anyway," Rainer retorted, and there was a release of laughter. Again, that thickening in the air. Emil tugged at his tie. He seemed as surprised as the rest of us that the conference had veered in this direction.

"I was in the Hitler Youth. We simply all were—the boys my age. It was compulsory, you know."

A scribble of pencils.

"As for regret . . . How can I say this properly? This is the main thing I feel, looking back. It was a terrible time, and we—I—played a part. And yet, it allows me now to look at this brainwashing and say to myself, *Never again.*" His face was strained. It was interesting to watch, in a terrible way. "This is why I must now say no to any new mass insanity. This is why I oppose the deployment of nuclear missiles on West German soil, with their first-strike capacity, their hair-trigger responsiveness. We must learn from the past."

Scribble, scribble, scribble, scribble.

Then off he went, talking about NATO's double-track position from a strategic and military point of view, and this wave of grey dullness soon made the media flip their pads closed and wrap up.

"What was Rainer trying to achieve?" Jürgen asked, as he, Emil, Petra and I drove towards a meeting after the press conference.

"I suppose he felt it was worth asking," Petra said cautiously. She was in the front seat, beside Emil, who was driving. I couldn't see the expression on either of their faces. "Still, it took attention away from our news." Her voice was soft, as though she was discussing a faraway star.

"We ask it of other politicians," I said. "We ask it of judges. We ask questions. It's part of a healthy society."

"Of course," she said.

"It was indecent." Jürgen leaned forward. "A divisive tactic to undermine us. I was pleased by how you handled it, Emil."

"Oh, well," Emil managed.

"What do you think, Emil?" I asked.

He had both hands carefully placed on the leather steering wheel, and he didn't turn or look in the rear-view mirror. "It's their right to ask questions," he said at last. "I'm not afraid to answer any of them."

I felt a sort of pity for him at that moment, mixed with respect. Not only must he give everything to get us elected, called on daily to provide gravitas and middle-class respectability, but now he must fight on a new flank. Nevertheless, when Jürgen suggested that, for the next conference, we put Freya up front with Petra, I said no, not a good idea. Better to let them go at him again, if that was what was in the air.

So at our next briefing, Emil was again at the table, a small, nervous frown on his face. Rainer threw the question on the table again, like a large and trembling fish. Every member of the press looked up from their notebooks, involuntary smiles on their faces. I heard the clock ticking at the back of the room.

"How old were you when you joined the Hitler Youth?"

"I wouldn't say 'joined.'"

"When you were recruited, then."

"Not that either. There wasn't much free will involved."

"How old were you?"

"Eleven. Twelve."

"Did you see anything wrong with it?"

A sigh. An actual sigh. "*Now*, of course. *Then*, we didn't have your gift of insight."

Narrow laughter. People weren't quite sure how to take this.

"Were your parents members of the Nazi Party?"

"My father died in the war. My mother raised me alone. And yes, she was, in fact, a great believer in Nazism. I'm sorry to report this. It causes me pain to remember. She was a believer in 'the Führer.'" He made quote marks with his hands around "the Führer" and then dropped his hands abruptly. "I volunteered for the army. I would have been drafted into it, but I joined on my own. I wanted to be a soldier. I suppose one could say I was pleasing my mother. But I was also pleasing myself. This is the truth."

"You wanted to be a soldier in Hitler's army."

"Yes, Rainer. Exactly."

"Why did you want that?

Sigh. "We were a brainwashed culture. It is hard to look back and make sense of it."

"Where did you serve?"

Petra looked like she wanted to break in and speak. Yet she was also searching Emil's face. What was she looking for? Something definitive. Something that allowed her to breathe out.

He recited his rank, his battalion—45th Panzer Division—and where he'd been stationed, the Don. He paused, then leaned forward. "I was among countless other German soldiers. The same story. It was an unremarkable war experience."

Unremarkable. At that word, a shiver ran down my arms. For some reason I heard my mother's voice, how she would explain my father to me: *He means well. You must love him and forgive him.* I almost wanted to put up my hand and ask, *Unremarkable? What does that mean?* I looked at Petra. She had a small frozen smile on her face.

Now Emil began to describe what he meant: gruelling travel across the steppes with his battalion, documented by countless others. Training for tank action at a town near the front, then deployment. A battle in a winter wilderness, terrible clothing. The struggle for winter boots.

"Town?"

He paused.

"What town or village were you deployed to, Herr Gerhardt?"

"It was a medium-sized town in the Ukraine called Krivoy Rog. I believe the name means 'Crooked Horn,' because of the shape of the river." He was wounded twice, he continued. Once in the shoulder, once in the leg. He was awarded the Iron Cross.

Afterwards, I followed Petra into the hallway and found her hovering over a table of peace buttons.

"That was odd," I said. "*Unremarkable.*"

Her face, when she raised it, was carefully blank. "I don't see why."

"Such a strange word to use. I can imagine war being many things, but unremarkable is not one of them."

"That's because you're not a soldier. For a professional soldier, everything is different. I'm amazed you cannot see that. Really, Manfred, you're always looking for the worst."

"No, I'm not."

She deposited a mark in the can, picked up a large sunflower button and attached it to her coat lapel.

"What are you so afraid of?" My voice came out with more force than I'd meant it to.

She frowned, then shook her head. "It's you," she said. "You who bring fear into every equation. Your jealousy distorts you, Manfred. It's unbecoming." She turned and went back into the room.

That night in bed, I thought about what she had said, and her tone of voice—cold and angry. Was my jealousy distorting me? Or was I right to applaud this sudden turn of events? Emil was trying so hard to be Green, to discover, as he'd said, a new way to be German. All well and good. Yet, said another voice in me (one with the weight of history behind it), if he wants to be Green, maybe he needs to feel the plough a bit. Get dug up. Why should he wander into our generation's garden, make use of the power and sunshine of our new movement, and never have to account for his life before?

I turned on the light and got out of bed. I sat naked at my desk and put paper into my typewriter.

To Whom it May Concern. No. *Dear Friend in Truth.* Definitely not. I settled on *Dear Sir or Madam.*

The letter was to Yad Vashem, the Jerusalem library that holds the world's largest repository of Nazi war crimes. Could they shed light on a town named Krivoy Rog in western Ukraine? It had been a station for the Wehrmacht, including the 45th Panzer Division, and I was writing to find out if there were any reports of misdoings from that region.

With kind regards, etcetera.

The letter spilled out within minutes, and I realized, as I walked to the village mailbox, that I'd had it in my mind, pre-composed. I opened the mailbox and slipped the envelope in. I felt my mother watching me, reproaching me for my lack of tenderness. *Leave the old men alone. They mean well.* I could hear her voice, suffering like the sea, urging compassion.

I stood at the corner for a long time. It was a cold, ugly little village without even a proper coffee shop. I was pretty sure it had looked roughly the same for five hundred years. The houses were stone, the cobbles ancient beneath my feet. Not that long ago, some of the older people of this town must have gotten into their cars—Volkswagens or maybe even horse carts—and headed to Bonn to see the Führer. Not that long ago. The past felt like it was pressing against my skin.

Fathers. Lately, my own father had been trying to reach me, leaving messages at the farmhouse, his voice more frail than I remembered. He'd seen my name in the newspaper, he said, and he wished me well in the upcoming election. I knew I ought to call him back, yet each time I erased his message.

The last time I'd seen him was three years earlier. Dear god. What had I screamed at him? I'd slammed the front door so hard the adjoining store window shook, and for an awful minute I'd thought it would shatter. I had shouted something about his treatment of my mother. I'd insinuated—this came to me clearly, out of a cloudy miasma of remembered anger—that living with him had made her want to die, to give up and succumb to death. The two tumours, one in the brain, one in the bone. It seemed almost impossible that I'd yelled that, yet I had, the words seeming to belong not to me but to a fire in my stomach that demanded expression.

I walked briskly to the next corner, where there was a telephone booth. One bold action deserved another. I stepped inside the rank-smelling box, inserted my coins and dialled Freya's number; Katrina was staying with her. I felt loose in my skin, unsettled.

When Katrina picked up, I said her name, and she knew at once that it was me. "What?" she said. "What do you want?"

"Can I come see you? I want to talk."

But that was a lie, I didn't want to talk. And she knew it.

I was a little surprised she let me come. But there was a logic, and Katrina had left her own sort of trail: her fury at me was actually a signal that she still cared. As soon as she opened the door, she began in on me with righteous anger: I was to leave my shoes by the door, not track in mud, and why was I visiting so late? She wasn't just someone I could come and go from; she had work in the morning. And where was Petra? Why not bring her along, and the general too—or was Petra busy tonight? "Women aren't just puppets, Manfred."

"It's nice to see you too."

I followed her to the couch. Her hair was platinum, cut short in a stubbly fuzz. It looked good.

"I hope you know I spent most of last night discussing you in a feminist support circle."

"Did you come to any conclusions?"

"We just decided that men are useless. Why are you here?"

"I wanted to see you."

"Great, just what I need."

But I could tell she was pleased.

In the kitchen, Katrina reached for the teapot on the windowsill above the counter. I put my arms around her and held her against me, and I could feel her relaxing, responding. I pressed myself against her, and she pushed her butt against me. There was something horse-like in how she did this, and it turned us both on. She turned, and I grabbed her and pushed her against the kitchen counter, then hoisted her up, and it felt animal and raw, and she kept saying, "Careful, don't break Freya's dishes," and I kept saying, "Shush, don't worry, they're safe."

Basically, I fucked my way out of my depression.

20

My Brush with the Spy World

Now I must take a detour into a story from my past.

In 1968, when I left my father's house in Freiburg at eighteen to go to the Freie Universität Berlin, I was barely on speaking terms with him. My mother caught the brunt of my anger. She was always between us, wringing her hands. *He loves you deep down. He has trouble expressing things. Remember, he was a prisoner.*

"He beat me, Mutti. You remember? The butter you put on my skin?"

"And the bandages," she sighed. "Yes. I learned later you must never cover a break in the skin, as I did. There was infection. I didn't know any better."

"So it was your fault? Don't you see what he does? And you, too. Everything twists around so that you are to blame. Where is he tonight? Where was he last weekend?"

"Oh, stop, Manfred, please!"

And I did stop, because she looked so crumpled and defeated. But I took my anger with me to West Berlin, where it became fuel for politics. I was there to study political science and history, eventually intending to write my master's thesis, reading books that isolated, like a virus, the German postwar malaise, but suddenly all hell broke loose. Classes were cancelled, and the words on everybody's lips were: *Benno Ohnesorg has been murdered by the police.*

They said this, and I thought, *Who is Benno Ohnesorg?* But I couldn't ask the other students without looking ridiculous; besides, as it turned out, nobody actually knew him personally, famous as he was to become. His fame was in his death. Alive, he was merely a boy in the wrong place, a young protester running from a demonstration against the shah of Iran, where the police had wielded batons and the students responded with stones. Benno Ohnesorg was cornered by a police officer who shot him, point blank, in the head.

We boycotted classes. We sat on the floor instead of sitting in classroom chairs. We shouted at the professors. We cried out, *One of us has been murdered!* Patrice Holms, an exchange student, sat cross-legged near me, weeping openly. I realized I wanted to cry too, that the coal dust in my body was being released, that my generation would release it.

Then we were on the streets and the police were descending on us, raising their truncheons. They brought their sticks down on Patrice, and I saw her startled face and then blood flowing from a gash in her head.

But how do I get from there to a daycare—and one of the seminal moments of my life?

In the weeks after Patrice was hospitalized (when she recovered, she fled back to the States, to raise her children on American cheese and Tang), in that time of political confusion when taking to the streets and the long march through the institutions both looked useless, my politics of protest sputtered and ran out. I wanted a hammer with which to smash the system that had smashed my friend's head, but no hammer was to be had. I dropped out of school and took work in an alternative kindergarten (children, the sixty-eighter creed ran, were our only trustable future), and I joined the Communist Party and swore my allegiance (briefly, all this so briefly) to the socialist workers' system of East Germany. Briefly, I actually believed in it.

Magnus Isaacson was my main colleague at the daycare. He was a tall man in his late twenties, taller than me, even, with a great head of sandy hair like a lion's mane, which he tied back in a ponytail, revealing his strong, freckled forehead. I was very taken with him, as I think most everyone was, particularly the mothers who dropped off their kids. He could spend hours on all fours pretending to be a horse, for instance, yet he was efficient when need be, good with the diapering, quick with the washing up, and never seemed to be bothered by the mindlessness of the work.

Still, Magnus also had an air of the adventurer about him, in his velvet jacket over an old waffle-weave T-shirt. Sometimes I thought his name should be Hercule or Constantine—that he should be travelling to remote places for archeological digs, not stuck in a baby-and-toddler room.

The two of us fell into a pattern of going for beers after work. Now here it comes.

After a year of dull but oddly satisfying meetings in basements (a kind of Marxist flagellation, if you will), I decided to quit the party and the daycare to go to Wyhl, where big nuclear power protests were brewing. *Yes, do*, the party said to me. *Do leave us, and would you mind doing it publicly? Express some vociferous disgust.* A signal, of course, that they wanted to make use of me.

Then they moved their chess piece—and guess who it was? My very own co-worker, Magnus Isaacson. We were changing diapers at the diaper station, if you please, and I'd just told him I planned to quit, to go to Wyhl and join the anti-nuclear protests. Something was brewing there, I said. It was exciting to see the local community fight the nuclear industry. David and Goliath. And David might once again win.

He was, as I've said, quick with the pins, his broad hands freckled, the backs covered in soft blond hair. Up went the rubber pants, over the new diaper. Down went the child, to crawl among the pillows. He sniffed the next baby's behind, made a face, then laid him out on the change table.

He said, "It's not enough anymore to protest in the disorderly way that's happening at Wyhl."

I wondered where this was going. I wondered if Magnus Isaacson was going to advise me to stay in West Berlin, *because children are the future.*

"You're too smart to be working in a daycare for the rest of your life," he said.

"I'm quitting tomorrow."

"For Wyhl? You and I both know that these protestors will achieve nothing unless they have an inner direction."

I agreed.

"Do you want an assignment, Manfred?" he asked. "Something for the people?"

When he said *for the people*, I knew he meant for the GDR, for the East German spy network, for the Stasi's operations in the West. I felt a tug in my stomach. I looked up at his face, and he finished with the baby, picked him up and winked at me. Seriously! This large, attractive man, this man who did so much quiet folding of the cloth diapers, organizing of the wooden toys, who helped the children into their snowsuits with endless patience and was so successful with women—he winked at me, and I saw, just like that, that he was living a double life, and that it was precisely this double life that allowed him to be content with such a simple, unassuming existence. His secret endowed every diaper change with meaning. He was a spy.

He tried again later, over beers.

"We can stop this nuclear power plant," he said. "I do believe we can. This new group of activists has far more patience than we sixty-eighters ever had. So go and join, but don't forget that we are trying to replace systems. You can help us inject meaning into the movement. Do you know what I mean? Just make sure the movement understands that its purpose isn't just to protest nuclear power, but also to replace the system." He gave me his completely charming grin, the grin he'd used to seduce countless mothers. "What do you say?"

I was tempted. I wanted so badly to find Political Meaning, and here was a life of meaning being offered to me. My task? Just try to direct the mass movement to behave sensibly, and report their doings every quarter year on a free trip to West Berlin. A beer with Magnus.

I shook my head. "I think I'll pass," I said. "But thank you." I kept it polite. I didn't want to end up in a body bag in the Spree.

"Well, I must be going," Magnus said. And he tipped back his glass and finished the last of his beer, then stood up and walked away, like a giraffe that had finished mating and no longer had any interest in its long-legged partner.

That was my brush with the spy world.

I learned later that Covert Influence Operations was the Stasi category for the work Magnus had offered, wherein a network of cooperative agents attempted to keep the various Western movements for peace and ecology "on the right track." This meant gathering intelligence, subtly influencing the outcome of debates and "neutralizing" those who wanted to focus on Eastern Bloc weapons as well as Western ones, or on human-rights abuses behind the Iron Curtain. The movement should be serious, too, of course. Credible. Because the Western mass movements were only useful, according to the GDR spymasters, when they didn't fall prey to feminist, tree-hugging, chaotic loopiness.

But then came the Greens, rising to power out of the protests at Wyhl. And what were we if not the epitome of freewheeling criticism and "useless" tree hugging and feminist, anarchic, spontaneous love? The energy of the Greens was the very opposite of the squashed-flat totalitarian impulses that fuelled the GDR, so of course they wanted to control us from the get-go. But they found they couldn't, because we were powerful. Oh, yes. A force to be reckoned with. Uncompromising and real.

I mention all this because, in the late summer of 1982, the Stasi reached for us again.

But this time it was through the general.

You might say that at this point I was *playing* at disliking Emil Gerhardt, getting the taste of it in my mouth. I confided to Freya that I agreed with Rainer and his recent articles about Emil's Nazi past. We ask for a reckoning from our judges. We ask it of all the old fathers. Why not ask it of him? Freya agreed, though when I approached Jürgen, he shook his head, saying we needed the general to give us credibility and popularity. Then came an invitation in the mail—heavy paper stock, a Vienna address debossed into the thick, cream-tinted letterhead—that gave me an actual reason to dislike Emil.

He and Petra continued to plan to move in together, but for now he slept most weeknights at the farmhouse, with occasional weekends with Helena. One midmorning in late July, he arrived at the farmhouse looking flushed. "Something rather interesting has happened." He took a letter from his breast pocket and laid it on the table.

"What is it?" Petra asked.

"You'll see."

Petra and I read it together.

"Do you know these men?" Petra asked.

Emil nodded.

"Generals for Peace," Petra said out loud.

Naturally a very select group of retired top-level military commanders . . . informal working group . . . speaking at conferences, writing briefs and chapters for publications, promoting the ends of peace and co-existence between East and West.

I said, "You should check into this before you sign on the dotted line."

Emil glanced up. "The organization seems beyond reproach."

"It is!" Petra exclaimed. "Manfred, you're always so gloomy."

"Lots of communist front groups have Vienna addresses. You should find out if they're connected with the World Peace Council."

"Remind me again . . ." Emil said.

"It's the main Soviet peace front group. The front group of front groups."

"He's not a fool," Petra snapped. "He knows about the World Peace Council. But this group of generals—generals!—has nothing to do with that. Come on, Manfred."

"I'd check it out before I signed on the dotted line," I repeated.

"What's with this dotted line? There is no dotted line."

I read the letter spread on the table. The group consisted of eight ex-generals, all of whom had stepped away from NATO because of their reservations about its *dangerous and warlike policies vis-à-vis the nuclear missiles.* I could see no flaw.

Then I glanced at the signature. *Magnus Isaacson, Secretary to the Generals for Peace, on behalf of General Stathis Stathopoulos.*

I read it again.

I shook my head, more shocked than gleeful at being right. Magnus Isaacson appeared in my mind's eye—a face like that of a large dog lying by a fire, a noble retriever or other hunting dog. His brown eyes and sandy lashes and long nose, slightly bulbous at the end.

"I know him! He's renowned in Berlin circles. He's a recruiter for the Stasi."

"Listen to yourself. Don't be ridiculous," Petra said.

"He tried to recruit me!"

Both of them looked at me as though I was a madman. And then Petra laughed. "He has these flashbacks to being a sixty-eighter in West Berlin, and everything is spy this and spy that."

"I'm serious, Petra. He tried to recruit me just before I headed to Wyhl. He wanted an informant at the nuclear energy protests."

"How did you know him?"

"Actually, we both worked at a daycare."

"Terrifying." She raised her eyebrows. "I don't know how you survived."

"We were doing our bit for women and children. He was a serious GDR sympathizer."

"Big deal. So were you at one point, if I'm not mistaken. Besides, you're the one who always tells me we have to work around such groups. We all manage with the World Peace Council coming to demonstrations. But look at these names. Stathis Stathopoulos! He's the Greek commander. I've heard him speak. He's beyond reproach."

She turned back to Emil. "We'll have to put this immediately into a release. This will show those people who say it's only one type of Green who opposes the missiles. We have doctors and lawyers, and now we have Generals for Peace." She leaned forward and kissed him. "I'm proud of you."

"But—" I said.

She flashed me a glance, and then she snatched up the letter and read the generals' names aloud, military letters like small alphabets dragged behind each surname. "They give us credibility," she said. This was exactly what we needed to expand the movement and draw in centrist voters. Surely I could see the usefulness?

I left to sit in the garden. The ugly scarecrow of a broomstick with its motorcycle helmet watched me from the vegetable patch.

21.

The Die-In

"They want real blood, if possible."

It was two months later, mid-September, and Petra was talking about the Berrigan brothers, the famous US nuclear protestors. We were to drive with them the next morning to a field outside the US Army base where the nuclear missiles were to be deployed. A huge demonstration had been planned, at the height of which everyone was to fall down on the grass in a mass show of death. The Berrigan brothers, prominent Catholic ex-priests, had requested blood.

"It's a logistical nightmare," I said. "Just forget it."

"I don't know if they intend to douse themselves or fling it across the fence." She sighed. "I don't think they should splatter others."

I headed to the fridge to get another beer. "Those Berrigans ask for blood wherever they go."

"Yes, and always on short notice."

We had agreed to heighten the terror of the die-in by counting back from noon of the protest day, highlighting this "Explosion Time" to the media. As I lay in bed that night, I calculated that it was now eleven hours before "Explosion Time." *Death Time minus 11.* I stared at the ceiling, considering this number. It was a media gimmick to draw the media into the horrific drama of mass death through nuclear missiles. But the idea began to do its work on me. I normally felt cushioned from the horrors of nuclear war. Why? Because we spent our days describing it to others. My engagement created a protective shell, a well-known side benefit to activism. The children at demonstrations or mothers on the radio—average citizens—were much more afraid than I was. They lived with the dark thrumming, made their beds to its tune. But I was in the vanguard (ha ha—Petra would hate the word, so soaked in communist dogma), and so I focused on strategy, T-shirts, petitions, demonstrations. Not mass death. Radiation sickness. Nuclear winter. An earth plunged into desolation. Not a tree. Not a bird. Children with skin peeling from their bodies, plunging into rivers to cool themselves. Dying. In pain. Without their skin.

I checked the clock.

DT minus 10½.

The next day, the fine weather of mid-September was holding, and our Volkswagen van, covered in sunflower decals, headed south along the autobahn. Freya drove, with Gisela in the passenger seat. Emil and I sat in the middle seat, so Petra was lodged in the back between the Berrigan brothers. The blood rode at Gisela's feet, the only place the large vat could fit. It sloshed every time we took a curve.

The brothers were handsome, I gave them that, and oddly likeable, except for their dark-princely demand for blood wherever they went. Daniel Berrigan, the older of the two, had just gotten out of jail after famously breaking into an ICBM missile base and beating the nose cone of a nuclear warhead with a hammer, then pouring blood on documents housed nearby. Philip, the younger Berrigan, bearded and tented in a poncho like a desert preacher, was answering Petra's questions about the movement in America. He'd recently joined activists who had blocked the rail tracks near Spokane, Washington, to stop a shipment of plutonium.

"Satyagraha." He sounded the word with reverence. "You know what that means?"

"Of course," said Petra, and I couldn't help smiling.

"Petra lives satyagraha," I called back to him. I didn't mean this ironically, but it came out with an edge.

"Do you?" Daniel Berrigan asked.

"Manfred, don't put words in my mouth. I *try* to live it. Gandhi is one of my heroes. But of course living by such principles isn't easy."

"I don't know this word," Emil said, and Daniel explained that *satyagraha* was the Sanskrit word for *witness*. "It's what we're doing today, by travelling to this die-in, by imagining death by missiles. We're witnessing the suffering of those who died in Hiroshima and Nagasaki, and those who could die in a nuclear war. Every child. Every plant."

"Manfred, do you know the derivation of the word?" Daniel asked.

"No, I don't."

"*Satya* means *truth*, but it's also the word for *being*. And *agraha* means *to hold firmly*. So together they mean *we stand in truth*, but also that by doing so, by standing and witnessing, we become our truest selves."

"We become our truest selves," Petra repeated. "It's so key, isn't it, this act of witnessing? And not only with our eyes. We must witness with our bodies. With our hearts."

"Our souls, our guts," Daniel added.

This was one too many body parts for me. "If your beliefs run in that particular direction," I tossed out.

"Manfred doesn't believe in the soul," Petra said.

"Ah." They took this in, these two Jesuit priests. My Marxist past exposed with one sentence. Then Daniel put a large hand on my shoulder. "And yet you are witnessing today. So perhaps a belief in the soul isn't as important as an open mind."

We left the autobahn and rolled along a highway for half a kilometre, then turned onto an unpaved road beside an immense field next to the army base. Peace organizers with clipboards directed us to a mass of parked cars.

"We have the speakers for the demonstration in the car," Gisela said. "Can we park closer?" But the petite blond directing traffic shook her head. How long had she had this job—two hours?—and already she was officious. I was almost embarrassed for the Berrigans to see this Germanic trait. "Everybody has to walk," she said, "regardless of your role." When Gisela fumed that we had too much to unload, she shrugged. "Everybody has things to unload." I wondered if perhaps she'd glimpsed Petra in the back and was one of the many women who simply didn't like her. I even wondered if she knew Katrina.

Which made me fret.

Katrina and I had fought again, but this time over something serious. She'd recently told me that she was pregnant. She was less than six weeks in, and planned to keep the baby. When she took in my shocked face—we'd made love only twice!—she stood abruptly, dismissing me. "It's not yours. No reason to think it is." I really couldn't tell if she was saying this to protect herself or because it was true. "You're off the hook," she added. "Lucky you."

"I want you to be happy. You know that. But this is a huge decision."

"You can't take on a father role. You have your plate full."

She was right. Those were my thoughts.

And yet, if the baby wasn't mine, I *was* off the hook. At least as far as real responsibility, genetic responsibility, was concerned. How much did this turn of events even have to *do* with me if the baby wasn't mine? She had had other lovers. *She* was making the choice to go ahead with the pregnancy. And she had since surrounded herself with a shield of women, who shot me glances of ire whenever I came near.

The Berrigans carried their vat of blood, and the rest of us grabbed various peace signs. We were surrounded by least a hundred thousand peaceniks, about the same number of troops, I found myself thinking, as Napoleon had lost at Waterloo. But this group looked more like a peasants' uprising, in loose cotton and hemp, little dogs along for the day, children throwing themselves into haystacks. Dozens and dozens of hand-painted banners, and sudden blasts of tuba and accordion from the Green marching band. A death figure on stilts cruised by, hands full of black balloons. He was followed by three stilted figures in Ronald Reagan masks; they paused to hand us our own plastic masks, some black, some white. For each mask, they asked for a donation (my idea).

Then, all at once, I felt a bird of anger closing in, and I was sure Katrina was bearing down on me. But it was Gisela Fuchs, her long face close to mine. She'd been arguing with the parking attendant and panted as she caught up with me. "I'm glad I've got you alone. I need to talk to you about Katrina."

"Gisela, you don't really know—"

"I know enough. I know she's all alone."

"As a matter of fact, the baby isn't mine."

"Are you sure?"

I followed her glance and then I did see Katrina, on a small rise on the other side of the field, her cropped hair dyed parrot-green, a bright flare against the gold of the grass. I felt a pang in my heart, but it wasn't my fault! She knew exactly what she was doing. She could have had an abortion.

Gisela leaned close. "She just says the baby isn't yours to protect herself."

"Well, it's working."

We were at our destination. I broke free and walked away.

Petra and Emil were standing near the stage. As I closed in on them, Emil recognized someone. He waved his hand, and I turned to see Magnus Isaacson heading towards them, clad in a white cotton shirt and black cotton trousers. He'd gotten rid of the velvet jacket, replaced it with beige linen: a natty dresser always, since his days in the daycare. He was older, just as I was, but I would recognize him anywhere.

I held back, watching as he shook Emil's hand and then laughed at something Petra said. She threw back her head and laughed too. Then Emil laughed, and they were all laughing, sanctified and more beautiful than the surrounding people. I remembered that this was what Magnus could do: he could electrify people.

I edged closer and heard Petra say, "I hope you will take good care of Emil at these meetings. He gets tired of us! He needs his peers."

"I am excited to bring Emil into the circle. It makes such a difference when generals speak against war."

"The article is coming along," Emil said. "I'm hoping to finish it by the end of the month."

"No hurry. We have time before it goes to print."

"What's this?" Petra looked from man to man. I heard

Magnus explain that Emil was writing an article on intermediate-range missiles for a book from the Generals for Peace.

"Ah, but I didn't know!" she exclaimed. "Why didn't you tell me?"

"It's only at the beginning stages," Magnus said.

Still, Petra looked surprised. Then someone appeared at her side with a message from the Berrigans, and she and Emil rushed off.

Magnus must have seen me as I wove towards him through the protestors, my heart beating in my chest, yet he waited calmly enough, pretending to review the contents of his clipboard.

"Magnus!"

"Manfred!"

Our voices expressed that we were long-lost friends, but we didn't shake hands or exchange a cursory, male embrace. He'd aged, yet what was odd was how deeply I knew him, even to the fact that his feet were freckled, his toenails a bit hoary—his most embarrassing feature. He'd once scratched a lover with a toenail, causing her calf to bleed.

"I'm escorting General Stathopoulos. Thought I'd collect a few signatures along the way." He gestured to the clipboard. "I suppose you know that I've changed my address to Vienna, and find myself a full-fledged member of the peace movement now, just like you. I'm secretary to the Generals for Peace. Your Emil Gerhardt is our newest member."

"So you've shifted your interests."

He lowered his voice. "Listen, I should say this: I left the Party shortly after you disappeared to Wyhl. So much of what we went through was a phase, wasn't it?"

Did he mean attempting to recruit me over the diapers or the entire sixty-eighter movement in West Berlin? He was perspiring lightly, and I knew that for him it was not a phase. I could only shrug.

"Anyway," he said. "I don't think you needed anyone to tell you what to do."

"What does that mean?"

"Your natural proclivities—I'm sure you're helpful in the Greens."

"How so?" I wasn't sure I'd heard right.

"Let's just say that many people have appreciated your reasoned take on things."

"Don't appreciate me too much!"

"Don't be angry, Manfred."

"I haven't been doing one thing to make your crowd happy."

"You are too hard on yourself."

I shook my head in disgust. "And now you're on to the general."

"I told you—I left all that behind, just as you did. You've got everything upside down."

"What does right side up look like, then?"

He paused before he answered. Then he spoke with open kindness, brother to brother, and I felt again how ably he disarmed people. "The Greens are a positive influence, Manfred. Or they could be, if they would control certain ludicrous tendencies. Surely we both agree on that."

I said nothing.

"However," he continued, "I don't worry too much, because it all comes out in the end. It gets massaged out of a group."

"You won't massage it out of Petra."

"No. But perhaps she will calm with time."

"Don't count on it. Look, is this why you've focused on the general? To try to get to her? Well, don't. And as for me, perhaps you're telling your bosses that you have the sympathetic ear of more people than you do. So report back to your bosses, if you please, that you don't have me."

"I wouldn't bother, Manfred. I don't think my bosses—these hypothetical bosses—would care!"

"But they care about Petra."

He smiled. "Everyone cares about Petra. She's a wild card. If I *had* bosses, they would most definitely care about Petra. They'd care about her influence. And they'd care about her crazy positions, and they'd want them tempered. I've heard that Marcus Wolf himself, the head of Stasi operations in the West, has a crush on Petra. Did you know? Apparently he keeps a very large file of clippings and can be seen perusing it for no reason. She's a flame, that's for sure, but some of her ideas are nuts, and when they are aimed at the GDR and the Soviet Union, many people, East and West, think they are dangerous as well. She supports some real counter-revolutionary elements, you know, and builds them up as heroes."

"I heard you say you're getting Emil to write a chapter for a book. I'm sure that comes with a nice paycheque."

"We're paying him, yes, and all the generals who contribute."

"You're paying them to stay in line."

"Not at all."

I walked away.

"Counting backwards from ten."

Daniel Berrigan's American voice came through the microphone.

"By the count of three, please don your face mask. Does everybody have one?"

The people who'd made a donation began to pull on their plastic masks; others covered up with balaclavas or scarves.

Then Berrigan intoned, "Please be aware. Please be aware. A Pershing II missile is flying towards us at this moment. And who and where are we? Are we on the Soviet side of the wall, or are we on the Western side? It doesn't matter. Dead is dead. In dying, let us witness the violence of the weapons, and the sorrow of every human, every animal, every plant, captured in the agony of ground zero. Ten, nine, eight, seven, six, five, four, three, two . . . one."

A thudding as bodies hit earth. I think I stood longer than the others, and this gave me a view as the elder Berrigan hoisted the container of blood and poured it over his brother. The brother looked appalled, as though caught in an ancient brother fight, then the elder lifted his face to the sky and poured it over himself, and down the two of them went.

Down I went too.

Dead.

Theoretically.

A helicopter beat overhead. News cameras flashed. The field seemed to breathe softly with the weight of so many bodies draped under the sun. The dead were colourful, I thought. *The dead could use some sunscreen.*

After a respectful moment I turned my head to locate Emil and Petra. Emil had spread his coat for her, so she could die in comfort. Emil met my eyes. *Yes, it's ridiculous*, he seemed to be saying. *We aren't really dead.*

Emil, in fact, was thinking about how itchy his forehead was. Would he scratch it or wouldn't he? The news cameras were searching the fallen people to take pictures of Petra, Emil and the Berrigan brothers. Now they were above him, a flock of cameras, so if Emil moved even slightly he would become ridiculous. The General Who Would Not Die.

The side of his nose had begun to sweat. Was there a bug there? How long would this go on? It was ridiculous. A ridiculous piece of theatre. Almost as ridiculous as those two mock-Catholics in the car, going on about Gandhi, impressing Petra with their knowledge of Hindu words.

Yes, it was ridiculous, and uncomfortable, too. And what was the point of pretending to be dead? What did it mean to these people? What were they "witnessing," as the Berrigans kept calling it? *All we are witnessing,* Emil thought, *is our own fatuousness.*

And what of that Magnus Isaacson? The secretary at Generals for Peace. He was a smooth one, a talker, a lady's man; Emil knew the type. There had been awkwardness about the article. Petra had seemed surprised, as though Emil was keeping it from her. But he wasn't. Or was he? No, he wasn't. He'd spoken quite freely about it just now; he didn't have to reproach himself in any way. Still, there was a *feeling* about the money he was being paid. And what was it? It was the fact that it was too much, a little too much, for writing an article. And there was a certain nebulousness about his deadline. Yet, on the other hand, they were paying him because they valued his opinions. And why shouldn't they? It felt good to be appreciated.

His mind went to Helena. He didn't want to think about her, but he felt unguarded on the ground, as though his thoughts could go anywhere they chose. She'd been drunk when he saw her the week before, and he wondered if she was drunk again right now. As he played dead, perhaps she was playing dead too, lying across the bed, the curtains unopened though it was midday, her hair unkempt, her lips slack and her eyes bleary. If she was in that state, the room would smell. Yes, he'd noticed how this happened, how she stunk of alcohol and female smells that at other times she kept under lock and key. What a good imitation of death she could bring on. And yet, last week, after he'd walked her to the bathroom, helped her run a shower, unwrapped her peach kimono, he'd seen a glimmer in her eyes:

a deep, atavistic triumph. "You're a fucker," she'd said. "Such a fucker." A word he was sure had never before passed her lips. And why that glimmer of triumph? Because she'd extinguished herself, and in doing so she had finally shown him what he was. What he'd caused. What he was capable of.

With a sense that his head was now frozen numb, almost as if the back of his skull had opened to the ground, he was back, standing at the parting in the trees, in the place he never wanted to go, at the edge of the clay pit. His sight rimmed with tunnel vision, closing in steadily, until he could only see through a pinhole. He looked into the pit and saw the freckled calf of a woman, then her naked body, face down. Her calf was covered in spattered mud. Beside her, a child's hand poked through the dirt. He could see the lines on the knuckles.

Then Emil was standing and shouting, ripping off his mask, gasping for breath and seeing nothing.

He's choking. Emil Gerhardt is choking!

He heard voices, felt Petra holding his arm, but he batted her away. All he could see were blotches of darkness and pins of light.

Make space for him.

Let him breathe.

Give him space.

He should sit with his head between his knees.

Emil sat, and his vision cleared. Petra knelt beside him. Cameramen had closed in and were filming, as though his behaviour was a worthy part of the "die-in" spectacle.

"For god's sake, stop filming!" Petra shouted. "Can't you see there's something wrong?" Then, more quietly, "Emil, should we find a doctor?"

"It's nothing." He rested his forehead on his knees. "But I may be ruining the die-in."

"Don't worry about that."

"I should find a quiet place."

"I'll come with you."

"No. Stay. You need to speak to the press. I'll find the van."

"What happened?"

"Later."

"I'll come."

But he gestured for her to stay. He found he was able to stand, and he began to step around the bodies, making his way towards the parking area. There seemed to be a thousand cars, but at last he located the van. It was unlocked. He climbed into the driver's seat and locked the door, then rested his head against the steering wheel. He could hear his breathing beginning to slow. He sat with his eyes closed until every vestige of the tunnel vision had cleared. Far away he heard the crowd clapping and cheering. The Berrigans' voices tearing open the silence. He could smell hay and dirt on his jacket. Night under his eyelids.

On impulse he lifted his head, took hold of the mirror and adjusted it to see his face. Dark eyes looked back. He thought of the meadow, his boyhood self running—yes, that helped. He wanted to expel what was in him, the other thing, expel it like a piece of snot, like something caught in his body. *Please*, he thought, *let me get rid of this heaviness. This is the basis of everything. If I can do that, something new will take its place.*

On the return home to Bonn, Petra tried once or twice to draw Emil out, reaching to touch his shoulder, but his face was drawn. He knew what was coming. He'd been heading to this place since quitting NATO. No, since seeing that apple in the pig's mouth at the banquet, the stretched and burnt lips of the pig, the shiny, round apple, greased and crisp. Then the postcard. Petra! Her eyes, her strength, even her breath, smelling lightly of jellied candies, that treat she'd grown up on in Günzburg. Only she could see into him, pull this terrible shard of glass from his heart.

We pulled in at a rest stop, and in the lineup to pay for gas and her chewy candies, I took Petra's arm. She glanced at my hand and said, "Don't."

I pulled my hand away. "I'm sorry for this," I said.

"No, don't say that. You *wanted* this. The press can't leave him alone, and you—you've primed the pump. I don't know what to say to you, Manfred. I'll be glad to move from the farmhouse, that's all."

"Petra."

"And all that bullshit about Generals for Peace, too, when Magnus Isaacson—I met him today—is a perfectly decent person."

"I spoke to him too, Petra. He as much as admitted it."

"Admitted what?"

"He wants to control our agenda. To neutralize what he calls 'the crazy element.'"

"He said that?"

"It's what they do, Petra."

"Well, it's ridiculous. I'm not afraid and neither is Emil. We aren't cattle to be prodded this way and that."

"I know that."

"Do you?" She spoke icily. "Anyway, it's all right. It doesn't matter. I can see what's happening now. What Emil and I need to do."

She turned and walked back to the van.

22

In Answer to Your Question

Shalom!

So began the letter from Yad Vashem, the Holocaust library. It was in the mailbox on our return. It began with this salutation and ended with the typed name and ballpoint signature of one Ada Meinbaum.

Ada Meinbaum, chain-smoker, for the pages seemed lightly dusted with ash. I pictured a portly body in a flowered dress, something made of light cotton for the desert weather.

She had attached, *for my further information*, three photocopied sheets listing in neat, alphabetized columns the names of Ukrainian villages, towns and cities where massacres had occurred. Bal, Buki, Bayer, Kiev, Krasilov, Novo-Vorontsovka, Novo Ziye, Vasilkov, Yuzvin, Zolotonosha. At three pages with fifty-two place names each that was over 150 sites. Then I turned over a page and saw that the backs, too, were covered in columns listing massacres.

Three hundred and twelve in all.

Shalom!

In answer to your most important inquiry, Herr Schwartz, here is information from our file on the town of Krivoy Rog.

"The first Jews settled in Krivoy Rog in the mid-1860s. Most of them were merchants or craftsmen. At the end of the nineteenth century and the beginning of the twentieth, the Jews of Krivoy Rog endured several pogroms. In the 1920s and 1930s, under Soviet rule, the Jewish farming community grew steadily. With the development of heavy industry in the 1930s, many new Jewish workers migrated to the city, while the traditional segment of the Jewish population continued as long as possible to work as craftsmen or to deal in commerce. In 1939, 12,745 Jews lived in Krivoy Rog, comprising about 6 percent of the total population.

Krivoy Rog was occupied by the Germans on August 14, 1941. Almost immediately, the Jews of the city were ordered to wear the Star of David and to hand over all their valuables to the German military authorities. Kosher slaughtering was banned. The municipal authorities confiscated the property of those Jews who had fled, and imposed a high tax on the remaining Jews.

On October 10, 1941, German soldiers and Ukrainian policemen assembled the Jews of Krivoy Rog, of all ages and both sexes, in the building of a former synagogue. On October 14, 1941, in the morning, the assembled Jews were arranged into two huge columns and taken to the railway station, where they were told to leave their bags and personal belongings. From there they were marched three kilometres farther, to the vicinity of an abandoned clay pit surrounded by trees. There the Jews were forced to undress and subjected to humiliations. Groups of ten to fifteen people were then driven between the trees to the edge of the pit, where German SS soldiers and Ukrainian volunteer policemen armed with submachine guns shot them dead and pushed their bodies into the pit. Children were thrown into the pit alive. The massacre continued on the following day, October 15. The number of victims of this two-day massacre was about three thousand on the first day and about four thousand on the second day. The perpetrators of this mass murder were members of the

1st SS Infantry Brigade, the Police Battalion 314 and Ukrainian auxiliary policemen."

In answer to your most important question, Herr Schwartz, eyewitness accounts tell us that involvement of the German army in atrocities across the Ukraine was by no means uncommon. At Krivoy Rog, a survivor has substantiated that members of a Wehrmacht division controlled the forced march to the pit and assisted in the policing of the crowd as they were stripped and humiliated, and that a Panzer team later buried the bodies— some still alive, blessed be their righteous memory—by collapsing the walls of the clay pit.

23.

Satyagraha

Emil and Petra are together in her bedroom. Petra sits cross-legged on the bedspread, teal and terracotta, bordered with a wide band of seahorses and starfish. She wears her ancient track pants and her Jonathan Livingston Seagull T-shirt.

Emil notices the saying on the shirt: TOUCHING HEAVEN. Then her earnest and serious face—the face of a youthful scholar in the age of Hamlet. The dark rings around her eyes.

He loves her.

She reaches for his hand. This gesture means *Emil, my love, we are in this together.* She closes her eyes, and an involuntary shudder passes through her. After it is gone, she sits up straighter. That familiar gesture: shaking the panic out of her body; how she renews herself again and again. For a moment he envies her. What would it be like to be so strong? Now she returns his gaze with patience, but he sees the fear lodged deep down. Yet she wants this.

"You've told me so little," she says.

"That's because you have never asked."

"I'm sorry. I know this. I think I trusted—I trusted something larger happening between us. I can't explain." She looks down at the bedspread, collecting her thoughts. What has gone on all this time? Why hasn't she asked? She feels as though she's been afraid to break a spell, skating on a lake, the two of them embracing and sliding together in a dance that has left her breathless. Who would want the ice to melt?

He looks at her face, the two small lines between her eyebrows. "Tell me," she says.

He wants to say, *I have done such terrible things.* He wants to bring out the worst part. Tell her about the rabbi. He wants to tell her about the girl and her brother, the rabbi and the apple. That was the memory that made him leap from his seat at the Rifle Banquet when the band struck up Hitler's march. He'd seen the roasted pig on its platter, the greased apple stuffed in its mouth.

"You were young," she starts, and he nods, for this is true. Perhaps she understands how little responsibility he had, growing up under that regime: ten years old when Hitler took over; nineteen when he went to war.

He says, "When Hitler came to power, my mother looked me in the eye, her expression very stern—she was a stern woman— and she said, 'I am sickened by everything we have suffered, Emil.' She meant cleaning rich people's houses and tending their gardens—the Kleiners, the Schneiders—all Jews. And our tiny apartment, which she hated, when she'd grown up with so much better."

Are you glad, Mutti?

Oh, yes, so glad.

And that night she said it all again to her friend Elsa: *This will set things straight.* As though Germany were a garden that needed to be dug up, a house that needed tidying. Ugly things had grown in their native land. But now they would make something new.

He is unsure how to go on. Petra is cross-legged, listening, kind. This he knows.

"I enlisted on the fourth of September, nineteen forty-one. My mother saw me off at the station. There were crowds everywhere. I wore my new uniform. I had my soldier's rations. My mother was suppressing her tears. I told her I was going to war at last for the Fatherland, and she hugged me and told me she had never been more proud. I was proud too. We'd been told that to fight and even die for the Fatherland was an honour."

"Brainwashing."

"But we didn't know it at the time. Do you see?"

"Yes."

"Or if I knew, it was only with one tiny part of my mind. The rest, well, I went with what people said, what I was told."

She frowns. Is this something she can earmark and then come back to? She doesn't want to stop him.

He describes the journey to the front, from Warsaw to Krivoy Rog, where his unit was to be trained in tank warfare before heading into combat. From the train window, he sees fields of flowers—sweet peas and blue flowers the colour of the sky. The land is huge, the destruction pocketed in villages: another burnt village, another. They see strange silhouettes in the distance, bodies hanging from trees. Friedrich, a member of Emil's battalion, explains that they are dead partisans. A champion of knowledge, is Friedrich.

Emil doesn't say that the bodies hanging from trees still fill his eyes. That walking in the English Garden in Munich or along the Rhine, he can see them lining the boulevard, feet pigeon-toed in their sad boots, body after body, so many of them women. How death makes people look like dirt. There is an obscenity to a body when it doesn't have a mind to direct it anymore. Instead, he emphasizes the flowers he saw from the train, because this too is engraved on his brain. Blue flowers to the horizon.

"Cornflowers," Petra says. She is with him, travelling towards the Eastern Front.

Emil wants to acknowledge Friedrich. They became friends. They lost their unit during the retreat from the Don. They shared food and walked across the frozen snow, almost died but found a village, warmed themselves at a peasant's fire. When the peasant refused them honey and bread, Friedrich shot him and his wife. He needed to eat. But Emil doesn't share this last part with Petra. He does say that they regained their unit and were ordered forward, and that Friedrich had his head blown off his shoulders. Emil witnessed this: the head of his friend flying through the air.

One hundred and fifty kilometres before Krivoy Rog, the train grinds to a halt because partisans have destroyed the tracks. They march the remaining distance, and this is exhausting. Some of the men need new boots after this slogging trek. "Yes, new boots, before even reaching the front."

At Krivoy Rog, the army administration has taken over houses, removed the occupants and sealed the ghetto. This is standard. The men sleep on cots in buildings commandeered from the Ukrainian townspeople, and this is fine, not uncomfortable. By day they forage for food, oversee gardens, clear people out of more houses. As soon as the tanks arrive, they will train and move to the front. At night Emil plays cards with Friedrich. In bed, Emil sees the steppes rolling past again and again: flowers, fields, burnt villages, hanging bodies.

Emil begins to tell Petra about October 14, the march to the clay pit. This is where they have both been heading. She gives him a faint nod. *Yes, go on.*

Soldiers from his battalion are ordered to support the SS and the Ukrainian auxiliary police. The soldiers spread out along the line of people being marched from the synagogue to the railway station. Bare lacy branches reflect in the ditch. At the train station, everyone assembles, and Emil assumes this is the destination, but the police order the Jews to drop their things and keep moving. Several Jewish men argue, say they will go no farther, and the Ukrainian police beat them with their rifles and then shoot them in the head. A mother falls to embrace her son's body and is hit across the face with a rifle butt.

Emil reaches for Petra's hand, and she takes his, weaving her fingers into his.

There will be no train journey. The people have been marched to the station so that they can drop their suitcases, take off their coats and dispose of their valuables. They are forced to cross the tracks and move along a cart road towards a distant grove of trees.

There is a different feeling as they walk along the cart road. The crowd gives off an animal smell of adrenalin. One old rabbi (Emil can tell her this part) has a large wart on the side of his nose, but many of the women are handsome, with hair held by coloured scarves. They have arms around the elderly, or they carry children. One girl wears a cotton dress with a pattern of dark-green ivy leaves. She walks with her smaller brother, holding his hand. Her hair is in pigtails. Emil watches her slender body, her legs and thin feet. She has a tender, exceptional beauty.

They reach the trees, which shimmer and have a subtle mottled bark, like pig's ears, inky blue and pink. The SS soldiers give the order to strip, and the girl unbuttons her dress and folds it at her feet. She undresses her brother, who is crying. Then she picks him up and they go between the trees.

"You saw this? You were right there?"

"Yes."

"Telling people to strip." The hardness of her voice surprises them both.

"Not me—the SS."

"But you kept order."

The girl strips with her back to him. In his memory, her skin glows like the moon. She hugs the boy to her before they go between the trees.

"Petra, you must understand. It was war. There was only one choice, which was to follow orders or be shot myself."

"Yes, but."

"But what?"

She says nothing. They sit like that for a full minute. Everything in the scene is terrible, and she can't shake the feeling that if she had been there, she would have said, *Shoot me*—yes: *Shoot me—I cannot kill these innocents.* Died with the girl and her brother. Held hands with them and walked between the trees.

"Did you think—Emil, I know this is terrible, and forgive me if I don't understand, but did you think of refusing?"

A startled look flies across his face. Irritation, almost. At what? Her failure to understand war? But also, this line of questioning is not what he expected.

"You don't understand."

"But I do. I'm so sorry. I do."

"We had *absolutely* no choice."

She nods.

"You understand?"

"It's so terrible. Yes. I do."

But in the night she wakes. She hears his breathing, and then all at once she is shaking him violently awake. He startles and flails his arms, and then jumps out of bed naked, breathing heavily.

"What is it? What's happened?" He comes to himself, then, and says, "You frightened me."

She—frightening him. "Oh, Emil, I'm so sorry. I had a nightmare."

They climb back into bed together, nestle close.

He has made himself so vulnerable. He has given her his secrets, the dark crust at his heart, every piece. She is equal now in every way to Helena, though she has no doubt that there will be a price.

THE WALL

I

Sing, Heavenly Muse

Petra Kelly has been dead for twenty-five years.

She is buried in a hillside graveyard outside Würzburg. It is a soothing place full of mature trees that now, in mid-May, are in full leaf, creating a canopy of shade above the gravel pathways and raised grave plots. Many of these plots are covered in flowers. Perhaps they change the flowers seasonally—pansies in springtime, chrysanthemums in fall—but I don't know, because I only ever come in May, the month Petra and I motorcycled to Günzburg together. What I see are grave beds of purple and white pansies, really lovely. Petra is under a blanket of these flowers; tucked in, as it were, by natural beauty.

I go to the spigot and fill a metal can with water, then return, feeling the weight of the water. I sprinkle the pansies, enjoying how the beads of water moisten their velvet faces, making sure to wet the plot from top to bottom. I return the can to its home beside the tap and retrace the fifty-four steps (I've counted them) to sit on the bench that overlooks her grave. Leaves filter the sunlight, creating patterns on the gravel path. Birds sing and call.

Her gravestone is a modest waist-high granite column, topped by cut-out stone figures of children dancing in a circle, holding hands. Are these figures supposed to be like paper cutouts, or are they, because of the thickness of the stone, meant to be like gingerbread children? I've never been sure. They convey a sense of innocence, but also, unfortunately, a sense of United Nations good cheer.

Beneath them, Petra's famous words are engraved into the rough granite: MIT DEM HERZEN DENKEN. Her suggestion to humankind. Our "takeaway," as people would call it now.

Think with the heart.

I'm not altogether sure why I come. I don't articulate it, never have. But I feel gentled by this place. I put in my time, then leave. Each movement has been ritualized, and I don't vary the ritual. I don't stir things up.

Frozen is what people call it.

You're frozen, Manfred.

Poor Manfred, he's frozen.

I've gotten used to it, over the years, accepted it. The abominable snowman.

He was so close to her—and now look: he never says her name.

Here's proof of how little I spoke of her. At one point, about fifteen years ago, I served lamb stew to my family. It was the same lamb stew I used to make for Petra, and I stared down at it, fork in my hand, realizing I didn't know if she had genuinely liked it or just ate it because it was there. Hannelore, my daughter, was nine at the time, and she stopped kicking the radiator and gave my arm a shake. "Papa's lost in thought," she said. I looked up at her and said, "Petra used to eat this stew all the time," and Hannelore must have noticed the change in my voice, because she looked at me with her bright eyes and said, "Who's Petra?"

Hannelore at age nine carried not a trace of Petra in her mind, though with every passing day she reminds me of Petra in her boldness, her fierceness.

———

I got the telephone call from Freya Fertig. It was morning. I had arrived at the office, hung up my coat and was standing beside my desk, preparing to open mail and review the day's headlines. I picked up the phone in a rush.

"Hello, yes? How can I help you?"

"Manfred?" Freya's voice through the receiver seemed covered in soft, feathery moss, and I remember I felt an aversion to it. When she said, equally softly, "It's Freya," I wondered what could possibly have happened. Had another of her beloved cats died? Freya had become quite a cat person of late. Three months earlier, one of them had fallen from her balcony, causing a long and (I privately felt) unseemly period of grief and talk therapy. If it was about her cats, then too bad for her; I was simply too busy.

"What's up, Freya? How can I help?"

"It's Petra. And Emil."

Their names dropped like stones, causing ripples of guilt.

She said, "They're dead. They were shot, both of them. Murdered. The police just called me."

There is a moment just after you hear about a death when the person is still there, still vividly with you, and the death you've just heard about is theoretical, a statement without meaning. That's how it was for me. "Dead" was just another thing that Petra was doing to be interesting.

I remember I stared at the floor, at the wrinkle in the grey-and-burgundy rag carpet. I'd brought it from home to cheer my small workspace, and I felt an urge to lean down now and straighten it, as though this problem with the carpet was my most pressing concern.

"Murdered?" I heard myself say. And I realized my voice was covered in feathery moss too.

"They were found at their place on Swinemünder Strasse. Both of them. Shot in the head. Come over, Manfred. Come now."

I actually don't want to relive it. This part I want to skip— have tried to skip for years. Yet I relive it in nightmares, where I am climbing the slender stairwell at Swinemünder Strasse because I have been called by Freya or some other urgent voice, telling me to *Come, come now*. Up I go, towards a tower room at the top of the stairs, but as in most dreams of this type, I can't make my feet move, or my knees collapse, my legs wobble as though boneless. Or I wake in the night with a queer feeling in my body, an electric current that comes from waking and knowing something is wrong. What is it? And then it lurches out of the shadows with its terrible face, or with no face at all—the no-face of something evil.

In the first days after the news, we were so confused. We suspected the CIA; we suspected skinheads or the group of neofascists that the anonymous hate letters had been traced to. We even suspected the Chinese secret police because of Petra's work supporting the Tibetan refugees who had fled to Dharamshala. We had theories and then dismissed them. All of this in a miasma of guilt. Guilt slowing down my body, so that getting out of bed felt like moving through molasses.

Of course I saw a therapist: he wanted me to heave something out of myself, hack my guilt and pain into a handkerchief. And sometimes I did cry, but it, the thing I was carrying, didn't dislodge.

I remember the rag carpet, its speckled lines of grey and burgundy. I remember thinking, *Petra, you've done it again. Never a dull moment where you're concerned.* Then I did bend down to straighten the wrinkle.

———

Now I sit on the bench and look at the dancing children. Birds sing above me, making looping threads of music, as though sewing patterns of light in the branches. I think of Freya again, that strange conversation I had with her about a year ago. I ran into her at Karstadt, buying cheese, driving the vendor mad asking for tastes. She has long grey hair now, buckets of it still, and she pushed it from her face and said something interesting. She said, "I see Petra all the time, as she was on election night. Do you remember?" And I said nothing, because at that point I still tried not to see Petra, ever. Then Freya said, "I love to see her like that." And she added, "The dead can be any age, because once a person is gone, they exist in all their forms. I often see my mother as a young woman, throwing back her head and laughing."

The dead can be any age, once they are dead. This went into the frozen river that was me. But whatever resolution was forming under the surface needed another catalyst, which came two months ago, at a political rally in support of Syrian refugees. These refugees are presently housed, ironically enough, in the former Stasi headquarters at Normannenstrasse, and of course some right-wing anti-immigration groups want them out, so down I went to protest. It was early March, and the weather was cold, flakes of snow in the air, but a freshness too, as though the season couldn't make up its mind. I texted Hannelore and met up with her near the front of the small protest, and soon I was talking to a male friend of hers. I found Petra's name on my lips.

"Who was she?" Hannelore's friend turned to me. "I think I've heard of her. She was famous for something, wasn't she?"

Then another fellow, heavily bearded and with one of those man-buns I see so frequently on my daughter's suitors, leaned in and said, "I know who she was—she was a figure skater!"

I stared from bearded face to bearded face. "You really don't know who Petra Kelly was? Political people such as yourselves?"

And they listened respectfully, as they would to any old man going on about things they don't really care about. How had this happened in twenty-five short years? And wasn't I partly to blame, I thought as I headed home that day, because of my silence? My refusal to turn and face her. To honour her.

Petra. Sucked from history. Replaced by a gravestone of dancing children.

I didn't want to unthaw at first. Bringing you back does hurt. It hurts the way my fingers once hurt after skiing, driving home in the back seat of our family car. How cold my hands were. *Chilblains*, my mother called them: "He has chilblains, Konrad."

"And what am I to do with that?" was my father's reply. "He ought to have kept his mittens from getting wet." And my mother was silenced, and my fingers hurt so much I thought they would crack as the warmth came back into them.

Yet here I am, the morning after my pilgrimage to your flower-covered grave in Würzburg, hovering over my desk at home, about to try to bring you to life. I perch my coffee cup on the windowsill, where it won't leave a ring, then I pause for a long time, staring at the wood grain of the desk surface.

I'm not going to let you be the corpse at the top of the stairs. This is what I say to myself, with some awareness that I'm being both grandiose and earnest. But still. There it is. You've been the corpse for too long. I've let your final identity define you, your murder turn you into a murder victim, as though that's who you were, your meaning, your *self*. As a feminist, how you would have hated that! All your complexity, your laughter, your fears, reduced to a dead body in a bed.

2.

Victory

But now we are back. March 6, 1983. Election night. Will we, won't we, will we, won't we?

The votes, as we waited in the conference hall, were tallied with agonizing slowness. We smiled, sometimes nervously, for the cameras. We looked exactly like the exhausted foot soldiers we'd been for the past year. We said to each other, *It was a good fight, regardless.* But then, as the results trickled in—could it be? It seemed we'd made inroads with voters. No. More than that. The final tally showed we had received more than two million party list votes and a further million and a half constituency votes.

We knew exactly what this meant, and so did the media, and so did Helmut Kohl of the winning Christian Democrats. We'd won more than 5 percent, enough to take us into parliament. And not just one or two of us, either. Twenty-eight earnest, crazy, earth-loving, missile-deploring Greens.

Petra, Emil and I were all elected, Petra by a landslide of love. Jürgen Wolff did very well, too, as did Gisela Fuchs. I saw them laughing together, Gisela kissing Jürgen on the lips and Jürgen bending her back in his arms, making her screech with delight. He had found Gisela's uncompromising positions a pain in the ass and often rolled his eyes when she spoke, but tonight they, too, were delirious with the shock of success.

People kept clapping me on the back. And the reporters swarmed me for quotes. *What next, what next?* I kept answering, *The missiles don't exist anymore. Consider them gone!* Then they'd laugh, and I'd say, *Yes—gone.* At one point we formed a conga line and snaked from the hall into the corridor, shouting, *Look out, Helmut Kohl, look out, Social Democrats—you're done, you're gone.*

People surrounded Petra and Emil, and I heard them saying to the general, *We couldn't have done it without you. Bravo, General. Bravo.* And he looked as though he'd found, at last, his safe harbour. Beside him, Petra was radiant. When I embraced her in victory, she smelled like sweat and apples. I gave her a long kiss and then touched her ears.

"Your little ears," I whispered, because I was very drunk. And she took my head and held it and said, "And your big ones," as though this were the most natural thing in the world, to congratulate both ourselves and our ears.

At one point I remember Gisela, equally drunk, leaning over me with her gaunt face and saying, sternly, "We are the force for the biosphere, that's what we are, as Greens—we are the party for the trees, who cannot speak for themselves." And instead of mentally recoiling from this image, I remember thinking, *Yes, so we are,* and that night I dreamed of a huge tree shoving its way through the roof of the Bundestag, breaking open the white concrete roof, and I woke laughing.

I dressed carefully for my first day as a member of parliament. Not in a suit. No, I was taking seriously the dictum of Thoreau: *Beware all enterprises that require new clothes.* But I combed my beard and put on a corduroy jacket, and I even pressed my jeans.

I was too excited to eat breakfast.

Spring. Crocuses were bursting into blossom. The leaves were unfurling, smelling of honey, and the Rhine shone like a clairvoyant strand of joy. Our group of elected parliamentarians formed a parade and marched towards the Bundestag, joined by the women of Frauen für den Frieden, and other cheering ecologists, and a group of organic farmers who, for better or for worse, had brought a goat. At the head of the congregation, a half-dozen children pushed a human-sized inflatable globe. Jürgen bounced along in his running shoes. Emil smiled like a prince and waved to the crowd. He had given up power—and now the world, in its beneficence, had given power back to him. But good power this time. The power to make things right. A pretty young woman ran up and threw her arms around him and kissed his cheek, leaving a lipstick mark, which Petra wiped away with a laugh. For every girl leaving lipstick marks on Emil, there were ten others in the crowd shouting Petra's name. At times so many people wanted to hug her that we had to stop the parade to wait. *You've done it! Amazing! We love you, Petra Kelly!* She was the charismatic centre of West Germany's new politics—the earth's new politics. How we loved her that day.

Still, as we neared the Bundestag, with its unblinking windows, its facade of innocuous bureaucracy, we felt a chill. How would we manage in this building, which we'd dubbed "the Refrigerator on the Rhine"? Greens in a bone-white building. Then the tethered goat broke free, butting one of the children to the ground, and the spell of the building dissolved in the mother's rush to comfort him and the crowd's laughter as the farmers chased and caught their goat.

Inside, we gathered in the foyer. The same chill, but now rising through our feet from the polished granite floor. What next?

Some members of the Christian Democrats showed us into the elevators and took us for a spontaneous tour.

Even our opponents were excited.

3

Swinemünder Strasse and Tulpenfeld

Petra moved in with Emil after the victory, leaving the farmhouse forever. Their duplex, at the end of Swinemünder Strasse, in the Tannenbusch neighbourhood, was clad in stucco, with a black tile roof to match the neighbours. Some of the pebbled front gardens even had ceramic gnomes—a suburb dying of quaintness.

As I stepped out of my car, I realized how unruly the farmhouse must have seemed to Petra; and her stepfather's family was so far away and uninterested in her; and her ever-missing father was never coming back, was he? But here was an answer. How deeply she must have wanted this.

Petra had been mostly aloof towards me since the die-in. Was *aloof* the right word? Something had closed inside her. I pictured a pine cone pressed tight, not letting loose its numerous seeds. As we planned the campaign, she was just as pleasant on the surface, just as driven and businesslike, but she no longer allowed me in.

At the doorstep, I held out the potted plant, with its fuzzy, delicate leaves. Petra took it and kissed my cheek. "I'll even water it. You'll see."

As she showed me into the narrow flat, I kept up my smile. A part of me ached, watching her slim figure go ahead of me up the stairs, but what more did I need to convince myself that she'd moved on? As she made me tea, she even mentioned getting a cat.

"Who would look after it? You work until three a.m. every night."

"Right. I'll stick to plants."

It was a relief as we sank into politics, the Bundestag, our upcoming challenges. We still had that, and as we made our plans, I enjoyed the re-emergence of the hungry political animal.

Later, as I was leaving, I ventured to ask, "How are you, Petra? I mean, really?"

"Me?" She turned at the door. "As you can see, everything is as I've always wanted it. Now it's just a question of the missiles, isn't it? And our thousand and one other demands. But the missiles first!"

She began to talk about the demonstrations planned for October, the month before the missiles were to be deployed. She spoke with rapture about the all-women encampment at Greenham Common in the UK, the thrilling solidarity and parallel direct actions. She kept me at a distance, and then she stepped aside, releasing me into the sunlight.

I drove back to Tulpenfeld, the tower where we Greens had our offices. It was a truly terrible place, sterile and airless, with windows that couldn't open. I parked and crossed the quadrangle, along a walkway of cement pressed with circles to imitate cobbles. Rose bushes flanked the walk. We were too far from the Bundestag; Petra and Gisela had both officially objected, but they'd done so as they unpacked their copious boxes, complaining and settling simultaneously.

"The Green Chaos," the Christian Democrats called our offices, because it seemed like we'd never truly settled in—books and papers and press clippings overflowed every surface, reminiscent of the flooded rooms in *The Sorcerer's Apprentice.*

My mind turned back to Petra's little house, with its cozy cuteness. She really did want all the trappings of domesticity now. She wanted it sewn up all around her. A place to come home to. A place to dream in. The problem was, Emil was still married to someone else, and Swinemünder Strasse wasn't changing that. It was just masking it. Was that why she'd seemed so brittle?

As I stepped across the polished lobby floor to the elevator, I thought about how she had sidestepped my question—*How are you really?* Beneath the domestic act, there was steel. Something had shifted in her. But whatever it was, she was keeping it to herself.

The night of the die-in, she and Emil had sequestered themselves for hours, and when she had at last emerged into the kitchen, she'd averted her face. She'd made tea and placed it on a tray, which was highly unusual. She wasn't in the habit of serving people. Or using trays. I asked if I could help in any way, and she'd given me a strange smile, as if she couldn't actually see me, though I was sitting right there.

After that, the election had taken all our energy. There was no time for anything else. Or perhaps she avoided me. Finally, on a drive home after a late meeting in Cologne, a rare moment when I was alone with her, I took a chance and jumped in. I just said it straight. I had the letter from Yad Vashem. Ada Meinbaum's ash-covered list. I wanted Petra to understand that I knew.

There was so much silence I thought the car would die of it.

"Petra?" I couldn't see her face. We were taking the slow route, along winding country roads, and there were no street lights at all.

"You really don't stop, do you?" That was what she said. So sharp and blank it took my breath away.

"Yes. I do," I fumbled. "I can stop."

"You're like a child playing with puppets."

"I'm sorry if you feel that."

"You push and push. Anyway, to answer your question, yes, he's told me everything, just as it should be between two people who love each other. Now you can leave him alone."

On Tulpenfeld's seventh floor, Freya was overseeing the painting of a banner spread out along the length of the hallway. Women of all colours holding up a rainbow. We'd opened our offices to the peace groups.

"We're doing our best," Freya said, "to keep paint off the walls and floor of your corridor of power."

"But look, you've spilled. You know what happens now?"

"What?"

"They lock you in a windowless room and make you type memos for eternity."

"That's a fate some Greens might want."

"Is that a criticism, Freya?"

"Can't you hear it in my voice?"

"You're keeping me honest."

"Actually, you're not the one I worry about." She sat up. Nobody was around, and she whispered ardently, "Tell me you haven't seen the change in Petra! She's like a ghost."

"She's overworked."

She stared at me. "Keep an eye out for her," she said. "I can't. She won't speak to me about *him*."

"Emil?"

"Who else?"

I leaned in, noticing that she had a splotch of purple paint on her neck. "What exactly are you saying?"

"He's so crisp and well dressed—he fits right into this place."

"That's not a crime."

"Who said I'm looking for crimes? But there's something odd about him recently. Something cold."

It was true, I realized. Only the day before, at the door to his office, I'd come upon Emil searching his jacket pocket for his key, and there was something false in his smile, his very way of waggling the keys in the air, as though he was play-acting. I asked how he liked his new home, and he smiled broadly. "Oh, I like it immensely," he said. "It's a lovely little place. Of course, Petra has her thousands of books."

"You are surrounded by Anna Akhmatova now," I said, and he looked at me blankly at first, then laughed. "Yes, exactly. How well you put it. All those principled heroes of hers."

"And of course there is the way he jumps to obey her," Freya continued. "People comment on it. You know what they say, Manfred, when he follows three steps behind her, carrying all her things? *Oh, look—it's Petra's baggage carrier.*" She breathed out. A piece of her unruly hair fell in front of her nose, and I pushed it back for her. She softened with my touch. "Or maybe I'm just tired. But I will tell you something, Manfred. I don't trust him."

"Yes, but you never have."

"So I haven't wavered. His positions are so thin. He never speaks of the peace groups in the East. Our counterparts. Or any other issue of substance. It is only the missiles for him. And his group—"

"Generals for Peace."

She wrinkled her nose. "Old men around a boardroom table. They're not Greens—they should be called Greys. And people talk. They say they're an elaborate front group funded by the Eastern Bloc to criticize NATO."

"Yes, well, that could be."

"Where's their money coming from?"

I shrugged. "I'm with you, Freya. But you know how it is."

"What?"

I heard myself saying what Petra had said to me. "It's not that easy to manipulate eight generals."

She made a face of distaste, and I went to my office and shut the door. At my desk, I looked at the bare wall. Looked some more. It was absolutely true what she'd said. The Generals for Peace were conducting a clean, almost sanitized, version of our fight against the missiles. Dignified. Unified. Male. And with a tendency to spout statistics about firepower and missile strength in a way that was impressive yet—well, it lacked the chaotic green wildness of Petra's vision. It was another thing entirely.

But I didn't think that joining those generals accounted for the new coolness in Emil. And neither did being an elected official. These positions of political gravitas fit him like a good woollen suit. Yet he seemed stiff as he came and went with Petra, and he was too quick to smile.

Sometimes I heard them as they left late at night, talking softly by the elevator. And then the *shush* of the door opening, him attempting to keep it from closing while burdened with briefcase, umbrella, a box of files. A minute later, if I rose and went to the window, I would see them crossing the quadrangle towards his car, shadows lengthening across the square and up the neighbouring building like a single dark flame.

4.

Strange Bedfellows

What was happening in private was one thing. In public, Petra Kelly remained magnificent.

At every press conference, she warned that if Helmut Kohl went ahead with the missiles, it was going to be the autumn of our lives. The day she uttered the phrase, "The Hot Autumn of the Rockets," you could hear the frantic scribbling of pencils. "Will there be riots? Will there be bloodshed?" the journalists asked.

"Not caused by the Greens." She straightened in her chair. "We scorn the idea of violence—you know that. We are non-violent because that's what creates lasting change. Think of Selma, Alabama; think of Gandhi's great march."

"And so you would never resort to—"

"It is anathema. Violence causes violence. It's an endless cycle."

"And what about the confusion within the Greens themselves? Some don't hold your views."

"Growing pains."

They wrote that down too.

There *was* confusion within the Green elected caucus. We'd been thrown into the deep end naked, and the water was cold and shocking. We had to make decisions about how to function as elected members while managing the push and pull of the larger Green coalition, which wanted effective action but also warned against making compromises.

We decided that Emil should sit on an All-Party Defence Committee, while Petra would take her place on Foreign Affairs. I was given Immigration. We carried the weight of these committees on our backs, each of us the sole Green voice in a river of contrary opinion. Should we intervene each time something reactionary got said? How could we influence parliament? It was such a burningly obvious question—we'd worked so hard to get here—yet nobody could quite figure it out.

"What does it matter if we're the sole voice on a committee?" Gisela Fuchs said during one of our first caucus meetings, and glared at the others, daring them to contradict her. "We're not here to compromise with other parties, to get along. This isn't a tea party. We're here to start something new. And yes, these words are for you, Jürgen. I know you're plotting deals with the Social Democrats, meeting up with them in the beer cellar down the road."

Laughter. Jürgen leaned back in his chair, running shoes on the table, smiling like an elf. Unlike so many of us, who were floundering, politics suited him.

"The people who voted for us know we aren't here for coalition politics," Gisela said, and she got up and walked over to Jürgen's chair and took hold of the back. "We are here to fundamentally oppose what the established parties are doing." She gave the chair a little tug and Jürgen tipped backwards onto the floor, but he sprang up, unruffled, and took the stance of a boxer.

"Enough!" cried Emil. But there was no need to intervene. The whole room, including Gisela and Jürgen, began howling with laughter. We were giddy from our new position, the thrill of what we were heading towards.

"We are so different from each other," Petra marvelled, staring with genuine fondness at Jürgen, who gave her a little wink. "Nothing like us has hit politics before. Revolutions are built from such heat."

"Yes, but can we get Gisela to shut up?" I said.

"Stop it!" she poked me.

One day I walked into our Green meeting room to find Rainer Beckman of the *Frankfurter Allgemeine Zeitung* making himself comfortable in a chair near the wall. His notepad was open on his lap, and when he saw me, a smile played across his fleshy mouth.

"I'm sorry, but you'll have to wait outside," I said. "We have a lot of work to do today."

He bounced the eraser end of his pencil on his notebook and caught it. "You should pay attention to what your party decides," he said. "Your meetings are now open to all."

This was blatant craziness. I turned to Petra, Emil and Jürgen, who shrugged and showed me his palms, the pads of his fingers tobacco-stained. "We decided yesterday morning," he said. "Where were you?"

It was the single caucus meeting I'd missed, groggy from beer and a late night. "We can't do this."

Petra looked at me coolly. "Why not? It's an open party."

"But we have differences, which we need to thrash out in private."

"That's the way the other parties do it, but we're different. We aren't afraid of scrutiny." She was raising her voice for Rainer's benefit. Oh, yes. Her vanity was at work. She needed to be recorded, watched, made larger. In the parliamentary caucus, with so many other voices, she had shrunk ever so slightly.

"Oh, Petra. This is a very bad idea."

A cloud of concern crossed her face, but she brushed it away. "You're taking too bleak an attitude again. In fact, this isn't even a change—we've always been an open party."

"I don't need a slogan," I snapped at her. "I need some common sense."

I turned to Emil. "Help me here, will you?"

He was very still, looking at his hands. I could feel him weighing what he really thought against what Petra wanted him to say. I waited, relying on the slow churning of his gears, the truth emerging from him as it so often did, though it might take awhile. But Petra leapt in. "It's been decided, Manfred."

Emil gave me a bemused smile. Ah well. At least he was off the hook.

Jürgen had moved next to Rainer, lining him up on some point or other. He, of all people, should have known what a mess it would be opening the party to public scrutiny. I turned back to Petra and spoke quietly. "Do you think Rainer Beckman is going to write glowing accolades about our internal debates?"

"He might," said Petra.

"No," I shook my head. "No party can withstand—"

"But we aren't just any party," said Petra, firmly. "We're the Greens."

"I can't believe you all decided this without me."

Rainer finished with Jürgen and went to get a coffee. "It'll be a long afternoon," he called out cheerfully. I sat down beside Jürgen.

"Why?" I said simply.

He shrugged. "Petra wanted it too."

"Yes, but that isn't usually enough reason for you," I said. "The press will report every messy battle. And we're having them by the cartload."

"Perhaps," Jürgen said. "But then a voice of reason will start to emerge out of the chaos. People aren't stupid, Manfred. They'll start to notice which of us is making sense."

I stared at him.

"We need to become a reasonable party. Maybe this will help get us there."

I shook my head, and he reached out and touched my arm. "It's openness," he said, eyes sparkling. "Don't be so afraid of it."

The next bit of carnival madness seemed to happen in the blink of an eye. Our group, which had walked into the Bundestag a power-house of change, split into two highly public factions. We had always had divisions, of course, and consensus was hard work, but this split had a new intensity because it was about how we functioned on a day-to-day level as elected members of parliament.

The Realos, dominated by men, were led by Jürgen, compelling and always impish. Having ridden the Green wave into parliament, acting as though he'd swallowed the full agenda of feminism, non-violence and ecology, he now began to craft his own brand of deal-making politics. He wanted to forge compromises with the Social Democrats, to create a united left that could actually win the next election. *Coalition readiness* was the Realo buzz phrase. Why bother getting real political power if we didn't make plans to use it, to keep it? He argued that the more visionary notions of the Greens were just that—visions. The Greens' mammoth agenda was absurd. It needed whittling and organization. The Dalai Lama and the plight of Tibetan children weren't central to West German politics. That was so obvious! Must it be said?

Yes, apparently.

Gisela Fuchs, nose quivering with indignation, led the other faction, the Fundis. She rejected the Realos' "hierarchy of values."

How could they claim that protesting nuclear weapons in our backyard was more important than stopping the low-flying fighter jets from destroying the Innu's caribou hunting in Labrador? "To us in Germany it *feels* more burning," Gisela said to the caucus, parading her views before the press, "but the Innu would disagree. And who says the child in East Timor, terrified of Indonesian soldiers, is any less entitled to our help than a German child frightened of nuclear bombs?"

"But must we address all issues *at once?*" Jürgen called out, to laughter.

"Yes, we must," said Gisela staunchly. "Because to split the web into pieces is to debase the wholeness upon which the Greens are based."

Petra was a Fundi in her heart. Her deepest political vision was of valuing the interconnected web of life, and she was not a compromiser by nature. Despite this, she refused to align with Gisela, because she found the Fundis too divisive, too haranguing.

"But her politics are similar to yours," I said to Petra in her office one afternoon. "You've got to admit it."

"It doesn't matter. She's cold and arrogant."

Was she jealous of Gisela's new power or was she completely sincere? I didn't know, but she kept herself aloof from infighting, which often meant that she was not much of a factor in these internal battles. If, in a public meeting or a press interview, she was invited to explain the differences between the two groups, she could and did (she prided herself on being a quick study), but she considered the factions a waste of time.

As for me, I had more genuine sympathy for the deal-making Realos than for the principled Fundis, whose lack of compromise threatened our ability to build political power within the Bundestag. Still, I felt a loyalty to Petra that kept me from aligning myself outright with any faction. Often I found myself acting as a sort of go-between, interpreting one to the other, trying to keep peace. Which wasn't easy. The only thing they seemed to agree on was that Petra had too much power.

"Petra's not Realo or Fundi," Gisela said to the ever-present Rainer Beckman. "She thinks she's her own wing." When he asked her to clarify, Gisela shrugged. "She puts herself above us, and that's not how we Greens operate."

Rainer went to Jürgen Wolff. What did he have to say about this? Was Petra, he asked, too much of a star?

Jürgen leaned back in his chair, placed his feet on his desk and took a drag from his cigarette. "No, no, Rainer," he said at last. "Not at all. We all admire Petra Kelly."

He paused while Rainer wrote this down.

"And she's been politically useful, as charismatic people almost always are in party-building."

"And," said Rainer, "is she still, would you say, the leader of the Greens?"

A genial laugh. "Leader of the Greens." Jürgen mouthed the words, as if experimenting with their taste. "Have you asked Gisela that?"

"I have."

"Then she must have told you what the Fundis think of having leaders."

"She did."

"Ha ha. Then why ask me? You've got it from the horse's mouth."

5.

Enter Rufus

Now I must backtrack slightly, to catch us up on Katrina.

As the weeks of her pregnancy had crept by, and I'd been immersed in the election campaign, she had only become more stubbornly independent. She wasn't inclined to involve me in any way, although I had tried to talk to her at demonstrations or on the street as she hurried somewhere with a bevy of women friends closed around her like fierce dogs. And so I was surprised one morning in mid-April, about six weeks after the election, to see her filling the door of my office at Tulpenfeld. She was a full nine months' pregnant, wearing a red-and-black dress of horizontal stripes that made her look like an enormous beetle. Her hair was blue. She had dyed it her favourite colour, she said, for the birth. She stared at me across the piles of boxes, files, books and posters, unfurled but not yet hung.

I cleared a pile of files about Tibet from a chair—stories of refugees with frostbitten feet who had fled from the Chinese into northern India. Katrina sat down, massive belly pointing at me. I saw an enormous ripple pass beneath the fabric, like the involuntary flexing of a vast muscle.

"Oh fuck, oh fuck. Hey," she addressed her belly, "stop with the rolling."

"That's the baby," I said, rather stupidly.

"No kidding. What did you think? That it was something I ate?" Then she got to the point. "The baby's probably yours," she said. "But I don't want money."

This threw me: I had assumed money was the main thing I could offer her now that I had my new job, modest though the pay was.

"I don't know if I want you in my life," she continued, "and money may make you think you have a right."

I muttered that I was sure I didn't have any rights at all. I found a clear piece of desk and sat down. "Tell me what you want, Katrina."

"Here." She took several folded pieces of paper from her purse and thrust them at me. "Read this over. It's a baby contract. I need child-care breaks. I need time to study, because after my maternity leave I'm going back to school. You can take on these things yourself or you can arrange to have them done. I don't want your money, though at some point I'd like to discuss a long-term educational fund." With some difficulty, she pushed herself up to go. Her cheeks were red, and I saw how much coming to me had cost her.

"Think it over," she said, as she walked to the door.

"I don't need to think it over," I blurted. "Yes. Of course, yes. Yes to it all."

She paused at the door, then turned and sat back down in the chair, her face blotchy from the receding blush.

"All right, then," she said.

"All right."

"I guess you can't refuse me in my massive condition. I'm the Madonna to you now."

"Madonna with blue hair."

She laughed. "Just read the contract over," she said, "and try not to fuck up."

"And the birth?"

"The midwife will telephone you to let you know if it's a girl or a boy."

"Can't you have them phone me when you go into labour?"

She seemed surprised and then shrugged. "If you want."

She got up to go again, and I stood too.

"If you want me there, I could come to the hospital," I said.

"You at a birth? You'd be writing a brief while I had my contractions. No, I think I'll do this one solo, Manfred." Nevertheless, she turned once again at the door. "But thank you," she said.

Which is why we were *both* surprised, I suppose, when the midwife telephoned from the hospital.

"Katrina wants you here. She seems to think you might be of use."

That is how I ended up in the birthing room, holding my son in my arms. I touched the forceps marks at each temple—marks that framed his small, fierce face.

Moments before, as they had weighed him, I'd been at my designated station beside Katrina's head. She was clenching my hand while the obstetrician stitched where she'd torn. All at once, a jab of the needle caused blood to spurt onto the sheet. I must have looked faint, because the midwife took me by the arm and moved me away from my post, sitting me in a chair, while the doula handed me the baby, now swathed in a flannel receiving blanket. I was told to make myself useful. To sing.

It is true that, as I held my baby that morning, I sang him "The Internationale." Softly, of course. And it is true that my singing, through all the pain of the stitching, made Katrina laugh. But why her laughter at that moment was the best sound I had ever heard—that I can't explain.

With the baby in my arms, I came around the bed and stroked the wet blue hair from Katrina's face. She grimaced and the midwife shooed me away again. She and the doula were holding Katrina's thighs open while the doctor went at her with an enormous needle and suturing thread. Which was why, for the first fifteen minutes of his life, it was just us—Rufus Olaf Maximilian and Manfred Schwartz—while every now and then, from the bed, Katrina called out, "Can someone make sure he doesn't drop the baby?"

"The baby's doing fine," the obstetrician said. "Three and a half kilograms."

The size of a good-sized stone. A fisherman's buoy. A dossier of files on the problem of NATO low-level flight testing in Labrador.

A small enough weight, in other words, but destined to anchor my life forever.

6.

The Buddha Baby

Rufus's arrival threw me right off my trajectory. I had been so moved by the birth, by Katrina, that I felt overwhelmed—as though I couldn't take on even one additional piece of information. And yet, at some point in this blur, I did absorb one more thing: I realized that I hadn't thought about Petra at all. She had receded. The drama of what was happening between Emil and her had become less important to me, while life— LIFE—had, in fact, swamped me.

What should I do? Should I step up in some way for Katrina? What did that even mean? Should I change my life entirely? Should I marry her? What was happening to me?

And all the while, the baby, the baby, the baby! His softness, his face, his nose, so small and scrunched, the smell of the receiving blanket he was wrapped in, the little blue hat the nurses had put on his head. I was so in love, so incredibly in love with him.

I was in my office several days after the birth, preparing for one of our parliamentary caucus sessions, when the door flew open. There was Petra, positively beaming at me, with an expensive-looking shopping bag in her hand.

"Manfred!" she cried. "How is this even possible? *My* Manfred!" She danced around the desk to give me a kiss. "Why haven't I seen you? It feels like forever! You're a papa!" She hugged me. "And you will be a fantastic father. This I know." Her eyes were full of tears, and for a moment mine were too.

"I don't know about that," I managed to say.

"You do know! Yes, you do know. You will be wonderful. It is a role I have always felt you were waiting for."

I shook my head, thinking of all the complications with Katrina. But Petra said, "No, no—you'll work things out! You will have a good life!" And again her eyes got watery.

I opened the bag. Inside was a stuffed bear with a little red hat and a jar of expensive body cream for Katrina.

"The woman at the store told me the cream performs miracles with stretch marks!"

"Thank you."

(*What does she think?* Katrina said when she opened the gift. *That I'm covered in lines like a raisin?*)

I glanced behind her for the ever-present Emil, and she informed me that he had travelled to Vienna for a meeting with the Generals for Peace. "It's such a relief for him to be among his peers. He'll come back fattened with pheasant and caviar."

Did her face fall a little? I thought it did.

"Yes," I said tactfully, "they are one of our more lavish peace groups."

"It's an awful waste of money, but they want to keep the generals happy." For a moment she looked troubled. "There are rumours. Do you think there is truth in any of it?"

"Maybe. You know what I think of Magnus, and the group will be guided by him."

She sighed. "I think Emil will continue to consult his conscience. I think we can both give him that." But it felt like there was a question mark at the end of her statement.

She leaned over and touched me lightly on the top of my

hand, and a spark flew between us, a product of the carpet. "Look at that," she laughed. "The same old electricity."

When she was gone, I sat staring out the window. So there it was, at long last. Was she interested in me again? She'd tilted her head, laughed down at me, strode away with energy, knowing my eyes would follow her out the door. Well, it made sense—as I had moved away, she had moved towards me, as though she never wanted space to grow between us. But how subtle she was. How quickly she'd picked up on my change of heart.

That touch had said it all. She wanted to know that she could depend on me. She was asking, *Will you still love me, even when you are with Katrina at the hospital, even when you are buying groceries for her return home?* I was producing an ache in Petra at last. I could feel it just like it was in my own body.

The next day, Katrina was discharged. She and the baby moved into Freya's apartment. When I went to visit, she was in the rocking chair. Her breasts, now huge, had left two wet patches on the front of her smock. She pulled down the elastic neck and set Rufus to her breast with a bit of fumbling, while Freya pulled at her nipple to get Rufus to latch. It was intimate, almost workmanlike, to see the two women figuring out how to discharge the milk, which was backed up. Katrina's breasts were so hard they were almost like wood. When at last Rufus sucked, his entire head turned instantly red, even his little neck!

Once he was settled, Katrina sighed and looked up at me. "So," she said, "I think you know I'm heading to Lübeck for the next few months."

No, I hadn't. I felt at sea as she described how her parents were going to help her with Rufus, while she helped them out when she could with their bakery. A set-up that was possible, I realized, because they actually liked each other, an astonishing rarity in our generation.

She made no mention of me visiting Lübeck. Nor could I say a thing, except to murmur that I would miss them.

"You'll be completely swept up with the fight against the missiles. You won't notice we're gone."

"I will notice, Katrina."

"Ha, so you say. Well, I don't know, and I can't wait around to find out."

She looked up at me, and I wanted to say that things had changed between us, but what if it wasn't true? I asked to hold Rufus, and she passed him to me, milk-full and asleep. I stared down at his dreaming face, eyelids marbled with tiny veins. The smell of him. I put my nose to his stomach, breathing in the scent of his flannel receiving blanket, covered in tiny giraffes and elephants.

He had an extremely intelligent face, I thought. And wise. Freya had nicknamed him the Buddha Baby, and there was truth to that. He seemed to be dreaming of the place from which he'd come, a purple land, twilit and mysterious.

Now I was a father. And what was that going to be like? Would I hurt my son, as I'd been hurt? One day would he storm out, slamming my front door, shaking the windowpane? Was there any way I could stop the avalanche of anger, father to son?

7

Thank God for Vienna

Sitting in his hotel room, his first Generals for Peace meeting over, Emil decided to telephone the front desk and order champagne. A half bottle. His plan wasn't to get drunk, only to savour the final hours before he taxied to the airport and flew back to Bonn.

"Is that all, sir?"

On a whim, he asked for caviar as well. Ridiculous that the Greens had voted, almost as their first elected act, to take a pay cut. Just like them. Many complained afterward about the decision, and how hard it was to get by. Emil certainly could have used the money now that he had to support two households. So. A little taste of caviar before the return to Swinemünder Strasse and the lovely, complicated Petra, who kept proclaiming how domestic she was whenever she did anything in the kitchen, such as putting on coffee or rinsing a pot.

The flat was small, and yet it was cozy, and the two of them were acting like newlyweds, buying furniture and cast-iron pans and enamel pots with fitted lids so that he could cook for them and she could eat properly. How pleased she'd been when she saw that he had put the postcard of the Rhine on the mantelpiece! She had come to him and kissed him deeply, and they'd both felt stirred, abandoning what they were doing to climb the stairs to the bedroom. Like newlyweds, she had exclaimed, but of course it wasn't quite like that, because he was married to Helena and they both carried that knowledge, which made all they were doing sometimes seem a little like playing house.

While all of this was a difficult balance, it wasn't what was rankling him.

There was a hole somewhere, but it wasn't that.

Was it Helena herself, and his responsibilities in that direction? The old dog Felix was dead, and Helena had told him when they last met that she didn't want another dog. This was after he said he planned to live more of the time in Bonn, and she had said, "Oh dear, what does that mean? Are you setting up house with Petra?" And she'd seen from his face that it was so, and she had sunk to the couch. "So this is a lasting thing, then?" She'd said it with grief. And at that moment he had seen the dignity in her so clearly. "I thought we were 'for each other.'" That was what she said, and every particle of her, the silk blouse, the neat trousers, the grief and beauty, the high arched eyebrows, yes, every inch of her dignity was so different from the quarrelling Greens.

There was a knock on the door, and Emil opened it. The waiter. White gloves and a silver tray. "Yes, I'd like it uncorked. Set it there. Thank you." "Not at all." He had been assured that the tab was to be picked up by Generals for Peace. None of this done on the cheap, thank god.

Emil took off his shoes and sat looking at the bed, its pristine cover embossed with the hotel's circular insignia. Then he raised his glass and took a large gulp. Lovely. Not sweet, almost salty, with bubbles he could feel in his nose.

Was it only Helena that was bothering him? Manfred, that know-it-all, was warning him all the time about Generals for Peace, as though Emil couldn't see for himself the ways of the world. All his talk about manipulation. It was ridiculous. The meeting had been superb, with the eight military men sitting around the table. Affable General Stathopoulos had chaired. Next to him sat the bossy admiral from America, hair as white and full as Santa Claus's, but with a hard Californian voice, full of meaty privilege. Across from him sat General Baxter from the UK, with his meerschaum pipe. Emil wanted to laugh when Baxter pulled it out, like a prop in a play! But Baxter stuffed the tobacco into the bowl, cleared his throat messily and carried on with his point.

As for that fellow Magnus whom Manfred was so suspicious of, he'd been splendidly diffident, if one could put it that way, melting into the background, allowing the generals to debate and discuss each issue, proffering only occasional points of information. He was by far the youngest man in the room, well dressed in a cashmere sweater and jeans, paired with a lightweight suit jacket. A spy? Wearing something that looked like Hugo Boss? Surely not.

Over the past two days, Emil had been with serious men, making plans to intervene in the state of the world, to do good with the power they had accrued. It was a combination, the power and the doing good, that was like—like what? Like something you desperately needed in your system but didn't realize you'd missed until you got a jolt of it again. Like the first time you kissed a new woman. That first kiss with Petra in the Berlin hotel room, she completely naked and he completely clothed. Sliding his hand down her spine.

It was strange, of course, to compare the bliss of touching Petra with the bliss of talking military tactics with elderly men, but they were similar: some part of him was now twanging, plucked like a long-unused string, wanting to be plucked again.

Stathis Stathopoulos. You couldn't help liking the fellow. He had two children he absolutely doted on. Out came the wallet photos at the break. "They're my life. But oh—family life is complicated. And you, Emil?" Emil had murmured something about his own complications, and Stathis nodded. "Yes, a wife and a mistress—always in competition, eh?" Then he patted Emil on the back, laughing. "What can I say, my friend. You're in a fine stew now. No way out but forward."

"Good strategic advice."

As for their work crafting a basis of unity—their position on the nuclear Euromissiles was to remove all first-strike nuclear weapons from the European battlefield. East and West.

Emil had raised his hand. "Is this altogether wise? It does leave the Soviet Union with a three-to-one advantage in conventional forces. Perhaps we ought to mention the conventional disparity."

General Porter sucked his pipe. "Ah, but correcting the disparity in conventional forces must be addressed as stage two, don't you agree? We can't do it all at once."

Emil almost laughed out loud. Why couldn't the Greens figure that out?

As for nuclear reactors, that great and stormy issue, many of the generals openly supported nuclear power. Again, a door flew open in Emil—and how good the fresh air felt.

"I completely agree," he said. "Nuclear power is a viable source of energy. Though I'd be flayed alive if I said so in the Green caucus room."

Laughter.

Then Stathopoulos leaned forward seriously. "Emil, if we generals refuse to take a position against nuclear power, will that make it hard for you at home?"

"I'll manage. I often take a position that is more narrow, as they say, than my peers."

More chuckling.

"Very wise," said Baxter. "If you'll allow me to say so."

Emil did allow him to say so.

Then, in the afternoon, the thorny issue of human rights in

Eastern Europe had come up. Emil went over the discussion again in his head. The US admiral had unwrapped a tuna sandwich, saying he needed to eat every hour to balance his blood sugar. When Stathopoulos posed the question, the admiral answered testily: "Nothing to do with us. Plain and simple. Our credibility must rest on sticking to military issues."

Emil heard Petra gasp in his head. *Everything is to do with us!* Every outrage, every rape, every act of torture, every forced march. *We are them*—hadn't she said that again and again? *We must speak for those who cannot speak for themselves.*

"All right," said Stathopoulos. "Shall we call the vote?"

Emil looked down at his notepad.

"I'm ready to vote," said the admiral. "No controversy for me."

There was a murmuring of agreement.

They are us. But *were* they us? Wasn't that actually incorrect? A gross overstatement? In fact, couldn't such thinking make a person crazy? Perhaps it was even at the centre of the Greens' recent madness—a kind of grotesque over-empathy. Certainly, within the Green caucus, the Realos often responded with derision to the full web-of-life agenda.

He put up his hand tentatively. Stathopoulos gestured for him to speak.

"I suppose one might argue," Emil heard himself say, "that the human rights of anti-missile protestors in the GDR or the Soviet Union might be seen as part of our jurisdiction."

The American commander flicked his wax paper with his fingernail. *Oh, dear. Is this German going to be difficult?*

Did General Stathopoulos glance at Magnus Isaacson? If so, it happened in the blink of an eye, and then Stathopoulos was smiling broadly. He slammed both palms on the table. "Well done. Let's get this on the table. A good debate is always useful."

Hands shot up.

"We are generals, not human-rights lawyers. Or judges at the Hague."

"If we address this issue publicly, we could damage our credibility."

"From what I hear, there is a large and thriving movement for peace in the GDR—and it is an official movement. I visited Leipzig last year for a festival and saw thousands of peace supporters waving the country's flag. These others, who get arrested, we don't know who they are or who controls them."

Emil tried to clear his mind, willed himself to hear the soft rumble, like a heartbeat, that was his knowledge of what he thought and therefore must do. What was the formula again? Military manoeuvres, followed by cows. A boy running across a field. He felt flustered and, to make it worse, he kept hearing Petra. *They are us!* Her voice was filling his head. And where had that damned memory come from? Why cows? He could see their shining black-and-white hides. *Give me clarity*, he said to a cow, but nothing happened. And he shook his head. How had he been so ridiculous?

All the men were looking at him, the other speakers done.

"Emil?" Stathopoulos said softly.

Alone, he could sort out everything. Alone, he could find the steps. On a walk by the river he could do it. Or in the car with Helena. Yes, he felt a pang for Helena just at that exact moment, longing for the ripples of silence that spread from his wife.

"It seems," he ventured, "that my opinion is not of much importance. You've already arrived at the majority opinion."

"But do you agree?" This was the American admiral.

A pause. Then, "Yes, of course," he heard himself say. "I'm a military man. Our group should focus on military issues."

He'd meant it. It made sense. But could this possibly be the source of his distress? It seemed to be. Like a painful clock

ticking in his chest, it kept repeating, *You went along with them.*
You took no responsibility for your actions. And even: *You were*
manipulated. That glance from Stathopoulos to Magnus. From
one angle, he could see quite clearly that it had happened, yet
from another it was preposterous. And in between sat Emil, with
his idea about cows in a field, his memory of being young and
full of vigour and joy, with the sun on his shoulders and the wet
thwap, thwap of the grass against his calves. What did that
memory even mean? He had never been able to place it. It was
very strange, as though a rush of water flooded the sides of the
memory, so that he could never understand why the field, why
the cows, why the hillside in the distance, why the happiness.
And in the meeting, he hadn't been able to conjure it at all.

Emil lay back on the bed, tracing the ridges of the coverlet
with his fingertips.

It was wrong to think it—another wrong thought in a head
full of wrong thoughts—but he wanted to blame Petra for the
failure of his memory device. He had heard her voice in his head
just as he was searching for his personal sense of truth, and her
voice had covered up his own thoughts. *We are them! We are them!*
And then (here he sat up, because this was a thought he must
face), even as they decorated their house and cooked and honestly
enjoyed their new status, she was always watching him. A covert
activity. One part of her was as he had come to know her: gentle,
fierce, sexy, empathetic. The other was watching.

In the kitchen, in the hallway, in the living room. Question
marks were fairly bristling all around her, coming from her head
like in a comic book. Even standing in the kitchen, talking about
the baby birds in the nest outside the window, as they both had
been a few days ago. She was turned away from him at the stove,
but he felt her tracking his movements. Tracking his shadow. As
though it might part from him suddenly. Lunge at her.

In response to her unspoken fear, he had been trying to fold himself into a small, reliable package—a package of non-harm! Carrying bags. Checking that the coast was clear before they walked across the Tulpenfeld courtyard. Locking and chaining the doors. But what was he protecting her from? When he locked the French doors at night, what was he locking out?

He knew she was thinking about the girl in the dress with its pattern of dark-green ivy leaves, because one night, when neither of them could sleep, she sat up in bed and began to ask more questions. As though they'd both been waiting for the conversation to resume. How old had she been? A teenager? A girl, even? Or was she older? Did she seem educated, a girl who might find her way to a city, or had she been a farm girl? And as Petra asked these questions, the girl came into focus, glowing like a candle, slender and pale, with an inner beauty that hurt. It was as though Petra made her real, breathing life into the past without a care for the pain.

Witnessing.

Emil could never remember the long Hindu word for it. But that was what she was doing to him. She was witnessing his past.

He got up from the bed and went to the bathroom, pissed heavily and then washed his hands and looked at his face. Haggard and handsome. He remembered how quickly Petra had said to him, *I understand.* How she had held him in her arms.

Instead of thinking, *I understand*, she should have said what she really thought. She should have said, *You should have done right by them.*

But if I'd done right by them, he imagined himself saying, *I would have been shot myself.*

Then you should have been shot.

Was that what she thought—that he should have died like Sophie Scholl of the White Rose group, whose biography had mysteriously travelled from the bookshelf to the side table in the living room, as though to say: *She could do it, and she was a mere eighteen-year-old.* She knew the difference between right and wrong and stood up to Nazism with her pamphlets, she and her brother, Hans, and his friends. The pamphlets they dropped down the stairwell at the University of Munich. Their ardent tracts against Nazism were soon traced back to them, and their little group was imprisoned. Then all of them were decapitated. A swift axe, and off went their heads.

That's what noble people did.

And what was he to do? Could he tell Petra to her face, *I'm not Sophie Scholl. I'm not Hans Scholl. Don't you understand? I'm simply an ordinary man.*

8

The Hot Autumn of the Rockets

As we hashed out issues between the Realos and Fundis, or reported back to the larger citizens' groups, or put forward motions in parliament, or sat on all-party committees and tried to get our voices heard, the date of the Euromissile deployment crept closer. We'd promised a Hot Autumn of the Rockets, and at last, like the rising of a curtain for a play, autumn was upon us.

Every day now, we spun out the revolving doors of Tulpenfeld and raced to a new peace action, peace caravan, peace blockade. We startled even ourselves with a mass action of 400,000 people overflowing the Hofgarten, with 350,000 in Hamburg, 250,000 in Stuttgart and 100,000 in West Berlin—bringing over a million people into the streets on a single day. We rose against the nuclear missiles, and we felt it in the air, in our own determined grins: we were almost embarrassed to be so tightly bound to the making of history. We were living a myth. That was how it felt. The news reports said it all: *Largest protests Europe has ever seen.*

At Greenham Common in England, thousands of women had set up camp around the cruise missile base. At night they crept forward to leave webs of coloured yarn on the chain-link fence, knotted with flowers or pictures of their loved ones. Then they retreated to their campfires, chanting and holding each other, crying in grief because of the evil of the missiles so close by. Even now I can feel their power across the years, trying to transform the cruise missiles—all that mega-death— with the practical magic of a thousand female fingers, weaving a counterspell.

New York, a million on the streets.

Toronto, Paris, a hundred thousand.

But we, in Bonn, were the beating heart. And the only blot on our actions, which flowed spontaneously, again and again, shocking even ourselves—the only blot was the little man with his ferret, who kept getting into the news. He'd made a sign that he attached to the ferret's collar: FERRETS FOR FORNICATION WITH-OUT FEAR. He was driving Freya crazy. "Look," she pointed to the newspaper, "there he is again, grinning with his little animal. I think he may be a CIA agent trying to diminish our credibility."

"You think? Is the CIA so inventive," I asked, "that they would try to derail our protests with a *ferret?*"

It was the Hot Autumn of pink hair and protesting civil servants and angry professors and dogs wearing bandanas and ferrets for fornication. At the protests we were wrapped in Petra's voice; she kept managing to walk to the podium, the new, hollow look on her face, and then to do her mysterious shudder and begin the spell that magnetized us, so that years later, after her death, people would come up to me on the streets, put a hand on my arm or shoulder, and tell me they could still hear her voice in their dreams.

9

Come, Little Sister

As I crossed the market square, leaves skittered like mice, gathering in the gutters, shuffling against each other. I was exhausted after a long meeting at Freya's apartment, and was heading to the farmhouse. So cold, my house these days. My thoughts drifted to Petra, how she had leaned forward to touch me at the meeting, a hand on my shoulder. Her touch said, *Don't forget about me. Don't lose sight of me.* She was like a child, checking for my affections. Perhaps it was this child side of hers that I loved above all. Riding towards the sun, sword raised. Or looking at the man in the moon, thinking of her father. So wounded, after his vanishing.

Supposing I asked her to come with me. Leave him. Would she? Was this still a possibility? Perhaps she wasn't even aware of her fingers touching my shoulder, her hands grazing the back of my hand, while for me she created electricity and confusion with every touch.

All of this was in my head as I crossed the square and glanced, almost without thinking, towards the yellow-lit windows of the Stern Hotel. Framed in the window was a solitary figure, a veritable tableau of lonely drinking. Helena Gerhardt. The sight of her always came with background music, somehow, an accordion, perhaps, or the strains of a cello. I had heard that she'd taken Emil's final exodus hard. A body blow. Yet I also knew that she and Emil continued to see each other, and I had run into her dropping Emil off at Tulpenfeld.

She was to be pitied. Yet something in Helena Gerhardt did not inspire pity.

I swerved to avoid a cyclist barrelling across the square, and the motion must have caught her eye. She knocked on the glass, half-standing, beckoning for me to come inside. I pushed open the heavy lobby doors, then entered the bar, with its golden lighting and heavy chairs.

"Manfred Schwartz." She smiled, touching the syllables of my name as though she found them amusing. Her eyebrows were plucked alarmingly into two Harlequin bows, making her face look gaunt and exposed. "I would be delighted if you'd join me. I've had an adventure. Yes, an adventure, in Dinkelsbühl of all places, and I could use a little company."

She caught the waiter's eye. I ordered a beer and Helena asked for another glass of wine. She seemed to be vibrating lightly all over, a medicated high-frequency fizzing. I caught a whiff of dusky perfume and, for a moment, it staggered me. L'air du Temps. My mother's favourite.

"And so," I said, "what brings you to Bonn? Are you here to protest?"

She laughed. "Oh, dear, no. And not to see Emil either. He is away with the Generals for Peace." No, she was here to visit a friend who ran a flower shop, one of the little ones near Beethoven House. This friend thought Helena might enjoy a change of pace. Something new in her life. "She wondered whether I might like to work in a shop. So kind of her, but can you imagine? I told her no, but she's an insistent sort of friend, so I will visit her in her shop tomorrow."

She sat back and closed her eyes.

"Are you all right?"

"Oh, yes."

I wondered if Emil knew she had come to town, and how he would feel if he saw me sitting with her in her buzzed state. He'd hurt her badly, that was clear, but she seemed capable of hurting him back. She seemed to follow my train of thought, because she leaned forward then and said, "I tell him he needs to be careful."

"Emil?"

"Yes."

"Careful of what?"

"Ah, well. Who can say?"

"Careful of what, Frau Gerhardt?"

She hiccupped. "Of himself. He needs to be careful of himself."

"I don't understand."

She shook her head. "I feel him moving out of orbit. Like a planet at the edge of the solar system. He's held in place, but barely. She wants him to be big, Herr Schwartz—"

"Please call me Manfred."

"And me, Helena. She wants him to be big. Symphonic. Yes. I know this about her. I *like* this about her. She wants him to read poetry, but this can only lead to misery, and I'll tell you why. He's not big, Manfred. My husband is not a big man. At most he's medium-sized. Yes, like a good compact car, maybe a sedan. But she would have him be a bus. She would have him be a train."

She took a sip of wine. "I'm his wife, you see. I know this about him."

I had no response that I could give, so I excused myself and went to the restroom, paying the bill on my way back. When I returned, Helena was staring out the window. The square was quiet, the vendors long closed up.

"How close the past comes. How close it comes." She was wearing a queer smile that seemed to hurt her face.

"What makes you say that?"

"A memory. The Rathaus over there was absolutely hung with flags, and the square filled with girls. We had flower wreaths in our hair. BDM girls, you know: Bund Deutscher Mädel. We thought we were beautiful, but we were hideous." She shook her head, clearing the memory, and then she stood, swaying lightly. I gave her my arm and we walked to the elevator. We got in and she thought for a moment, then fumbled in her purse for her room key, a gigantic thing with the number printed on a copper weight. She pressed the floor. When the door opened, we walked to her door together.

"Are you all right from here?"

"Perfect. I'm perfect from here."

I left with relief, and it was only later, on the drive home, that I realized I'd never asked her to tell me about her adventure in Dinkelsbühl. What could it have been? My thoughts all ran towards the vacancy of her existence, as it had somehow been siphoned to me through Emil and Petra. I pictured a new purchase of nesting tables. Or a visit to a kennel, researching a new dog now that Felix was gone.

Dinkelsbühl was on the Romantic Road, a curving highway connecting medieval villages. Normally, coming from Munich, Helena didn't take that route, favouring the autobahn. But she'd been low on gas, so she'd left the main road. Eventually she pulled up at a filling station outside the picturesque walled town of Dinkelsbühl. After gassing up, she tried the station washroom, but it was closed, so she decided to walk into town to find a restroom.

She crossed the wooden bridge over the moat, admiring a swan gliding between willows. Once through the gates, the town looked the way it must have for a thousand years. Unbombed—a thing so rare for Germany. Almost everything had been laid to rubble, but not Dinkelsbühl. Flags hung from the timbered houses; lanterns decked the colourful building fronts. A market fair was just ending, and revellers jostled past her, pouring back through the gates and across the moat, towards their cars. She badly needed to go to the bathroom, so she walked quickly, though she felt the charm of this town in Central Franconia, its deep customs of neighbourliness.

She found her way to the toilets in the back of a beer hall. Afterwards, she stopped to order schnapps at the bar, to warm herself for the walk back. There was some slippage. Coppery light, soot-covered beams. A stag's head above the door. The clop of horses' hooves outside. She felt the grief she always carried. A spell—so it seemed, in this fairy-tale village—a spell wherein she must always carry the past, a painful bubble in her heart, and keep it safe, revere it, but most importantly, *carry it endlessly*. At the heart of that heart, the reeds of the River Elbe. Her handsome brother and his ridiculous, passionate need to know if his poem was any good. Or drivel. If it was drivel, he could bear it. He'd go to war, lay low in a trench, get attacked by enemies. He said this, but he didn't picture what was to come: not a trench but a freezing, crusted snow hole, attacks by Cossacks, the howl of their blades in the moonlight. He told her about the Cossacks on his first leave at home. By then he had changed. He was laid up in bed for a week with fever, and when he came down the stairs in his uniform, he wore a twisted smile. Alone with him after dinner, she begged to know how she could help, and he told her to shut up, just shut up. He couldn't stand her hypocrisy. Couldn't wait to get back to the front, where death was everywhere, but at least it was real.

What's real?

Just shut up. Will you?

He held up his thumb and forefinger, pinched together. *This is how much you know about life, Lena. You're a troll.* He was lost to her already. Lost before his return to the front, before the news of Stalingrad and his "valiant death." (That was what the telegram said. So many Dresden men were dying "valiant deaths," but not one of the acts of valour was described.)

Helena mostly tried to keep the Peter of the boat separate from the war-leave Peter. So she went back to the reeds at dawn, the *glub* of bird calls. She wanted to keep him in the boat so that what came later would never come; his beautiful face would never be twisted, and he would never call her a troll.

It was then, holding her glass of schnapps, picturing Peter among the reeds, that Helena looked up towards the end of the bar and saw Magdalena. The apothecary's daughter—Peter's love. She was sitting at the end of the bar, throwing back her head to laugh at something the bartender had just said. Her abundant hair was tied back loosely in a braid. A single thick streak of white flowed from her temple and showed in the braid. Her face was older, her jaw and neck heavier, but it was clearly and astonishingly her.

Did she feel Helena's gaze? Yes, because she turned and met her eyes. Magdalena stared right at Helena down the length of the bar.

It couldn't actually be Magdalena, of course. How could it be? That would take a miracle, because Helena had stood outside the apothecary while SS men carried the family's possessions down the stairs: clothes, candlesticks, the table inlaid with mother of pearl. A burlap sack full of clothing had been topped with the blue dress Magdalena so often wore to serve customers.

Helena had run through the streets to the path along the river, the reeds bending in the wind. She ran up the stone steps, across the lawn and into the kitchen, where her mother was dusted with flour. *What is happening?* Helena cried out. *Where are Magdalena and her family?* And she will never forget what happened next, how her mother leapt across the room to pinch her lips closed as though puckering her into a forced kiss—darting her head around to see who was there (only the maid, Greta). *You are too young to understand. You must never speak of them.*

And Helena hadn't.

Yet, here was Magdalena, in a red coat with a rabbit fur collar, briskly stepping past Helena, pushing open the door and going out.

Helena followed.

A cold breeze funnelled down the street. Helena looked left and right for Magdalena, but she was gone. No, there she was up a side street, pausing in front of a store, pushing open the door. Helena walked after her, stopping in front of the store, a flower shop with misted windows. She pushed open the door and was engulfed by its hothouse scent. She saw orchids and exotic flowers with long, penis-like stamens, a tall glass vase of pussy willows and dozens of potted chrysanthemums, russet and brown and gold.

Both women in the shop turned. They were caught in a conversation, bent together, friends gossiping.

"Yes?" said the woman behind the counter. "Can I help you?"

Helena looked from face to face and, with a mounting sense of slippage, as though coming out of a slight stroke, realized that neither of them resembled Magdalena in the least.

She fled: out the shop door to the square, through the deserted streets, out the town gates and across the bridge. Dear God—her own face! That was what tortured her as she fled. How her own face had worn such a simpleton's expression, so open, so naked with need.

She drove the rest of the way to Bonn without stopping once.

Only later, after drinks in the bar and her conversation with Manfred, had things begun to shift. Lying on her hotel bed, the memory swirled back, but now it had gained something golden at its centre. *I had a little adventure in Dinkelsbühl.* Something alive inside her, a bubble of warmth, like falling in love.

The cobbles. The stag's head and the medieval gates and the swan breaking the water. And at the heart, not a ghost, no, but a flower shop. Full of the scent of chrysanthemums and the soft heads of pussy willows.

How strange that she had been led in this direction. As though by fate.

She must meet her friend tomorrow with kindness. She must listen and consider. She mustn't think herself too good for a flower shop. If she worked in one, mightn't she wear her black shoes with the T-strap and silver buckles? She could do her hair high on her head so it lifted her features. She could glance up when the bell chimed, and in some way her small, erect figure might give satisfaction among the flowers.

In the night she dreamed she was back in the old house in Dresden. The hallway floorboards glowed with honey-coloured sunlight. Outside the window, she heard a Hitler Youth parade, boots on cobbles. They made the window rattle.

Her mother was there, right beside her: *Go to him, Mein Liebes. Your father needs you.*

And then Petra was there—oh, how strange. Helena sees Petra so clearly, bending towards her. She is as handsome as Peter. She might even *be* Peter, in that strange way dreams have of combining people. Petra holds out a hand, the palm oddly wrinkled. *Come, little sister,* she says, and the two of them walk towards a door Helena has never noticed before, a seamless crack in the hall wallpaper. *Yes, it's always been here*, says Petra, her face lit with shared joy. Then Petra turns the knob and they enter a vast ball-room, with ceilings and walls and floor of robin's egg blue.

Witnessing

Petra lies in bed, barely awake, surfacing from a bad dream—a wolf or an even scarier animal, a sort of faceless beast, bent over a pool in the forest.

Oh, how everyone wants something from her! The days of action are intensifying. And today's speech leads to tomorrow's mass protest, and each time something must be called out of herself with a great spasm.

She pictures hacking up an organ, her heart or kidney, presenting it to a meeting of NATO commanders. *Here's something special for you. Will this stop the missiles?*

If she described this to Emil, he would blanch, finding it both moving and overwrought. He might even tell her to rest, as he does these days. *Rest. Eat. You must take care of yourself.* So much gentleness—as though to gentle the furious part of her into submission. He tucks the bed covers around her feet, a little ritual of kindness near dawn, when she comes to bed and he has just risen. The two of them meet again at noon or one o'clock, when he wakes her with a steaming mug of coffee. Then they head off into the afternoon, to a demonstration or to the Bundestag or to parliamentary work at Tulpenfeld.

Even now she hears him coming up the stairs, the scratch

and flick of his slippers, a particle of stone engrained in the leather sole. He sets the mug on the bedside table.

"Petra? Are you awake?"

She hopes she doesn't look haggard, but what can she do? She can't be afraid of him seeing her morning face. She wonders what Helena looks like in the morning. Is her face beautiful day and night? Or would it be slack and drugged? And hurt. Hurt by her, by Petra Kelly. Now that Emil is with her all the time, Petra has time to consider what they have done to Helena, and it sits like a stone on her heart. Is it ethical? Is it right? But then she remembers the pledge Helena and Emil have, to live their old age together. When does that start? After all, he is in his sixties. What will be the hour of his leaving? It isn't fair to live this way, on the knife edge of abandonment.

"I'm awake," she says. As he comes close, she reaches for his hand, presses it against her cheek. "You're so good to me."

"You work too hard, Petra—I'm afraid for your health."

He sets the coffee down, then moves across the bedroom and down the stairs. Again she hears the grinding of that small stone lodged in the sole of his slipper, and she feels a flush of irritation.

She knows that the women in the caucus have been calling Emil her baggage carrier. He fetches and carries, and he locks the doors each night because lately she has become really afraid, and when she tells him that, he becomes protective, and that feeds something in her, a hunger. After he has checked the doors and windows, or gone into the garden because she heard a noise, they sometimes make love, the adrenalin scent of his body strong as he lies beside her. Yet later he puts on his clothes and waits—so it seems to her—rather vacantly for instruction. Will they go to the caucus meeting or to the protest? Wherever they go, he will open doors, carry her bags. She wants the man back who said no, he wouldn't read her books. No to Anna

Akhmatova. No to the Gnostics. The man who kept cocking his head, listening for an internal message.

Why has he folded inward?

She will not believe it is because of her questioning of his past. That past calls at her, especially when she sees him leaning back in his chair, looking ever-so-comfortable, about to reach for his newspaper. Then she finds herself thinking, *Look how he lives with it all. How easy it is for him to tuck what he does into a compartment. That's why he can have two wives.*

She doesn't attack. Of course not. She is gentle. But still, she must go close to the moment, because when she does, she feels this thing rear up—this thing in him—and she must never shy away, she must face it, this thing she sees inside him. She hardly wants to name it to herself, as she lies in bed, but her anger at the scraping of his slippers on the stairs brings the words to her mind.

Inner blankness.

There it is.

There is blankness in him. And so she questions him, and then notes each empty or dull response in the ledger of her heart. His insistence that herding that girl and her brother towards the pit, towards the endless gunfire, was *expected*. A fact of war. As though with these words he can be let off the hook. *Ah yes, war is terrible, but some awful things are expected.*

"But they weren't your enemies. This girl—she was . . . she was just a girl."

The pain on his face, again. "But you see, Petra, we were brainwashed. We were told."

"You thought a child was your enemy."

"Stop. Please, Petra."

And then she apologizes, she takes his heavy head against her breast, and she knows all he wants is to be absolved. Yet every single time, he justifies.

"Every soul is a world," she said to him once. "That is the grief of all this."

And he flinched—a look she wished had been understanding, but that instead she must call irritation. At her.

"I know that," he said. "I feel remorse for those souls."

And she would have left it—she would have—but then he added: "But it was war."

Oh, how she wants him to see. And *he* wants to see too. She knows this. But he justifies, and that isn't seeing. There is no justification. She still believes in him, and it seems to her, more and more, that if she can do this work of reaching into him, something will shift on a cosmic level, bringing peace closer. Or is that garbage? She isn't sure. All she knows is that she can't let go.

There is the layer in him that is blind and almost stupid (horrible word, but true), but beneath that there is something in him—she is sure of it—that is radiant and hot. Never touched. It is dark and light together, it is beautiful, it opens and sees, and then pours out tears of regret. An ocean of tears for the dead. Is this what witnessing is? To call that thing to the surface? Is that what she, Petra, must do?

But his quiet, complex nature almost has the better of her.

Take, for instance, this mess with the Generals for Peace. They keep paying him money, putting him up in lavish hotels, giving him honoraria and renewed contracts for his article (yet to be produced). God, she could have written three of them in the time it's taken him to roll paper into the typewriter. And for what? She has heard their position on the dissidents in the Eastern Bloc, heard they take no position against nuclear power. They are a narrow little group, grey, just as Freya said, and more and more Petra believes Manfred was right: they are, in fact, cosseted and controlled, bought by money laundered through the World Peace Council but coming from the Kremlin, or from some department in the Stasi for covert operations. And yet Emil refuses to see it. He is blind to his own fat place in the plush valentine box. He is being bought by caviar and the prestige of meeting with other generals. And he goes along with it.

Or does he?

Opening one eye, she can see the mug beside her selected works of Anna Akhmatova. Emil hasn't set the coffee on top of the book, though she suspects he wanted to. Now she must get up, which means getting dressed, presenting their constitutional amendment in the corridors of power, then putting on her puffy jacket and going outside to speak at the women's action in front of the Bundestag. It means figuring out what to do for the dissidents on the other side of the wall who are fighting the SS-20s.

The last time she brought up the dissidents, she was catcalled by the caucus.

She allows a surge of nausea to pass through her, remembering some of the men in Jürgen's faction pushing past her in the hallway, stinking of cigarette smoke.

Downstairs, Emil is moving pots with a clatter, making breakfast. The rub of his slippers on the floor makes her think of his naked feet. They inspire no lust in her, unlike his chest, his hair, his underarms. They are pale and well-kept. Old-world feet. They have poor circulation because of frostbite from the war. Yes, he wears the war on his feet. Like socks. The skin of his feet, all the way to his ankles, sometimes takes on a bruised yellow when he stands, and sometimes in bed his feet brush against her calves and they are stone cold. What does it mean to have feet that are so wounded?

She wonders if her father's feet were similar, realizes she has no recollection of them. Is he alive somewhere, with feet like that? Tender, but at the same time atrocious, cut off from the body, like they belonged to a different person, or to a different time.

II

Petra's Plan

Ten days before the date for deployment of the Euromissiles, Petra buzzed me on the inter-office phone line. I could hear excitement in her voice. She needed me at once, she said.

What did I expect? News on our push for a national referendum on the missiles, I think. It required a constitutional amendment to get to the floor, and was a long shot, but we were trying everything. We were exhausted, but also fuelled by adrenalin. It was us against those black vehicles of death.

As I pushed open her office door, I found Gisela Fuchs standing over Petra, who seemed trapped behind her desk. I stepped back into the hallway.

"You know you do this." Gisela was clearly in mid-harangue. "You say the words *military industrial complex* and acknowledge that the system of oppression hinges on male dominance, yet you can't cross the street without Emil holding an umbrella for you."

"But that has nothing to do with the patriarchy."

"You are the head of a movement, and women expect you to be stronger."

"I can be both strong and feminine."

"He carries your bags. He opens doors—"

"Gisela—"

"I'm saying, it's obscene."

"I'm saying, it's none of your business."

Gisela stormed out, shooting me a glance of hatred—hatred being her currency. "You!" she muttered. "Always lurking in corners."

Petra looked abraded. "You heard her?" She shook her head. "Perhaps I am that hypocrite she describes. Why can't I just walk clean and clear, as some women do? Tell me, Manfred: Why must I need him so badly? It makes me want to put my head down and weep."

"That's just Gisela's poison acting on you."

"But am I weak, the way Gisela is describing?"

I paused. The hypocrisy of Petra's dependence, looked at in a certain light, *was* astounding, yet now I wanted to defend her, and I found—once the words had left my mouth—that they were also true. "You're very strong, Petra. But always in your own way."

I pushed aside some papers and settled on the windowsill. Yes, something strange and ingrown had happened between Emil and Petra. Everyone felt it. Yet, a picture came to mind of her at Wyhl, sun on her face, enlivening the crowd. How sickly she always was before she spoke, and yet she could always summon the Thing that moved through her, whatever it was, the live juice that poured into her from the sun, the earth itself.

"You're a phoenix," I said, and laughed. "People like Gisela may write you off, but you always rise out of the fire."

She smiled, instantly captivated by the image. She even straightened her back, adjusting her invisible feathers.

"I've seen it a dozen times, Petra."

Gisela's poison now pushed aside, she reached for a letter on her desk and handed it to me. "This is why I buzzed you."

The waxy thinness of the paper told me at once that it was from the Eastern Bloc. But it wasn't anything official: it was in ballpoint pen, the writing heavily slanted. I turned it over to check the signature.

Petra exclaimed, "It's from Clara Pohl. It had no postmark. She must have had it smuggled out."

Clara Pohl. The well-known dissident peace activist, the organizer of candlelight demonstrations. On the most recent day we had blockaded the NATO base, Clara and two dozen others had held a peace vigil outside the Soviet embassy in East Berlin. The protestors sat in a circle with candles in front of them until they were violently disrupted, beaten and arrested by the Volkspolizei. All of this photographed by a visiting Belgian tourist, who managed to get his film across the border and gave it to *Der Spiegel.*

I read the letter. Clara Pohl described having been in a cell, worrying about her children, whom she was told might be taken from her, "an unfit mother." And then hearing from her husband that Petra Kelly of the Greens was speaking out everywhere for her release.

There is nothing, nothing our government fears so much as bad publicity. They must at least seem to be sticking to the strictures of the Helsinki Accords on human rights. In the third week of her incarceration, Clara was abruptly taken from her cell, given her clothes and told she could go home—*as though I had been interfering with them!* She was now in her apartment with her children. *They are having a bath. I can hear their voices in the next room, arguing over a yellow rubber duck.* She wrote that she wasn't sure what had caused this change in her fortunes, but she knew that Petra's constancy and good heart had helped.

Petra was beaming—looking exactly like the great-hearted person the letter described. "She's asking for my help."

"She doesn't say so."

"But she is, and even if she wasn't, it's what we have to do."

"But we're at the height of the Days of Action. We have to focus."

"Not you, too, Manfred! You sound like Jürgen Wolff."

"Focusing on one issue over another isn't the crime you say it is, Petra."

"No, it is. That's exactly what it is, Manfred. A sort of crime."

"Tell me why. I've never understood this point."

"We have to fight for Clara and the others even as we fight against the missiles, or we lose something vital in ourselves. Don't you see? *They are us*, on the other side of the wall. And we must imagine ourselves into their situation. That is our responsibility."

She was looking at me earnestly, yet I wondered if she was arguing with Emil, or even practising this speech for Jürgen Wolff.

She pushed back from the desk. "Anyway, I'm going to bring this letter to the caucus meeting today."

"I don't think that's wise."

"Why?"

"Because we have only a few days left, Petra, to stop the missiles. And everything we do counts."

"All the more reason."

"And suppose we did try to help Clara and the others. What could we even do? Realistically."

"Realistically?"

"Yes. Realistically."

"Realistically, we can furnish them with printing presses; realistically, we can circulate their samizdat materials; we can publicize every arrest; we can stand with Clara when the state threatens to take away her children; we can lobby Erich Honecker and the United Nations and the Court of Justice—and the Pope! Realistically, we can pass a motion of solidarity, create a petition, call for their rights at every one of our events."

"But you can't really intend to throw this issue at the caucus."

"We need to get this stuff into the open."

"It's a lion's den. You'll get eaten alive!"

"Yes, I will. So let's go have lunch. I should be well fed."

12

That Beautiful, Dangerous "As If"

"Where's Emil?" Petra flung her coat onto a chair in our parliamentary meeting room. "He should be here by now."

He had a toothache, apparently, but had told her he would come immediately from Swinemünder Strasse. It was only a ten-minute drive.

She glanced around, gauging the room. About twenty of our elected members had gathered and were going over briefing notes, or chatting and smoking. Lots of press, including Rainer Beckman. Far more Realos than Fundis. Lots of the Hamburg faction, too, and other Red-Greens. Some important women were missing, including Gisela Fuchs. *The Fundis had better show up fast*, I thought.

Petra took a pad from her briefcase and hastily began to write, while I made my way to Jürgen Wolff, who sat chatting with some Realo men. I noted the almost burly comfort they took in power. How quickly this self-gravitas had settled on them. I surprised myself by thinking, *I'm not one of them, the power guys*, and I wondered if this might, in some way, please Rufus. (Rufus—was I doing what I did these days to impress my baby?)

"Where's Gisela?" I asked Jürgen.

He shrugged, his go-to gesture. "They called a Women's Caucus meeting."

He had pitched his voice so that it carried all the way to Petra. "Without me?" she cried.

Was it Emil's absence that set Petra off course? Or was it the Women's Caucus holding a meeting without her? Or was it the room itself, another sterile box within the sterile complex, inadequate ventilation sealing in the licorice scent of Gestetnered papers, the occasional clandestine fart? Whatever it was, when the meeting got going, Petra was rattled. Her purple sweater, with its shoulder pads, dwarfed her slim body, making her look a little ridiculous even to me.

As I look back on it now, Petra's intervention feels like a piece of theatre: the intensity of the lighting, her solo presence at the front of the room. She was like a girl with a stick, wheeling this way and that, fending off bears. I searched out the meeting's transcript from the archives, and while I do not quote verbatim, I have leaned on it heavily.

PETRA: Friends. (*She clears her throat.*) Friends, as many of you know, while we have protested in Bonn, there have been candlelight vigils beyond the wall, in East Berlin. While ours are reported around the world, theirs are broken up by the Stasi.

JÜRGEN WOLFF: This is of concern to us all, Petra. But this afternoon, if I'm correct, we're speaking to business to do with the Days of Action. The missiles are slated for deployment in ten days.

PETRA: There's a connection, believe me, Jürgen.

JÜRGEN WOLFF: Our Lady of the Connections. (*Laughter.*) All right. Tell us how.

PETRA: When you focus all your energies on the Euromissiles, a narrow laser focused on one evil, and forget about the human beings beyond the wall, you are buying into a process of dehumanization—fighting for this, not that. Loving this, not that. We become—just ever so slightly—like the missile creators. To be Green, our minds must respond to the web that connects us to all living beings.

MAN 1 *(a Realo)*: Really? At every moment? That's absurd, Petra. I'm tired of this endless preaching.

PETRA: I'm not preaching. I'm saying that to act with love, we can never forget others just because they happen to be outside our range of vision. Let's expand our focus for these final actions. Let's embrace the Independent Peace Movement in the East. If we announce this at once, our efforts could have a profound effect on their lives, because everything we do gets publicity. Václav Havel—

MAN 2 *(a Hamburg Marxist)*: Here he comes, just when he's needed—

PETRA: Václav Havel, the great dissident poet of Czechoslovakia, has written about the power of the powerless.

MAN 2: (*Audible groan.*)

PETRA: What do the powerless possess in a totalitarian state? This is the remarkable thing he writes about. Despite complete lack of freedom, they possess a weapon of extraordinary subversive power. It is simply this: for each citizen to behave as though they are *not* contained and controlled by a closed system. To act normally. To act "as if" they are free. That's what Havel says.

MAN 2: This isn't a protest at the Hofgarten, Petra. We're meeting to decide our next actions on the Euromissiles. Your entire speech is out of order.

PETRA: (*Turning on him.*) Don't be ridiculous! We function by consensus, as you well know. Not by patriarchal rules of order.

MAN 1: Have you noticed? If you disagree with Petra Kelly, you're part of the patriarchy.

ME: (*Unable to contain myself.*) Let her speak!

(*A quiet temporarily descends.*)

PETRA: Thank you. Now listen. (*She takes the letter from her pocket.*) This is a letter that Clara Pohl has written to me.

ME: (*Under my breath.*) Oh, Petra—say *us*, not *me*.

PETRA: She has written to *me*, and this is what she says. Listen. In the state-run kindergartens of her youth, children were lined up at toilet time along a board with eight toilet holes in it, and told to defecate in unison. (*Laughter.*) This is true. Not one five-year-old was allowed to rise until every one of them had relieved themselves.

MAN 1: Tell us the connection between potty training and missiles!

MAN 2: Yes, from shit to missiles. Three, two, one—go.

PETRA: How are they connected? Through a million and one filaments. When people are controlled so tightly, it twists something deep inside, which affects their hearts and souls. This is the essence of totalitarianism. Clara knows this, and so does her husband, and they have the courage to resist. And so—*acting as if they had the right*—that beautiful, dangerous "as if"—six months ago they opened their own kindergarten in the neighbourhood of the Zionskirche. Friends and neighbours brought their children. It was an innocent act, agreed? To open a kindergarten? Yet it was also utterly subversive, because they did the one thing the state can't stand: they acted *as if* they were free. News spread. More children came. Then one day the parents arrived to find the doors and windows filled with bricks, the road blocked by the Volkspolizei. Tell me you can't feel the web of life that connects that moment—the children and their parents in front of the boarded building—to the darkness of the impending missiles. I feel it in my blood.

(*She looks from face to face, and another silence briefly descends, then . . .*)

MAN 2: You are the definition of naive, Petra. This is exactly what the capitalists who control the military industrial complex spend their nights praying for: a division in our ranks, a focus on the GDR's human-rights issues while NATO prepares to wheel its weapons of death across our doorstep.

PETRA: This is not about capitalism.

(Marxist laughter.)

MAN 2: Spoken like a true American-raised bourgeois.

MAN 3: Everything is about capitalism.

PETRA: Everything should be about life.

(She turns to Jürgen, who is watching these proceedings with a closed-lipped smile. When some of the blows have fallen a little hard, he has flinched, but otherwise his smile has been steady. She is about to speak again, but is interrupted by Man 1, 2 and 3, soon joined by others, chanting her name in a rising singsong.)

MAN 1, 2 AND 3: Petra, sit down! Petra, sit down!

(Man 2 takes off his shoe and bangs it on the table.)

ME: *(Disgusted.)* What is that? A tribute to Khrushchev?

A WHOLE CHORUS: *(Taunting.)* Sit down! Sit down!

(Petra glares at them like a cornered animal.)

JÜRGEN WOLFF: You see, Petra? It isn't enough for you to want something very badly. It also has to make sense for our party.

PETRA: Since when are we a conventional party? Aren't we beyond that?

MAN 1: Quite right. We are different. But that difference doesn't come from Petra Kelly directing us to do whatever she wants.

(Shouts of approval.)

PETRA: Enough. You've all made your point. Shouted it in my ears. *(She throws herself into her seat.)*

(Blackout.)

13.

The Follower

As we crossed the Bundestag grounds towards Tulpenfeld after the meeting, Petra was angrier than I'd ever seen her. "Jürgen has become a little Stalin! And the Hamburg Greens—they are appalling. But it's Jürgen who has them all by the nose."

The attack had been so personal, driven by disdain for her ego and drive, for her being female, even. I suddenly remembered Petra telling me about being in her bedroom in Virginia as a teenager, working on an essay on levels of government, and knowing she was going to ace it, as she aced all her homework in this new country, this new language; but then hearing her mother and stepfather in the living room, laughing, enjoying themselves, warm and happy, and realizing, all through her body, that she was an outsider even inside her own family.

Power is a tool, and it must be used carefully, and she had gone at the caucus without any strategy. I saw this, and something else, too: she would never be able to return to her previous place of power. This kind of contempt, so publicly stated, marked a definite shift.

Up the elevator we went. Down the corridor. There was Emil in her office. He'd pulled her chair to the window and was gazing out at the sliver of Rhine.

"I'm so sorry I missed the debate," he said.

"It wasn't a debate," Petra answered. "More like a frontal attack. What happened to you?"

Traffic. Tooth. A probable abscess.

"Oh, Emil, really?" She shook her head.

"I should go," I hazarded.

"No, don't." She turned to me. "I need both of you." She ran her fingers through her hair. "I have a plan."

We were all silent for a moment: Petra by her desk, looking from one to the other of us; me near the door; Emil with his arms tensely aligned along the wooden arms, as though strapped to an electric chair.

Petra turned to him. "I know that we have differences in our politics."

He breathed out. "We have differences, yes."

"But we are at a moment when I simply cannot back down. The East German dissidents must be part of our programme."

I reached out to jiggle a plastic box of push-pins on the desktop, then stopped my hand.

"Well? Emil? Are you with me? Do you support Clara—who could be thrown into prison at any time for doing precisely what we do here on this side of the wall? Or should we all turn away, go about our business?"

I watched Emil—we both did. His face was darkened by inner concentration, as it always was when he was asked for a commitment, but this time a dog whistle of panic seemed to reverberate in the silence. At last he said, "You know the position of the Generals for Peace."

"I do, but I'm not asking what the official line of the generals is. I'm asking you."

Emil stretched out his fingers, as though the answer was under his nails. I could almost feel his heart beating through his sweater. Then, in a whisper, he said, "Petra. You are so passionate."

"No!" she cut him off sharply. "My passion is not the subject!"

They began again, he in the chair, she looking down at him, the sharp little V of the Rhine behind her. "I know you have Generals for Peace to think of—and Realo sympathies—and Jürgen is always hiving you off to talk man to man. But what I'm asking you is more important. I'm asking what your soul says. Please." A small word to finish, a plea, yet there was ice in it.

When he answered, in a soft tone I find terrible to remember, his words were simple enough: "I agree."

"But what do you agree *with*?"

"I agree with you," he said, and she collapsed into a chair and put her hands to her face.

"Thank you, Emil," she whispered. She reached for his hand. "We're in this together, then?"

"Of course. I'm with you."

That was when I saw a look cross his face—so fast. So fast. I recognized it, because it was the expression my own face held, I was sure of it, when my father bullied me. *What is this?* he'd thunder at me. *This mud in the hallway? This record left outside its sleeve?* And behind his back, I'd flash him a look of sly hatred, because that is what we do when we cannot reason with those in control.

14.

Cosmic Laughter

That night I couldn't sleep. I tossed in bed, all alone in the cold farmhouse. At about three a.m., I gave up. I got up and went to the kitchen and opened a beer. All at once I wanted to telephone Petra. I felt such an urge to lay bare what I'd seen, warn her about her own self, how she'd been scraped clean of grace or kindness. Her despotism. And all at once I saw Katrina, her hair blue or orange or platinum or jet black, throwing back her head, laughing, and I thought, there we are: she isn't pinpoint smart like Petra, she isn't scintillating or vivid. She doesn't break my heart with her lonely childhood stories, or make me feel more alive just being with her—but she can laugh. At herself and at me.

Petra worked late almost every evening: if I telephoned her at Swinemünder Strasse, she might still be awake. I got the phone, set it on the kitchen table and sat down in front of it. I felt heat under my skin.

What did I want to say?

I remembered seeing a Shakespearean comedy with my mother. How she'd laughed with delight! At every point the characters seemed about to veer off into chaos and tragedy; all the elements of destruction were there, just as they were in the tragedies, yet miraculously hatreds got resolved. Brothers kissed. The father took the hand of his alienated son and gave him the keys to the dukedom, and everyone prepared for a wedding, rather than the multiple funerals of *Hamlet* or *Othello*. There was something so graceful and light in the ending. As we left the theatre, my mother said, "He has tapped into a cosmic laughter." How she looked as she said that—really happy, and so knowledgeable, so clear. I was surprised enough that the words stayed with me, right to this moment.

Was there still time to turn this situation into a comedy? That was what I wanted to put to Petra. *Let's stop, let's rest, let's start again tomorrow with more gentleness. Let's try to find the cosmic laughter.* Words I felt would intrigue Petra, draw her in. *And your mother said this to you? You have never told me! What did she mean?*

I was so close to telephoning her, or perhaps that's what I tell myself now. Instead, I decided to sort out my thoughts in a bath with another beer, which, as it turned out, was one beer too many. I woke naked in the tepid water, leaning against the horrid mound of concrete I had once poured into the tub to stop a leak.

The telephone was ringing and ringing and ringing. I made my way to the kitchen and picked it up.

It was Petra. I searched my head for cosmic laughter, but the words now meant next to nothing, like a puzzle that had reknotted itself in the night. Besides, Petra wasn't calling to chat.

15

Alexanderplatz

I won't enumerate in too much detail the logistics involved in Petra's plan: an invitation dug up from the papers received at the office to a conference of "official peace groups." We had no intention of actually attending, but it served as a smokescreen.

The day before, we travelled by train to West Berlin and I rented a car. I stayed in a friend's apartment in Kreuzberg, where I woke before sunrise, dressed, gathered my bag and let myself out. Dawn outlined in bare limbs, a chill in the air. I drove through the quiet streets. When I pulled up in front of the hotel, Emil and Petra were waiting on the sidewalk, also holding day packs. Petra, who'd been determined but brittle on the train, now emanated the fierce intensity I knew so well.

As he got into the back seat, Emil gave me a quick smile. This action could ruin him with Generals for Peace, yet here he was. We started down the street and I watched him in the rearview mirror; he didn't meet my gaze, but stared out the window, an expression of polite involvement on his handsome face. Petra frowned slightly, then looked at me. A stoplight luminously switched from red to green.

"Did you line up the photographer?" she asked me.

"Yes. He's from the French embassy."

The full moon appeared from behind a building, then it was

gone. We arrived at Checkpoint Charlie, and I could hear the blood in my ears. We passed through the American part of the checkpoint. Ahead of us was the watchtower, and beyond that, blocked by a vehicle shed, the floodlit death strip.

The GDR guard bent to my window. "Passports."

I handed him our papers. He perused them carefully, leaning to peer into the back seat.

"Purpose of visit?"

I passed him our invitation.

"A peace conference?"

"An *official* one."

He licked his lips and then stamped the passports. "Proceed."

The rental car lurched past the sign: *HERZLICH WILLKOMMEN IN DER HAUPTSTADT DER DEUTSCHEN DEMOKRATISCHEN REPUBLIK.*

Clara Pohl closed her building door behind us and led us quickly up the stairs to her apartment. After that door was also firmly closed, she hugged Petra. "It's been too long," she said. "Too long to get to see your beautiful face for myself."

Clara had one hazel eye, the other a grey-blue. Wild sandy curls against a sandy complexion. She stepped back to take in Petra, who was grinning hugely. She led us into a kitchen with bamboo-patterned wallpaper, explaining that the children were with her mother. She must have caught my worried look. Was our visit putting her at risk? She reached for my hand. "After this one took to the stage," she indicated Petra, "I was released from prison, and the children—well, I believe they are safer than they have been since they were born. Though we shall see, of course—we shall see. It's the Helsinki Accords," she added. "Honecker is feeling the heat." She wore a knee-length suede tunic, cinched with a mannish belt with a bronze buckle, over a scarlet shirt and tights. Clara clearly dressed to express her individuality, a kind of Bohemian "fuck you" to the GDR's conformity. As she moved around that small room, flashing her colours like a bird, it struck me as brave.

"Manfred Schwartz," she turned to me. "I hear so much about you."

"I don't see how."

"Memos and briefs illicitly smuggled. We follow you and Petra—and you, too, Emil Gerhardt. We thank you." She settled us at the table and set a mug in front of each of us, pausing to kiss Petra on the forehead. "But this one is special."

The kiss set Petra beaming. "I brought books for the children, and some toys. And some coffee for you. Emil, do you have our day packs?"

Petra watched as he brought them out and handed the gifts to Clara. The look of pleasure on Petra's face, a melting. I watched as she glanced around the old-fashioned kitchen, its out-of-date wallpaper and pale tiles, then back to the artistic-looking Clara: Petra's mirror activist across the wall. *See? She is real*, she might have said to Emil—the words were painted in the air.

Clara smelled the package of coffee lovingly, then leaned forward and kissed Emil's cheek. "You don't forget us."

Emil smiled a little wanly.

"How could we?" Petra cried.

"Oh, plenty of others do."

I leaned forward, put my mouth close to Clara's ear. "Any chance we're bugged?"

Clara shrugged. "Do you know how you can tell if the Stasi have bugged your apartment?" She turned off the flame under the whistling kettle, poured water into the teapot.

"How?"

"There's a new chest of drawers in the living room."

I laughed, but Emil looked puzzled.

"It's a joke." Clara laid a sympathetic hand on his arm. "They are horribly obvious, the Stasi, almost always. But we must continue to behave normally—that is how Ulrich and I try to live. And since my imprisonment, they've been leaving us alone. A temporary reprieve? We can't tell. I walk down the street, and where there used to be two men who followed me everywhere—they even stole my stroller from the front porch— now there's nobody. Something has shifted, and it's not just the Helsinki Accords: they know they are under international scrutiny. So," she turned again to Emil, "yes, they know about your visit. But not," she mouthed the word, "Alex."

She placed the teapot on the table, then went and turned on the water, a loud rush of it. "Still, a little extra noise never hurts." She sat back down and leaned forward, gesturing for us to do the same. "If you want to get serious about the Stasi spy network," she whispered, "you'd be very naive not to know that they're on your side of the wall too. In your ranks, in your 'anti-party party,' causing some of the noisy bad press for your Greens."

"I know that," I said.

"Wreckers and saboteurs," she said, unaware that to my ears the words reeked of Communist dogma. "They will never leave the Greens untouched. They'll try to control the Western peace movement every way they can." She looked from face to face. Then abruptly she stood and turned off the water.

Petra reached into her day pack, bringing out cookies with lemon custard centres and placing them on the table.

Clara sighed. "You remembered."

"I can send you even more."

"The border police eat them, every time."

Petra stood and placed the package in one of the kitchen cupboards, beside a container of dried milk, some depressed-looking pickles. "There. Not to be served to us. Also, Clara, I must tell you, I can never eat before—"

"Then all the cookies are for me! Or perhaps I'll give one or two to the children."

I glanced again at Emil. He had barely spoken, though he had moved swiftly to perform each of Petra's requests regarding day packs, toys, and his legs were stretched out comfortably under the table. I thought what a figure he must seem to Clara: the ex-general, Petra's consort. "Clara," he said suddenly. "Do you happen to know the name of a restaurant that used to sit near *Hackescher Markt*, on the corner? Red geraniums in a window box? It was a very famous little place in its time."

We all turned to take in this question, which seemed to have floated free from another time. Clara looked at him quizzically, narrowing her eyes. "Ah yes, of course. You would have known Berlin before the war."

"Very well indeed. This restaurant—I went there once. So long ago. Being back here has put me in mind of it."

"When was the last time you crossed through the wall?"

"I have never before crossed the wall."

"Ah."

"But I have memories of all of these streets. I came to Berlin on leave three times. It's where I met my wife."

Petra flinched. And for a moment I was astonished. Here we were, on the flip side of the wall, the other universe—on Petra's mission—and still he could hurt her with that single word, *wife*.

If Clara noticed, she was too polite to say so. Instead, she named a restaurant. Then another. "I can't go to any of them," she said. "They're expensive—for officials only. They serve food we never see. Things my children don't even know exist. Pineapples. Pizza. Real chocolate."

Petra's face looked bleak. "I'll bring you chocolate next time."

"Of course you will; that's who you are." Clara reached for Petra's hand. They laced fingers. "All right," Clara said abruptly. "Enough of this love-in. If you want to be there soon, you'd better go."

It was morning now. The sun had risen, the streets smelled of creosote and burning plastic, yet everything felt fogged by an underwater light. Petra pressed her palms against the leather passenger seat, and then lifted them to check if she'd left palm-shaped sweat prints. She turned to the window, which she'd opened a crack, and I could smell the dampness outside. What had I read once? *Ghosts collect in watery places.* Was that why I had felt, ever since Emil mentioned her, that Helena was along with us now? Not Helena as I'd seen her at the Stern Hotel, out of focus, peering at her drained glass of wine as if willing it to refill, but in her youth, as she walked these streets in the last days of the war. We passed buildings that she and Emil must have known, architectural beauties that had escaped bombing, interspersed between monsters of cement.

Petra started in her seat as I slowed the car and then stopped.

"What are you doing?"

I fumbled in the glove compartment for the map. I'd become confused, lost in the three kilometres between Clara's apartment and Alexanderplatz. It was ridiculous. The final thing Clara had said to me as we'd left her apartment—a laughed whisper in my ear—was that nobody could get lost on their way to Alex: just follow the TV Tower. But it had disappeared behind the buildings on this narrow street.

Just then, three men in vinyl jackets emerged from the wrought-iron entrance of a park. One of them met my eye and seemed to pick up speed. I grappled for the gear shift, but they crossed and passed us.

I turned to see if Emil had noticed them, but he was gazing towards the corner, his face lit by a shaft of morning sun. "It's impossible," he said. "But look. There it is." We followed his gaze: just ahead of us on the corner was a quaint, half-timbered restaurant. As if on cue, a slender woman in a knee-length black skirt emerged and began to sweep the sidewalk.

"That's remarkable!" All the recent greyness on Emil's face had dropped away like ash. He checked the view from the other window. "And I know exactly where we are, Manfred! If you continue straight ahead, then turn at the intersection, it will lead you past the market." He caught my eye in the mirror, smiled helplessly. Happy. A happy man. We could feel the change in the car, as though happiness took up less volume and mass.

"Oh, Manfred. Please drive!" Petra cried out, and we headed on.

I parked behind the S-Bahn station and we walked into Alexanderplatz, which was now full of people headed to work. The space-age needle of the TV Tower loomed above us—the GDR's ode to modernity. Alexanderplatz was the nightmare of agoraphobes, a huge expanse of pavement gawking at the sky, surrounded by slab-like buildings of glass and concrete. The only human elements, besides the people rushing across it, were supplied by the smell of piss, and the cigarette butts swept into the tram tracks that bisected the square.

In my memory it takes us hours to reach the World Clock, our destination, but in reality it must have been a minute. Looking up, I saw the hive-like mesh of iron on top, hung with planets representing the solar system, and below, the fat tablet of the clock, which turned every twenty-four hours, listing cities in their time zones: Belgrade, Mogadishu, Havana, London.

Petra looked like she might actually vomit. She took Emil's arm in a slow-motion gesture. "The bullhorn," she mouthed. "We've left it behind. It was in the second day pack."

"We can't get it now," I said. "We have to do this quickly."

"My voice isn't strong enough to carry here."

Emil's voice seemed sharp in the surreal atmosphere. "I'll go," he said.

"No!" Petra still held his arm. "I need you."

"But you also need the bullhorn, and I will get it."

He gave her hand a pat, disengaged it from his arm and hurried across the square.

Time slowed and perception heightened. Small things. An old woman rushed by in a kerchief, a real Baba Yaga type. She cast us a glance, then ran on like a winter witch.

"Why is he taking so long?" Petra gritted her teeth to stop them chattering. I glanced again towards the edge of the square where Emil had disappeared. Petra turned to me. "This is it, you see. He will not stand by me."

"He'll be back," I said, though I truly wondered.

"Has he deserted me because of what we're about to do? Or is he searching out that place where he and Helena were so happy?" She peered across the square, her face yellow-white, her eyes dark. She turned to me then. "But we're here. You and I. You don't run, you don't flee. You don't tell me one thing and mean another."

Behind her I saw two Volkspolizei near the entrance to the S-Bahn.

"Police," I said. "Petra, they've got their eyes on us."

I looked in the other direction. More Volkspolizei at the edge of the square. One spoke into a walkie-talkie.

Petra: "Do you think he *told* them?"

But what did it matter? We were in so deep, we had no choice. I undid the day pack at my feet, pulled out the rolled banner and began picking at the knots that bound it. They weren't tight, but the string was twisted. A woman with thick braids and eyeliner slowed to watch me. Others picked up their pace, averting their eyes, but an old man in a pale suit stopped, grinning broadly as though at a circus act.

Then the banner was free. Petra grabbed one end and I the other, and we stepped apart to unfurl the cloth, revealing the words of the illegal East German peace movement, SWORDS INTO PLOUGHSHARES. Somewhere in the crowd, the flash of a camera. I was shouting at Petra, "Say something! Speak!" but sirens buried my voice as a police van screeched onto the square, opening its side doors to let out three policemen in grey-green uniforms. They sprang into a run, pulling out truncheons. Suddenly the little witch woman was there—I'll never forget this. Her face seemed to come towards me with superhuman speed, as though her neck were rubber. "Now we'll see some fun!" she cackled.

Then I was knocked forward onto my stomach, a cold circle of steel pressed against my neck. I thought, *I'm going to die*, and to my mortal humiliation, I pissed my pants.

"Don't move, you fuck." A push with the rifle barrel.

Still I managed to turn my head and find Petra.

I was looking at her upside down. So things weren't all that clear. I always tell myself this before going over the memory. As anyone knows who has looked at a school friend upside down, the chin becomes the nose, the face clownish and absurd. As I lay on the ground at her feet, she was turned from the Vopo, and from me, towards Emil, who was running in our direction—with no bullhorn in his hand. "Where were you? Tell me you weren't looking for that restaurant!" Her entire self shrunken to this one jealous question.

Then I heard Emil's voice, very official: "I am an ex-General of the Federal Republic of Germany. Please be aware, if you manhandle these people in any way, you will have cause to regret it."

And the Vopo listened, like fucking servants, to the voice of authority. And the point is this. The point is this: I am on the ground, a gun shoved against my neck. I am like a piece of Alexanderplatz concrete. I am like the gum stuck to the cement. I am like the cigarette butt next to my face. I am wet with pee and at their feet, and it seems to go on for a long time, because in my life it has done exactly that. It has gone on for a long time, with me looking at this moment and seeing myself flattened there, on the cement.

16

Stasi Headquarters

Like me, Petra and Emil were taken to the Secret Police head-quarters at Normannenstrasse. Unlike me, they were escorted upstairs to the office of a senior official, nothing on his desk but a grey telephone and a bust of Lenin. This representative of the GDR, handsome despite his pocked cheeks, encouraged them, over tea brewed in the adjoining small kitchen, to *reconsider their relationship* to the peace movement of the East. A pause, while he took a sip. The sun slatted through the blinds. He reached for a pack of gum from his breast pocket, offering sticks to Petra and Emil.

I wasn't at their tea party, because I'd been extracted from the square by different means. Petra would swear later that she called out to the Vopo, "Be careful with him," but as far as I was concerned, she forgot about me the moment I went down. Everything was Emil. And then the arrest brought on a panic attack, and she had to sit for many minutes on a bench, surrounded by the Vopo, with her head between her knees.

I, meanwhile, was dragged across the square and pushed into an unmarked car. From there, I was taken to the basement of Normannenstrasse, where—steeped in piss and sweat—I was asked, cordially, whether I'd care for a cold cell or a warm one.

"Warm," I murmured, which was why I was squatting, wet with sweat, in the corner of the cell, as far as I could get from the scalding ceiling pipes.

During the ten miserable hours that I spent in that cell, stinking it up with diarrhea, the toilet unflushable, our aborted action in Alexanderplatz flashed into my mind again and again. I saw myself led there by a ring in my nose. Petra was leading me, wearing a long fairy-tale dress. I go where she leads me, the flesh in my nostrils aching from her soft pull. I see her face so close, have loved it so deeply that I have been inside her, *been* her. Then I see her turn to Emil. *Tell me you weren't looking for that restaurant!* I see something so tiny in her being, seeing her upside down from the pavement. She has turned herself into nothing but jealousy.

Is that right? No. No. No. I am crying again. I am thinking of my mother, quietly darning upstairs by the window. Now I am thinking of my bereft father. He is hot in the room, pacing, he is longing for me, in words that cannot come because the war cut out his tongue. My heart aches, it is all so simple, the blanket of suffering that covers all of us, it is just like the night sky, and we are all under it. And then I am back. I hear the long pull of the door bolt rasping against metal.

A small, dapper man in a grey suit enters. He murmurs apologetically, looking at his hands, "We don't know what to do with you, so we've decided to shoot you."

I can't remember what I say. I believe it may be: "I don't think you should."

"You're sixty-eighter scum."

"I'm a Member of Parliament."

"Then you should have stayed on the other side and acted like one. And you should shave."

"Where is Petra?"

"Your colleagues have been released. But we've been told on good authority that you could go missing." He sniffs with distaste. "Ugh. You've stunk up this room with your shit. Come."

I follow him along the nameless corridor of the Stasi headquarters and out a metal door that lets us into a courtyard. It is night. We are met by three more men and, without a word, I am loaded into the back of an unmarked car. "I'm an elected official," I plead.

"Tsk-tsk," says one of the men, amiably, from the front seat.

We twist and turn. I expect the car to stop, expect to be pushed out and then shot, my only warning the steel against the back of my neck. And all the while my unlived life, the love of it and the huge pity of losing it, create a pressure in my body. This is me.

I hear myself say, "I have a wife. I have a child."

The car stops "Please," I say.

"This is all the free service you get."

And when I don't understand, another one says, "Out."

I stagger from the car, and they gesture for me to walk into the headlights: "Get going before we change our minds." They laugh as I stumble towards the guard station.

I am at Checkpoint Charlie.

Across the wall again, I find a telephone booth on Friedrichstrasse. I can barely draw the change from my wallet, can barely dial. I steady my hands. *Concentrate. Dial zero.*

The operator puts me through to the hotel, and after a couple of rings, Emil is on the other end. "Hallo, yes? Is that room service?"

Room service!

"You're there," I say into the telephone. "They let you go. And Petra?"

"We're safe, yes. But we've been worried sick about you. I'd put her on, but she's having a bath."

A bath.

"They were actually fairly decent to us," he says. "How did you fare?"

I hang up.

17

Post-Alex

I didn't hear from my French photographer friend, and I supposed the photographs—if he had indeed taken them as we struggled with the banner—had been ruined or seized. But then, three days after the action, they appeared on the front pages of many newspapers and were blasted around the world by the Associated Press. They showed a grainy but triumphant Petra in front of the World Clock, SWORDS INTO PLOUGHSHARES banner in her hands, then the uniformed Vopo rushing in to yank it down. No sign of me, except for a hand clutching the banner. Classic.

Everyone in the media wanted to interview her.

That morning, Petra walked into the caucus room looking very tired. She sat down next to me and complained of both a cold and a pain in her kidney. Not a word about how I'd fared. She was a narcissist, I remember thinking, bitterly. Despite all her talk about *We are us*, she didn't have the capacity to see things from any point of view but her own.

"Where's Emil?" I asked coldly.

"At home. He's also sick."

"Poor him!"

If she caught my sarcasm, she didn't acknowledge it. The room was filling around us, and before we could say another word, the most vociferous of our colleagues began to hurl questions at us. I say they hurled questions at "us," but in fact their fury was aimed at Petra. What did she think she was doing with this unilateral action? What had she—the Great Petra Kelly—been thinking? Or did she think at all these days? What would this media stunt do to East–West relations? We'd played into the game plan of Ronald Reagan by giving credence to one small group of angry Eastern dissidents. Gisela Fuchs was furious about the lack of consultation, while the men from the Hamburg faction kept up the line about how Petra had played into NATO's hands. They attacked Petra as though she were the greatest single obstruction on the road to world peace. Any time she attempted to speak, they shouted her down. While Jürgen leaned back in his chair, fingers pressed together, an unlit cigarette in his mouth.

After awhile, the meeting mercifully moved on to protests and resolutions, but the worst wasn't over: that afternoon, Gisela called together the Women's Caucus, once again without Petra. Petra was a diva, Gisela said, dangerously ego-driven and far too dependent on men. She was a woman—they had to grant her that—but she was not really a feminist; only when it suited her purposes. They decided to change their name to the Feminist Caucus and tell Petra she was no longer welcome.

Gisela's gang were like children at a birthday party who decide to torment one particular girl. Perhaps she is the one with asthma, whistling when she breathes, or the one who has worn the prettiest dress but cries too easily. This was Petra. Most of the Greens, Realo and Fundi, began to treat her as a figure to snicker at, though still dangerous because of her inexplicable popularity outside the inner Green chamber.

Gone was the gallant girl in sneakers who had captivated the world. Once both sides began to bay at her, to bring her down, she seemed to emanate vulnerability like a pheromone. Soon even those who had been indifferent, or on her side, switched over to join the pack.

As for me, I stayed silent when the others joked about her or derided her for her outsized ego, her grotesque sense of self-importance.

I didn't defend her.

Five days after Alexanderplatz, she came to me. She looked pale and thin; her cold had gotten worse, she said, and moved to her chest. She sat down. She could sense the shift in me, but I don't think she knew why. She had lost the ability to see into me, if she'd ever had it. After a few moments, as though to prove my silent indictment, she turned the subject to herself and Emil.

"He'll have to answer to the Generals for Peace, though of course he was absent for the actual action." She paused, watching my face. "Manfred," she said at last, "Emil was gone for a long time, wasn't he? At Alexanderplatz? It felt like forever, but he's saying time must have shrunk for me because of the—"

"It was long," I said shortly.

"Where did he go?"

"I don't know, Petra. If it matters to you, you must ask him."

"But what do you think?"

"I think you need to ask him."

Our eyes met, and I saw that she was at the bottom of a well.

"Of course I have asked him," she said.

"And what does he say?"

"He says he got confused and couldn't locate the car. So many side streets. Then he got worried and came back."

"But you don't believe him?"

She looked towards the window. Somewhere out there, the Rhine was magically flowing, full of barges and boats moving cement and toxic substances and joy riders who didn't know about any of this.

"When I ask him—this will sound ridiculous. When I ask him, he pauses and looks to the left and up. I've heard that's what people do when they lie. You know what I think?"

"What?"

"I think he loved being over there, because it reminded him of falling in love with Helena. It was all about that restaurant. Can you imagine? I think he's still in love with her. I think he can't help himself, and now I've made it all come closer by insisting we cross the wall."

"Maybe," I said. "Or maybe he left us because that was what people had asked him to do."

She didn't shake her head. She took it in. "Can you help me figure this out, Manfred? Please. I can't do it on my own. I feel like I just can't slice through to the truth." She put out a hand, touched the top of mine with the slender pads of her fingers, setting in motion the desire her touch always caused. I pulled back my hand. She looked at me, startled.

"How is Clara?" I asked.

"She's fine. I don't understand your tone. Are you angry?"

"Isn't *she* the reason we risked so much?"

"Yes, of course. It was always for Clara. She's not in jail, which counts for a lot. She says Honecker himself has told the Stasi not to touch her. An order from above, and they—Jürgen and his gang—well, you heard them in the caucus. They say I've personally weakened the fight against the missiles. And Jürgen told Rainer that I have no strategic sense, and that's what came out in his newspaper. I am sickened by them."

I am sickened. Always *I.*

We were silent. There seemed to be nothing more to say, because I wasn't going to say the obvious. That the Vopo had pointed a gun at my neck and threatened to kill me, and she hadn't once mentioned it.

18

The Derringer .38 Special

Three days before the scheduled deployment of the nuclear missiles, Jürgen Wolff stopped me in the hallway. I had come from outside and hadn't yet taken off my puffy jacket, and was sweating as I emerged from the elevator. Jürgen looked me up and down, a coffee mug in his hand. "You look like you're being boiled alive in that thing."

I shrugged.

"Listen." He came closer. "I've been meaning to talk to you. Can we have a moment?" He led the way to his office. He had a full ashtray on his desk, beside an Inuit carving of a hunter spearing a walrus. Of course he'd weaseled a big view of the Rhine. He sat down and gestured for me to do likewise. Pushing away papers, he stuck one running-shoed foot on the desk and lit a cigarette.

"So?" I asked.

"I'm saying this as a friend. I think you should be careful."

"Careful of what?"

"Careful or you'll lose your credibility. Get painted with the same brush. And that would be a pity, because we like you."

We. By which he now meant the Greens.

"Emil takes reasonable positions," he said. "Despite this last bout of madness. I've talked to him, and he'll have to prostrate himself before the generals, kiss a little ass, but he'll get through.

That isn't the point. I think she listens more to you. Here's the thing." He swung his foot to the floor. "I'd like to offer you a deal."

This hardly surprised me. Deal-making was his language.

"What kind of deal?"

"We call off the dogs. She can speak again in caucus."

"And?"

He shrugged, a rather French gesture that went with the unfiltered Gauloises. "It's tit for tat. If she wants protection at the party level, then she needs to bend herself more to the aims of the party. It's basic courtesy."

"What would that look like?"

"No more long-winded motions on Tibet, for starters—not when so many members of the party find it a waste of resources. And no more publicity stunts on the other side of the wall. It creates chaos among the Red-Greens, and you know that this woman—Clara Pohl—between you and me, I've heard she's impossible."

"How so?"

"That group she belongs to, in East Berlin, they aren't in a true sense *political*. They're Christian martyrs. Their entire raison d'être is to disrupt the GDR so that it pounds down on them. They then get jailed or put under house arrest, and they can scream about the Helsinki Accords and the entire Western peace movement buzzes with outrage. Yes, they're martyrs—Christian martyrs—with an impulse to impale themselves. Which isn't a strategy, by the way: self-impalation isn't a strategy."

"So if Petra comes under your wing?"

"Then she has to stop prancing around providing legitimacy to Clara and the others—and every fourth word that comes from her mouth can't be *The Dalai Lama says, blah, blah blah*."

"Great." I stood up. "I'll pass this on."

"Will you?" He stood too.

I was at the door, breathing heavily, my head down, as though I had just been in a boxing match, which I suppose I had.

"We can count on you?"

I turned. "Of course not," I said.

He shook his head to the side, as though to clear his ears. I had actually surprised him. "Excuse me?"

"I'm not going to pass this on to Petra Kelly."

"Because?"

I reached for the doorknob, but he came towards me. "Don't go," he said. "I want to hear your reasons."

"Because there's no point, Jürgen."

"And why is that?"

I turned to face him. "Because she'd never agree to silence herself. Because your politicking means nothing to her. Because she actually believes in the rights of Clara Pohl. Because she wants freedom for Tibet. Because she mentions the Dalai Lama because she thinks he's worth mentioning, not because she is trying to advance to Go, or move her pawns forward in a chess game."

He too was breathing heavily. Then he shrugged. "I was trying to help."

"Jürgen the Benign."

His eyes met mine. "I see how you watch her."

"What does that mean?"

"How long ago was it that you two were fucking? Isn't it time to move on?"

"Oh, fuck off."

"You've always been her big bear of a shadow. Yes. Her shadow bear." He gave me a quick, terrifying smile—a smile with absolutely no mirth in it, so that it inhabited the territory of a smile without any of the emotion. He said, "Do you know about his guns?"

I wasn't sure I had heard right.

"Emil Gerhardt. He has a gun in his glove compartment. Gisela found it when she was driving with Petra somewhere. A gun in the car. Another in their place in Tannenbusch. And our feminist friend *wants* this—that's how twisted the whole thing has become. Our peace diva is begging for a weapon to protect her." He shook his head.

I felt winded, and he saw that.

"Don't tell me you're the last to know about this? Even I blanch at the hypocrisy. First he opens doors for her, then he carries her briefcase, and now he's protecting her with a .38 Special. Tell me, Manfred, *what has happened?*"

I went to my office and telephoned Petra. *Petra, pick up.* I let it ring and ring, then hung up and called back. On the sixth ring she answered, voice groggy. Yes, she'd been sleeping; she'd been up until five a.m. compiling stories of Tibetan refugees, their fight for their homeland in that high, cold land, so they could be presented to the International Court of Justice in the Hague.

"We can never forget Tibet."

"Why not? The missiles are about to be deployed. Why not forget Tibet for one week?"

A pause. "I can't, that's all."

"Never mind about Tibet. I need to see you."

"Now?"

"Let me come, Petra. It's important."

My voice was demanding, I knew that, and I felt her pause.

"All right." She sighed. "Come and tell me everything I'm doing wrong."

As I waited at the elevator, Emil appeared. I had seen him a few times since Alexanderplatz, but across rooms, down hallways. He gave me a facsimile of a smile. I smiled back, my own masklike offering. When the elevator arrived, he stepped back to let me to enter first. Manners. Always his forte.

The elevator stopped on the fifth floor, admitting a secretary with a mail cart. I glanced over at Emil, and he raised his eyebrows to indicate, man to man, that the secretary was pretty. I caught a whiff of his aftershave. My throat clamped. Oh fuck, how I hated him at that moment, eternally civil in his well-made suit.

The elevator stopped, letting people out and in. I remembered how he had come to us with such an intense desire for renewal. His face at some of the rallies raised up to the others, grinning and smiling in the rain, all those *völkisch* feelings of being joined in community. To stand on the wet earth singing, to protect the homeland, to be a part of something bigger. I'd admired him then, our eyes meeting in the rain, his baffled happiness at belonging. But that was before Alexanderplatz.

The elevator reached the ground floor and we stepped out.

"You've been very silent," he said.

"I have a lot to think about."

As we crossed the lobby together, I looked at him sidelong, catching his smile of calm detachment. He stepped back to allow me to pass first through the revolving doors. Then we were outside in the cold Tulpenfeld quadrangle, that place of symmetry meant to arouse no emotion, a Bundesrepublik monument to conformity. *We will not cause harm again: look, even our buildings say so.* We continued across the parking lot. There, waiting in his car, was Helena, her leather-gloved hand poised on the leather-clad steering wheel. Had he told her he'd found the restaurant in East Berlin, the place of their early romance? He smiled at me suddenly, a wide, bright smile, the smile of a man whose next words are going to be *I just can't help who I am.* Then he broke from me and went to the car. I could just make out Helena's profile through the window, her fragile beauty glimmering like a flower petal on water.

19

Death Fugue

The suburb of Tannenbusch is a quiet enclave in a quiet city. I pulled in front of Petra's house, with its stucco walls and solid black door and black tile roof, like all the rest in the row of duplexes. White stones in the tiny front garden. *This is the place*, I thought as I got out, *where black-and-white things go to die.* The only spot of colour came from a ceramic gnome nestled among the next-door neighbour's stones.

I pressed the doorbell, hearing its cuckoo chime on the landing stairs. After awhile there was a fumbling at the lock. Petra's face appeared in the crack. "Ah, it's you."

She closed the door. I heard her release the chain, and then she let me inside. She wore her Adidas track pants. Her hair smelled like apple shampoo, her breath of the jellied candy she liked, but in the close hallway, these scents seemed to mask something unwashed. She was clearly still sick from the cold that had plagued her since Alexanderplatz. Her face looked thinner.

"It's a fortress here, Petra."

"If your life was threatened daily, you might consider chains on your door too."

"The ugly notes, you mean?"

"And phone calls." She coughed, and it turned into a spasm of coughing. When she caught her breath, she said, "Last night we thought someone was in the back garden. I saw a face through the window, I'm pretty sure of it. Well, not a face, the shadow of a face, right up against the glass. Emil had to search the garden. And the notes don't stop. They just get more disgusting."

"The police have their suspects."

"They think they're coming from that gang of right-wing crazies, the Lyndon LaRouche league, but I think it could be the CIA. Or the Chinese government. But most likely it's the Stasi. Though sometimes I even suspect Gisela Fuchs and the Feminist Caucus. I wouldn't put it past them."

"Gisela wouldn't stoop so low."

She was on the stairs, and she turned to me with a small smile. "We don't know how far she can stoop; we've never been that far down."

I followed her upstairs into the slender kitchen. Stark branches of a bare elm tree crowded the far window, a few brown leaves holding on. Against the wall, a red table with two bistro chairs. A pair of oven mitts hung from a hook by the stove. Jollity, in other words.

"Do you want coffee? I think we have enough. Emil said he would pick up more. He'll be home soon."

"Really? I just saw him meeting up with Helena."

She paused, the bag of coffee in her hand, and closed her eyes. Then she gave me a rueful smile, the kind my mother used to dole out. "Well, he's evidently forgotten his promise to bring coffee. We'll have to make do with this." She fetched the French press from the counter. "Sit, Manfred," she said over her shoulder. "You make me nervous, towering over me like that. And the kitchen is small—you'll break something."

The red chair felt small under my weight. Like a fake chair, I thought. A prop. Perhaps not for Petra—she was so slender—but wouldn't Emil feel the lack of heft in this flimsy thing? Had he gone along with her silently, or actively helped her pick them? Either way, it was another thing to hold against him.

"Let's get coffee in us, at least. I cannot be lectured before coffee."

"What makes you think I'm here to lecture you?"

"Don't I know you well enough by now?"

Dim light filtered through the elm branches. We sat in silence, waiting for the water to boil. I felt a drip of sweat along my hairline and wiped it away with my fingertips.

"How is Rufus?"

"I'm not sure. He's with Katrina in Lübeck."

The kettle whistled. She poured water into the French press and set it on the table, along with a carton of cream. "We may as well have cookies too."

As I poured coffee, Petra made conversation, pulling it in familiar directions: Clara and Ulrich Pohl, the power of our action; the candlelight vigil against the missiles slated for tonight outside the Bundestag; a speech she would make tomorrow to the full parliament. "I just hope I get my voice back."

Then she talked about the Tibetan doctor whom she had yet to meet face to face but who was proving to be such a help drafting the intervention at the International Court of Justice in the Hague. She mentioned her correspondence with an Innu elder in Labrador, how her people were fighting back against NATO fighter planes destroying their nomadic way of life. But then she took in my expression. "All right," she said. "Go ahead, Manfred."

"I spoke to Jürgen."

She put her cup down. "No, I can't drink this. I was up all night working, and after you go, I'm going to try to sleep for another hour."

"He told me a rumour."

"That's what he thrives on."

"He says there's a gun in this house. Another in your car."

She gave me a surprised, false smile. I had seen many expressions on her face, but until now never falseness. I didn't like it.

"Is that all?" she said brightly. "Manfred, yes. He has a gun."

I stared at her across the table.

"What? Why the shock? It's for our good."

"Listen to yourself."

"It's for protection."

"Protection! Since when do weapons protect us? And tonight, what will you do? Get back up onstage and speak about the power of non-violence?"

The skin under her eye twitched. She got up and went to the window and looked out. "There was a nest in the crook of that tree, in a little hole. You can't see it from here. But I sat here all spring, just after we moved in, and watched the mother bird bring worms and bugs to the babies. Then one day the baby birds were gone. At first I thought they had flown away, but now I think the neighbour's cat got them. It's blind, you know. But absolutely ferocious. And quite able to climb trees or get at the nest from the second-floor gutter."

"They probably flew away."

She turned to look at me. "You only heard about them this second. How can you know?"

"I don't want to talk about the birds."

"Neither do I."

We glared at each other.

"All right," she said, returning to the table, pulling her coffee cup towards her. "This is a conversation you are intent on having, so let's have it. Yes, Emil has a gun. In fact, Emil has always had a gun, but he kept it at the other house. If you think about it, it makes perfect sense. Now that he is living with me, he has brought it here. It's his, from his years as a military man. What is a soldier without a gun?"

"But, Petra—"

"I will admit that the first time I saw it in his hand, I was horrified. He'd heard noises in the garden. But then I keep getting those disgusting notes. The police may know who's sending them now, but it doesn't matter. Don't stare at me with those big eyes, Manfred. You're making me nervous."

"Violence causes violence, Petra. I've heard you say it a thousand times."

"Well, maybe I have. But maybe I'm also against people spying on me through my windows. And hounding me with hatred."

She looked sallow and broken, but beautiful still. I wondered if others would think so too, or if it was only me.

"I accept Emil's protection," she said simply.

Protection. What a stirring word. I thought of how he'd been in her office after the caucus meeting: hollowed out and bending to her will. Then I pictured him blown big again, responding to every imagined sound from outside, all that faceless evil brought to life by their joint assent. *What? You heard a noise?* Him slipping away to get the gun from upstairs, sliding open the door to the garden, his resolute circling of the tree, like the hero in a film noir.

"You know," I said, "I think he wants you afraid."

"Why would he want that?"

"To right the balance."

She cocked her head, considering. But this idea, which seemed to me of burning importance, hardly interested her at all. "Perhaps," she said at last.

I'd hit a wall. She wasn't going to let me through.

"All right," I said. "Show me the gun. I want to see you with it."

"Why would you even ask such a thing? Now you're frightening me. Anyway, I never go near it."

"Yet you live with it every day." I stood up. "Tell me where it is. I want to see you touch it, Petra."

She looked at me fiercely, ready to refuse me again, and then shrugged. "It's upstairs in the cupboard on the landing, above his desk. Back of the second shelf, behind his sweaters. Go on," she said. "A wooden box. You'll see it there."

And so there I was, a minute and a half later, standing beside Emil's desk on the small, cramped landing. A diminutive table held their fax machine, and a set of narrow stairs led to the bedroom. I opened the cupboard and felt among the sweaters, bringing out the wooden box, which I placed on the desk. It was made of walnut, buffed to a high gloss. I pulled back the catch. The derringer lay in a velvet pocket of forest green. I picked it up. The weight in my palm seemed to hold meaning. My index finger curled around the trigger, and a flicker of excitement twitched down my arm. Was it loaded?

I heard her call my name from downstairs.

"I'm coming."

"I need to get back to drafting my piece on Tibet."

"I'll be right there."

I placed the gun carefully on the table in front of her. We both stared down at it. A weapon of destruction—a small stick of death. Polished. Inviting to the hand. She didn't turn white or reel back in fear. She raised an eyebrow. "Now you've seen me with it. Will you take it back upstairs?"

"No."

"You can't leave it there."

"Then you pick it up and take it back."

"I won't play this game. You must realize you're frightening me."

"*I* am not frightening you," I said, like a schoolteacher with a simple lesson. "The gun is frightening you. And *he* is frightening you, making you feel you must depend on him—"

"That's not what he's doing—"

"—when, in reality, you're one of the strongest people I know."

"Also not true."

"You are." I leaned forward. "You need to shake this off. Like you do every time you stand up on a stage. He's got you pinned somehow—"

"Again untrue."

"And the gun—you know what the gun is. You can't touch it because your soul tells you it's wrong."

"My *soul?*" She laughed. "This must be important to you if you're referencing my soul." She was watching my face. Then she smiled and shook her head. "Manfred, I know you're trying to help me."

I breathed out carefully.

She let her gaze fall on the gun, a look of sorrow, as though seeing it from a long way away. As though one day the message would get through and it would break her heart.

"So you think he's doing it to right the balance?"

I nodded.

"A general with a gun. That's what he is, after all this time with me." She laughed once, a small, dry bark. "The more I want of him, the thinner he becomes. Please take it upstairs."

This time I did, resting it again in its velvet pocket, the gun-shaped hole. Then closing the latch, tucking it among his sweaters.

When I returned, she had poured us both more coffee. She tasted it and made a face.

"Whenever I drink cold coffee, I think of the Paul Celan poem—you know?"

I did. We all did—our generation. *"Black milk of daybreak, we drink it at evening. We drink it at midday and morning, we drink it at night."*

Petra added: *"Dein goldenes Haar, Margarete."*

"Dein aschenes Haar, Shulamith."

"Such beautiful words." She was frowning down at her cup. "I asked him a question the other day—just a question. I wanted to know what he did on Kristallnacht, that traumatic night. He said to me: 'You're not a lover, you're a detective.' Can you imagine?"

"Well, he loves detective novels. That should please him."

"I'm just trying to bring the pieces together, and he wants that; I know he wants that too. But we get so exhausted. Then we don't speak, and we are just like Helena and him, no different: a silent house all around us. Then he says something I don't like, like he's visiting Helena for the entire weekend, and I feel distrust rising like vomit in my mouth—really! And it makes me think of all the rest, and then I ask him something—something small, even, about his mother, or about the Hitler Youth, and he just looks at me and shakes his head. Then out comes this line about being his personal detective." She pushed her coffee away. "But I want to believe in him. I actually *do* believe in him. I think I believe in him more than he believes in himself."

"What do you believe?"

"What do I believe? What do I believe? I believe," and here she straightened her back, "I believe he is a fine, fine person, that's what I believe. But I think he must go through fire to become that self. I want him to love me, but to love me—for us to love each other—he must somehow burn this stuff away, like a ritual cleansing. It has to be burnt away."

There was a hard clarity in her eyes. This was her task—I saw it. She was riding towards the sun, sword raised.

And then I saw more. What I saw was so strange that, looking back, I wonder if I recognized it fully at the time or only later, after her death, and then backfilled the moment with my subsequent understanding. It was like two illustrated pages in a book laid flat, divided by the spine. One half of her sat across from me and talked of burning, but the other was hovering above the pit of Krivoy Rog. When Emil tried to lead her away, down the cart path, her answer was to rise like an angel, beating her wings above the scene, so that the air thickened and transformed with their pulsing. Witness to the world. Oh, he faced that world every night, but in silence, in the darkness of his mind, which gave him a sort of protection. He never broke on the wheel of it. But she saw everything. The girl in the ivy dress raised her face and said, *Do not let him move past this, not until he knows the hairs on my arms, not until he knows the hairs on my head, the mole on my brother's thigh shaped like the tiny face of a mouse. Then—only then—can he go free.*

"Petra."

She was looking at the red tabletop.

"My dear," I whispered. "My dear, dear Petra."

She glanced up. The hardness in her eyes had softened to something sad, but the resolution was still there, beneath everything.

I took her hand. "This is a difficult question, but I'm going to ask it anyway. Is this love?"

"Is what love?"

"This cleansing. This—what did you call it? Ritual cleansing."

"What a strange question." She pulled her hand away. "We love each other deeply."

It wasn't love, I thought, but I wasn't sure. Maybe it was, and of the truest sort. Like the fiercest of mothers holding a child to account.

"And now I have to work." She stood up.

Dismissed.

I descended the stairs in a sort of daze, Petra behind me. I kissed her on the cheek and stepped into the cold sunshine. I heard her turn the lock and pull the chain into place. I had been inside for less than an hour. The garden gnome was still grinning from its place among the stones.

20.

Night

Two days later, November 23, NATO trucks crossed the French-German border, carrying the guidance systems of the Pershing II and cruise missiles. Despite our protests, our die-ins, our Days of Action and conferences, pledges and petitions and candlelight vigils, the Euromissiles were deployed exactly as NATO had planned. Not one day, not one hour delayed.

That night we gathered in the tens of thousands in the Hofgarten.

Petra spoke brilliantly, Emil in the shadows behind her. She pledged to keep fighting, to bring criminal lawsuits against NATO, to go to the Hague. We would create non-violent peace camps, surround the missiles day and night, with humour and sabotage, vigilance and love. I closed my eyes, swaying in the crowd, holding my stub of a candle, and felt the weight of the missiles on my heart.

Then I made my way out of the Hofgarten. I found a pay telephone on a shadowed street. I phoned long distance, then realized I didn't have change. I hung up and fumbled for coins, but I simply didn't have enough. I picked up again and dialled the operator. Arranged a collect call.

Katrina answered after the third ring.

"Yes, I accept," I heard her say. "Yes, it's all right. I will accept the charges."

21

More Night

Outside Bonn station. I nestled the six-month-old Rufus into the rented car seat, then fixed it safe with the seat belt. He'd grown. Yes. He had grown.

"How are you?" I whispered to him, but he looked past me into the sky. I followed his gaze and saw the waning moon above the station, between two sets of telephone wires.

"He can't take his eyes off it." Katrina settled herself in the front seat. "He's been watching it through the train window ever since Cologne."

I got in and turned on the car. Right away, Katrina started in on the missiles. "It's terrible. Total shit. I ask myself, what world will Rufus grow up in? What's coming next? It's total shit." She shook her head, and then took off her woollen hat. Her hair was the mint green popular with anarchists. I reached out and touched a strand of it. She didn't move away.

"At least he's here," I managed to say.

"Yes." She smiled out the side window. She didn't intend to share that smile with me, but I felt it anyway, and I knew its meaning. Roughly speaking, it was: *When I think of Rufus Olaf Maximilian, I fill up with softness and joy, despite the fact that the missiles are deployed and the world is shit.*

I knew this, because I felt it too.

———

And, in fact, this will become the very first of our family stories: how the night after the missiles were deployed, Rufus raised his face to the moon and just couldn't stop looking at it. Mesmerized! What a remarkable child. From Cologne to Bonn, then gazing through the car window all the way to the farmhouse, then in my arms, squirming to look at it over my shoulder as I carried him inside.

You gave us hope, Rufus. That's what we said to him all through his growing up.

Your bearded father. Your green-haired mother.

You gave us hope.

THE TURNING

Die Wende

That should be the end of it. We've pushed forward by hair-breadths towards both conclusions: we will have wedding bells and funeral bells; love will triumph and destroy. Some of us, it seems, are destined, ultimately, to accept our ordinary lives, while others will move on a tragic trajectory towards the heavens. I'm picturing a comet roaring into black space.

There will, in other words, be the *Gemütlichkeit* of bratwurst affixed on barbeque forks, even to infinity.

And there will be cities of frosted ice, watched over by blazing stars.

There are various ways to count off the passage of the next years. They were marked by birthday parties with piñatas, school report cards, worries about Rufus's ability to make friends. There was the joy of Katrina's second pregnancy, followed by the sorrow of her miscarriage, and then the birth of our Hannelore. We were carried on a sea of Lego pieces, pick-up sticks and morning rushes: diapers, juice boxes, jamming children into car seats.

We marked every change within the walls of our apartment, and our own family dramas were at the forefront of every conversation, but they were acted out against a background of convulsive political change. The Turning Point, the *Wendezeit.* Reforms in Hungary and Czechoslovakia spurring East German demonstrations for freedom, reaching a crescendo in the Monday vigils at Nikolaikirche in Leipzig; Clara Pohl coordinating parallel demonstrations in East Berlin; crowds of more than half a million gathering at Alexanderplatz, shouting "We are the people!" Then the moment when the Berlin Wall fell: thousands dancing on top of it, then going at it with sledgehammers. Then the reunification of Germany, and, six months later, Clara and Ulrich Pohl helping to form the new party, Alliance 90, the East German partner to the Greens.

In the federal election of 1990, the new Alliance 90 took 6 percent of the vote in the Eastern states, and Clara and a number of others were elected into Parliament. However, the Greens—with dynamic prescience, perhaps, or a complete and arrogant disregard for the European moment—ran a campaign that focused on global warming.

"Germany is in the process of reunification *now*, we are living history *at this exact moment*, and we're focused on something—what?—twenty, thirty years in the future? We'll go down in flames!" Jürgen predicted to the caucus.

And we did, of course.

Not one of us was re-elected.

All at once we had to scramble for new jobs. Petra, who still maintained some popularity far from home, took to the international lecture circuit and agreed to some teaching stints, piecing together a living as best she could. Emil had his tiny pension and bits and pieces from lecturing.

As for me, to my surprise, Clara and Alliance 90 asked me to stay on and help them as a parliamentary secretary to the party. I leapt at the job. The money was actually better than our wretched pay as politicians; the status wasn't much, and the hours were long, but I—supporting two children and a wife who worked part-time at a women's shelter—was at least employed.

I didn't see Petra at all. Our paths simply didn't cross, or perhaps I took steps to avoid her. I had no place in whatever destructive myth she and Emil were living. I wasn't part of their story, and perhaps never had been, had only grafted myself onto it, a humiliating extra. Jürgen had called me her shadow bear, and I resolved never to be that again.

Whenever her name did come up, it was attached to fierce and ugly rumours: that she was thin to the point of anorexia; that she was fat. A woman from the UK Greens visited our offices and said, "You wouldn't recognize her, Manfred. Her nose is oddly flattened." But she couldn't tell me why.

The stories varied widely, but there was uniformity to what lay behind them. Petra was ridiculous now, in a certain very political way that was a cautionary lesson to us all. She had failed to adjust to the *die Wende*. She had failed to catch the zeitgeist. But (and this was the worst condemnation) she could not even *see* how out of date she was. She continued to act as though she ought to be the star of every event, wanting to make a stir as she entered a conference, Emil at her side, unable to realize that she had been supplanted by other leaders, other women such as Clara Pohl. The Greens had moved on, ruthlessly and without sentiment, and the days of Petra and her "cult of the individual," as Jürgen ironically put it, were over.

One rumour I heard, a real urban legend, came to me first from Clara Pohl as she and I were collating papers on the carpet of her office. She was looking as much like the Clara we'd met in East

Berlin as ever, in a knitted garment cinched by an elasticized yellow belt. She told me she'd heard from a reliable source that the night the Berlin Wall fell, people gathering at the checkpoints in disbelief, Petra and Emil had actually been in West Berlin but hadn't left their hotel room.

"I heard they watched from the window. Emil was afraid Petra might get hurt." Clara sat back on her heels, allowing me to picture the scene, the screams and tears and laughter, the crowbars and sledgehammers and victorious climbers—all of this seen from behind a double-paned hotel window. Petra, fingers on the glass like a ghost.

Emil: What's happening?
Petra: More dancing.

It was unlikely. And yet there were stories like this from all over Berlin, of people who had missed the entire night of jubilation because they were in bed nursing hangovers or hadn't turned on the news.

Clara had cared about Petra in the past, and worried about her now. Yet I could also feel how she wished to hold herself aloof from Petra's grotesque ossification. The whole of Germany had shifted, the entire world, but Emil and Petra had remained in place. I told Clara her story was impossible, given everything I knew about Petra, but she shook her head.

"I would never have believed it either," she said. "But Petra is no longer Petra."

Katrina and I bought an apartment in the old district of Bonn, assisted by money from my father. I wasn't utterly delighted by my first trip to Cologne's IKEA, or by the days we spent searching for a medium-sized chair with wooden arms to place in front of our (non-working but beautiful) tiled fireplace. Not delighted.

But still, I found it pleasant. At IKEA we would drop Rufus off in the ball room, and Katrina and I would wander the market-place section, pushing our toddler, Hannelore, in an umbrella stroller. I remember turning to Katrina among the rugs and waxing poetic on our "flight into forgetful consumerism."

"You should write a paper on that," she said, and gave me the stroller to push.

Our raging Hannelore had come into the world with a grudge in her eyes and fury coiled in her tiny body. At two she ate only white foods. At three she wept through an entire dinner when she found out that the chicken on our plates was the chicken of her *Barnyard ABC*. She was also fiercely brave. Was and is. (She is now the executive director of an international organization fighting oil and gas companies.) She has always reminded me of Petra, but of course I've never been such a fool as to say this to Katrina.

Father. Homeowner. Husband. Son.

Yes, that last is important to mention too. Several times a year, we visited my father in Freiburg, and to my surprise, when Hannelore pulled on the pleat of Opa Schwartz's trouser leg, demanding to see the birds, he led the children outside quite calmly. He even let them try on the hawking glove and hold the leather hoods.

Later, when the children were sliding down the stairs on pillows, I braced myself for him to spring from his chair and yell, or pull out his belt. If he did, I would spring too. I would defend them; my heart and mouth were full of what this final standoff would look like, the bird feathers flying, the screaming as we pecked at each other's skin.

The children ran into the room, and he held out his hand, age-spotted but strong, and said, "Hannelore, Hannelore?"

And she stopped. "Yes, Opa?"

"I have something for you. Here." He reached into his pocket, held out both hands.

She took hold of his fist with her smaller hand, just as though it weren't frightening, and he opened it, and inside was a black licorice coin.

Katrina watched from the couch. She wore a soft lavender T-shirt and a pair of low-waisted jeans that were unflattering to her stomach after two pregnancies. But she didn't think that way, and so her lounging body became sexy all at once, in its patently rich, milky oblivion.

I kissed her in the kitchen. "You're so good at this."

"He's not so bad, Manfred."

As we left the house, my father leaned forward and kissed Katrina's cheek. "Take care of this great blunderbuss, my son."

"I will, Papa."

"Tell him that I admire him."

Did that happen? Did those words come from his mouth?

In the car, Katrina shrugged. "Why not? Of course he admires you—he's your father."

Oh, that wall of blandness, just as I was counting myself blessed and lucky. Her lack of imagination was a palpable *thing*, like a great opaque window of snot. And I felt, even with all this familial happiness (Hannelore in her car seat, singing a song about Christmas, and Rufus reading his comic book by the car light and telling her to shush, shush, in an automatic way, every ten seconds), all this family life could not heal me. The car was full of milk, and we were floating in it. The wandering moon followed us along the autobahn, just as it had the night we were reunited. And though I knew myself to be happy in my daily life with Katrina, all I could think about at that moment was Petra. As though she were the answer, still, to my bliss and to my boredom. As though she sat in the sky—pocked and graceful and terribly sad.

2

Flower Shop

That brings me to a final rumour from this period. One day, as Freya and I sat in my little office, editing a joint release on the outbreak of war in Bosnia, she told me she had heard from someone who had heard from a good source, a source close to the couple, that Emil had gone to Helena in Bonn to beg her to take him back. "He wants out. Badly."

"But how do you know?"

"I don't. But it makes sense to me, Manfred. Think about it." She turned to look at me. Her red hair was getting some grey in it. She had pulled it into two pigtails, and this made her sharp chin look like a jutting exclamation mark.

"But, Freya," I said carefully, "Emil and Helena have always had a pledge—I know this from Petra—to return to each other regardless of his infidelities. That their old age belongs to each other."

Freya shuddered. "Well, apparently that's not the case. Because what I heard is this: Helena has independence now. She manages a flower shop with another woman and is quite happy where she is."

Later I checked this story with Clara Pohl, and she had heard it too.

A picture formed in my head of that final scene in the little

Bonn florist shop near Beethoven-Haus. A bell rings as Emil pushes open the door. Helena glances up from behind the counter, where she is arranging the twisted branches of witch hazel in a tall glass urn. He comes towards her, smiling broadly. At last. His Helena. His heart is clear, and he wants to say so, but he must start slowly—he has so much to make up for. He invites her for lunch, a neutral place with good linens, where he can begin to explain.

"Are you hungry? Can we hang a sign on the door?"

"I can't. There's no one to tend the store but me today."

"Ah—they are harsh taskmasters."

"I don't have 'taskmasters,' Emil." Her voice is surprisingly clipped. "I simply cannot come."

"Tomorrow, then?"

"That isn't possible either."

"When, then?"

He sits heavily in a wrought-iron chair, and Helena stops arranging the branches. Her lips are pursed, her hair quite grey and pulled back at the base of her neck, a severe style Emil has never seen on her before. In the corner of the shop is a smoky mirror flecked with gold, a three-way mirror that makes a person go on forever. Looking into it, he sees a hundred Helenas, all looking at him with pity. All shaking her head and telling him no.

3.

Now We Will See

We were riding the wave of change that came with the lifting of the Iron Curtain. I felt exultant and optimistic one moment, then aghast the next as I read reports of East German skinheads with swastika tattoos raping an African woman in Leipzig. Followed by more incidents, then more. It seemed that a thuglike neo-Nazism had been released like a gas from beyond the demolished wall.

Editorialists struggled to explain. Years of repression in the East—heavy metal bands banned, even safety pins in ears and nostrils a sign of "oppositional thinking"—*all this could lead to* . . . blah, blah, blah. The neo-Nazis didn't give a shit what the editorialists said.

Katrina and I watched this new chain of events with disgust and fear. The Iron Curtain had been lifted, the wall demolished, but now an old evil had leapt from behind the rubble, grinning wildly.

It was at this moment that the issue of the files came across my desk.

What to do with these files soon became *the* burning issue in the reunified country: what to do with the files of the Ministry for State Security of the former GDR, the Stasi, which revealed those who had been spied on and those who had spied. The amount of material was enormous—people talked about a billion sheets of paper. Most files documented the lives of East German citizens, but many hundreds contained information on spies for the East who had operated in Bonn.

Some people wanted these files destroyed, citing privacy and worries about violent acts of revenge. *Let the past stay in the past—* that old argument. Others, including the Greens and Alliance 90, wanted the files opened and the past revealed.

A long story short: the files were put under the control of the Federal Commissioner for the Records of the State Security Service of the Former GDR, and this organization decided to make the files available, but not to everyone. Each individual citizen could fill out a personal request for their documents. Requests soon flooded the authority, and the released files led to stories of others whose files might still be off limits, but whose names and positions could be triangulated to reveal what they'd done. Professors had spied on their students, husbands had informed on their wives.

And so I woke one morning, fumbled my way to the kitchen and spread out the newspaper to read that evidence pointed to one peace activist and one Green Party member engaging in covert operations orchestrated by the East German secret police. The peace activist was no surprise to me. It was Magnus Isaacson.

The Green politician was Jürgen Wolff.

His elfin face stared from the newspaper. The photo showed him in an iconic pose, leaning back at his desk, running-shoe treads in the foreground. His bad-boy smirk. I felt the floor and walls lurch, the tremor you might expect from a small earthquake. I read carefully. *Engaged in covert influence operations . . . access to power within a rising political party . . . ongoing attempts to "neutralize hostile elements."* The precise tactic, according to the report, was called divisionism. Divide and conquer.

I sat back. I remembered the time he'd asked me to try to control Petra, to bring her into line. How he'd leveraged his position in our caucus, charming everyone with his antics, building his cadre of supporters. What a double game it must have been for him, what a dance. I had downed beers with him countless times, drafted resolutions with him into the night. How much pleasure he must have gotten from the deception. And from going after Petra. How successfully he'd ostracized her.

Careful or you'll be painted with her colours, he'd said to me.

The past was spinning like a merry-go-round. Everyone needed to talk, to try to process the shock of the news. What had he done to us? What would we—our party—have looked like without him at the centre, the worm in the apple? There was outrage, questioning and tears. A journalist managed to contact Jürgen where he now lived in Switzerland, but he would speak only through his lawyer, though apparently he'd had the temerity to state that no damage had been done: after all, the two Germanys were now united. I could imagine the contemptuous shrug of his shoulders.

After a few days of reassembling my universe, I started to calm down.

Yes, Jürgen had been influential, but would we have behaved so very differently without him? He hadn't made the Greens tear Petra limb from limb. That impulse had already existed, in the air, in the hatred for her personal power, her strange, fragile strength. He'd simply directed the hatred and then presided over the carnage. I remembered how he would drop chance remarks, creating waves of male laughter. It seemed, looking back, that he had succeeded far too easily, working the back scenes like Iago. His duplicity went into the core and twisted there, and it made me consider who else had played a double game.

And, of course, I thought of Emil Gerhardt.

Not long after this, Clara Pohl and the Green Party–Alliance 90 decided to organize a special conference on spies and informants. They put me in charge of paperwork for a group information request.

I must have known I was spreading a net for Emil, but I told myself it was political, not personal. Clara and the others from the East were eager for their personal files, and there was such furious debate in the party, and hysteria in the press, too, as other political parties were hit by their own revelations. Clara wisely suggested that, as a party that valued openness, we should lead the way and make a blanket request for the files of all Green parliamentarians, past and present.

It was quite natural that I took on the job of compiling our collective request. It was only in the most distant portion of my mind that I thought, *Now we will see.*

Sure enough, soon after, on an overcast and muggy day in late September, I picked up the telephone and heard Petra's voice, watery and strange, but definitely her.

"Manfred! I feel like we haven't spoken for a very, very long time."

"Petra."

"Yes, it's me."

She congratulated me on the birth of Hannelore, which meant we hadn't seen each other for two-and-a-half years. Could it really have been that long? She had a little present at home, she said, something she'd picked out ages ago when she'd first heard the news, but had neglected to bring by. But she would put it in the mail that very day. Her voice still managed to shoot an electric spark down my spine.

"How are you?" I asked.

She paused and then laughed. "You don't want to know," she said, which was at least partly true.

"And what do you think of this news of Jürgen?" It seemed inconceivable that she hadn't heard about him, but unlike the rest of us, she hadn't opened the conversation with her outrage.

"Yes," she mused. "We all trusted him." Then, more sharply, "I told you he was a little Stalin."

"No truer words were spoken," I said.

"It hurts to be betrayed," she said. "But it's good that this is all coming out."

Clues. There were clues there, and if I'd listened, I would have been able to hear them.

"Life is strange," she continued. "And Magnus, too. Just as you always said." Again that distance in her voice. Perhaps she realized I'd noticed, because she added, "The biggest change in my life is that I've been practising Tibetan meditation. It teaches one to have compassion, and to let go."

"Both at the same time?"

"Yes. It seems they are linked."

She then briskly outlined a few of her recent projects. She spoke of a women's conference in Madrid, then of the acclaimed Tibetan doctor, now living, like so many other exiles, in Dharamshala. His personal experiences were helping to build contacts with farmers and villagers in occupied Tibet.

She might have made more political small talk, but that was not her way. She had heard I was in charge of the party's official request for Stasi files. "Explain how it works. Have you put the requests in?"

I told her I was almost ready to, but that I needed signatures from every member of the old Green Party caucus. "I will courier the documents to your home early next week, so that you and Emil can sign and return."

"And without our signatures?" Something sharp in her voice made me pause. "I'm only curious," she added.

"Without a signature of authorization, each person's personal file remains sealed. But naturally everyone wants to sign. That is how it stands now. Why?"

"Oh, I just wanted to know how these things are done."

I couriered the lengthy forms to all of my former Green parliamentary colleagues for signatures of agreement, and within three weeks I had received back all but Emil's and Petra's. I faxed a message to their home. *This needs to go ahead now*, I wrote on the cover page, adding that their slowness was holding up the process. *Yes, we are reading the forms over*, came Petra's handwritten response, also by fax.

I could have left off. It would have been strange in the extreme not to include requests from Petra and Emil—our most famous Greens—along with the others, but we might have been able to weather it. But I had no stake in being helpful to them anymore, and when I sounded out Katrina on the subject one evening, she agreed. "There's far more at stake than their strange relationship," she said. "There's justice." A big word, coming from Katrina, who didn't favour abstractions. I wondered at that.

"Justice?"

She walked out of the room. I followed her into the kids' room and found her searching a drawer for children's pyjamas. Hannelore was lying on the bottom bunk, playing with her mini dollhouse, soft murmurs of agreement coming from her two plastic dolls, while Rufus was on the top bunk, forcing out burps.

"Don't do that," I said irritably.

Katrina swung around. "He has a right to burp."

I followed her back into the living room. "What's wrong?"

She let out a huge sigh of frustration.

"What?"

"What yourself. I'm sick to death of this. You say you're over Petra, but she hovers everywhere in our life."

She stood in front of me in a pair of torn jeans and a sweatshirt with the name of her women's shelter across the front. She had let her hair grow long, and it was feathered with grey, with bangs she had cut herself. She looked tired, as she often did, but then I did too. I usually attributed our tiredness to our work and the children, to eating too many meals of hastily prepared frozen sole (one of the white foods Hannelore liked), to the extra weight we had both put on, like desert animals packing it on for the long journey. But as she stared at me now, I thought, *I am what's making her tired.*

I felt very sorry, and I said so. And if I could have let go at that instant, I believe I would have. That was what she was asking me to do, and she was the mother of my children and she had that right: to ask for my faithful thoughts as well as my faithful body.

Katrina left the room to check on Hannelore's bedtime progress. I went to our own bedroom and switched on the fax machine, which was set up in the closet. I removed one of Katrina's sweatshirts from on top and stared down at the machine. I took a piece of fax paper and wrote on it with haste and anger: *Dear Petra and Emil. This waiting for your signatures has gone on for too long. I plan to send the requests to the authority on Monday morning, even if yours are not included.* I placed it in the paper tray and pressed the Send button.

The machine made its customary two-note sound, high and then low, and then began chuffing, copying the scrawled message, scrolling quickly when it hit white space.

At three in the morning, the fax machine sprang to life in response. I heard its long note, then the series of grunting shuffles. I got up and crossed the rag rug. Trees cast shadows of bare branches onto the floor. A baby bottle of curdled milk sat on the windowsill above the radiator. I closed the closet door, so as not to disturb Katrina, and pulled the light switch, then read the faxed response. Petra and Emil were attending a two-day conference in Berlin on global victims of radiation, but Petra would meet me on Sunday, the morning after their return, in the market square. Eleven a.m. She would bring her signed papers.

4

After the Global Victims
of Radiation Conference

Freya Fertig attended the Global Victims of Radiation Conference too, and she told me later that she'd been surprised by how few of the old Greens showed up. They'd moved on from the core issues, following the trends. "From radiation to retrofitting," she said. "We'll kill ourselves with these small steps." Looking around at the plenary session, she'd spotted Emil and Petra at the very back of the conference room. She'd squeezed in next to Petra, and when Emil got up to fetch something, Freya tried to find out how Petra was doing. Petra pressed her hand, but then Emil was back. He sat on the other side of Freya, so that she was sandwiched between them.

"He made me nervous," she said to me later. But this was after their deaths, as we talked in the thick of our mutual grief. It's possible that Freya's discomfort had grown larger in her mind because of what had happened.

I asked if they had mentioned the Stasi files. Were they feeling pressured? But Freya said she hadn't picked up on that. They'd nodded in agreement with the various speakers. The only sign of stress was a new tic of Emil's: tapping his foot, a quiver of motion that shook them all in their seats. He told Freya he was suffering from sciatica, which made it hard to sit still for long periods of time; the concrete floor was making it much worse.

Driving home from Berlin, Petra and Emil took the A2, not bothering to find a scenic route. They passed fields of winter barley, which moved and darkened with the wind as though pressed by a giant's hand. They talked about the victims of radiation, the speakers from Micronesia, Chernobyl—so much suffering—and then Petra mentioned her upcoming trip to Dharamshala. The conference she was co-organizing with her Tibetan doctor friend.

"And these papers," she added calmly. "The documents."

Emil noticed that she kept her voice calm. But why bring it up at all? Must she speak of every distasteful thing at once?

"Yes. What of them?"

"I'm meeting Manfred tomorrow morning."

"Good." Emil said it grimly, attempting to cut off conversation, but she continued with the same dispassion, as though it were all a thing of air. He could sign too, and give his papers to her to take, she said. She looked at him with her large, almost black eyes, calm on the surface but haunted and fierce below— and with not a scratch of love for him in them. He had the feeling of being dropped through space.

How he missed Helena. How he longed for her. She'd turned her face away from him at the flower shop after he had begged her to come for a simple lunch. Just lunch. Because he knew that if he got her out, he could wheedle and convince, order a bottle of something lovely. *Come with me.* She kept fiddling with the twisted branches as though they were the most important thing in the room. He felt an urge to throw the vase to the floor, send it crashing. *I have no rights*, he had faltered. He meant no rights as a husband, that he'd given them away, yet even as he spoke, he felt something else in her stance, the way she kept the counter between them. He knew her so well. She could feel that he wanted to sweep the vase to the floor—it was in the air between them—and she stayed behind the counter because she was afraid. She who had known violence, had felt it crush her. He might have pleaded, *I would never hurt you*, but that was so palpably untrue that he couldn't speak the words.

After awhile Petra took out her briefcase and began to review some papers. Did she know what was roaring in his mind, these memories of his destroyed marriage? Of course not. She was oblivious, in her nest of fucking compassionate, mindful Tibetan self-love. Emil checked the fuel gauge and pulled over at the next rest stop for gas, a typical well-maintained autobahn Rasthof with a bay of fuel pumps and a convenience store. Petra, of course, didn't volunteer to pump gas or wipe the windshield.

As the wind gusted across the field, Emil felt the burn of sciatica shoot down his right leg. He shook the leg, crouched and stretched, but the pain made him think of the papers to sign. They were on the landing table, beside the fax machine. He had put them out of his mind, but now, thanks to Petra, they loomed like an onset of flu, a wave of nausea in undefined parts of his body where nausea shouldn't rest. The backs of his knees. His hair.

Yet why feel so cornered? It was true that he had, at times, loosened by the luxuries of the conferences in Vienna or Helsinki or New York, so pleased and relieved to be again with his peers, recounted some of the Greens' more egregious errors and fights. Was that a sin? If so, he had committed it. String him up. Make him dance. Like the bodies of the partisans, dangling like terrible Christmas decorations, always in the back of his mind's eye, with toes pointed inwards, as though death insisted that the dead, reduced to nothing, must also be pigeon-toed. Was what he'd done a sin? He couldn't say now. He had no inner compass, did he? (Just one of Petra's many insults, before she gained Buddhist enlightenment.) Magnus Isaacson (a spy, just as Manfred had warned) had encouraged Emil, and, yes, sometimes Magnus took him for drinks in this or that posh lounge, to pry and poke. Info gathering. Emil had known it, but so what? Had it mattered so very much? The cognac was good, and the news, if he carried any, was already common knowledge in Bonn. So what? So what?

I was interested in what you said, Herr Gerhardt. Is that what Petra thinks of the Red-Greens? And tell me, who supports Jürgen in his new positions in favour of nuclear power? He remembered that Magnus wrote these answers down, but again, so what?

He saw the bar, warmed by a fire in the grate, the green walls the colour of the lining of a velvet box. He saw Magnus taking out a notebook, jotting down a few lines. Pausing and smiling ruefully.

"Why are you writing?"

And Magnus slipped the notepad back into his inside pocket. "Because your opinions matter. But I won't, if you'd rather I didn't."

"I do rather. I would rather."

"Really, it's just because your views matter to me. All of you." He meant the generals.

And this had mollified Emil. In the end, was that what it came down to? Emil threw his goods on the table because the man said he was important? Well, that and the money, enough (barely) to keep Helena and Petra going for awhile, each with her quiet taste for luxury.

Magnus had led Emil in other directions too, which, in the queer, still light of the rest stop, he saw now. Saw. "Don't fool yourself," he said, as the gas pump clicked off. He placed the nozzle back in the stand, sciatica burning through him like a message from the earth. *Don't fool yourself*—as though that wasn't his prize ability, his forte, his language. He saw himself after how many cognacs—five? six?—sketching out the CENTAG tank force deployment, defence scenarios, for the interested, the calculating, the unctuous Magnus, who had, as though in celebration, produced a couple of cigars.

Not the gravest military secrets. But information that, while somewhat out of date, could still be used. This evidence would be in his file, along with some unflattering name. He imagined it there—his code name, given to him by some functionaries having a good time. Emil would have been "The Pawn."

Wind flapped his trouser legs. He went in to pay, staring with dull eyes at the maps for sale in the turning stand and then at the turbaned cashier. He handed over his money and went outside again, but he didn't want to get back in the car. He was split in two, and a bird was eating his insides. And this bird was Petra, who had not let him alone from the day they had met, but had gone after him, relentlessly drawing his hidden life into the sunlight. Dear god. She had made him feel, night and day, like a stunted man, a terrible human being. Not on the surface, but underneath. As though his very heart were riddled with worms.

And now what? What had she said in the hotel as they were packing to leave the conference? *The words—say the words out loud.*

"We will always be close friends, my dear. We will always love each other. But love has to evolve."

Love kills, is what he had wanted to say. *Your love ripped me into pieces and fed my heart to the birds, only the bird was you, hungry for my flesh. And when you ate it, you got strong, while I became nothing. How's that for evolution?*

And then there was the loss of that sweet thing that had briefly held him in place. It was hard to look at that one. *Innere*

Führung. Oh, don't get me started. He almost laughed, it was so awful, so ugly. The meadow. The memory of running, sweat drying on his sticky arms, sunlight smacking the hides of three dappled cows. He had located the memory at last. Wouldn't she love to know it? He was ten, coming from picking hops with the other boys, running towards a traditional farm parade. He could hear music echoing, smell hay and warm earth, spring becoming summer. To be so excited, so young and alive! Farm men and women in Bavarian dress wound up the hillside road, leading their cows, each one decked with a floral wreath on its bony head. The smell of milk and manure, the women with scarves wrapped at their waists, and many in dirndls—they were celebrating their homegrown culture, the glory of the land. He'd been running towards a Blood and Soil parade! Cows and horses draped in swastikas. Oh, yes. All his life he'd carried the feeling of the sun shining down—and now? He felt tricked by his deepest self. It filled him with disgust, all the joy sucked out, deflated like the sickly grey skin of a balloon.

He crossed at last to the car, stealing a glance at Petra through the passenger window. Her head rested on the glass. With her eyes closed, her thin face with its vast eye sockets looked just like a bug's. Yes, she had a bug face. She looked exactly like a cartoon ant.

The next night, at four in the morning, I sent Emil a final fax. I don't know why I did it so late, but I was up, and in the paper went. To this day, I do not know if it was the hum and beeping of that message that made him decide, as he sat at his desk on the landing, that he had had enough.

———

What surprised Emil was the blood rush he got from pushing back his chair. (It tumbled to the floor, where it would be found, days later, by the neighbour, Irma Schwab, and then by the police.) Back went the chair, and what surprised Emil was the cold, intense pleasure flooding his body, knowing that he would take Petra with him.

In all her laying claim to his soul, day and night, this was the thing she had never seen. She had never seen that, with a gun in the hand, there was pleasure. Pleasure in controlling a person at your mercy. The rabbi with his hideous wart, pleading for his life! Pleasure in knocking the life right out of him. Emil really ought to wake Petra and tell her.

Emil opened the cupboard, pulled the walnut box from between his sweaters and placed it on his desk, remembering the old rabbi undressing at gunpoint. All those people, cowed by the orders, doing what they were told. Then the adrenalin shock, noticing a bulge in the man's jacket pocket. Was it a grenade? The moment of fear, of terror. *Halt! Halt! Hands up!* Then reaching forward, tentatively, to put his hand into the man's pocket, feeling the thing inside, bringing out the wrinkled red apple. Blushing because he was so close to looking ridiculous. The soldiers had all stopped to watch this piece of theatre. Everyone curious, even the old man, who was looking up at him as if to say, *Yes, it's true: I too eat apples.* And Emil, with anger, had handed the apple back. "Put it in your mouth. Yes, yes, quite right, like that." Bending to fix the apple between the man's stretched lips, as though doing him a service; putting the gun's muzzle to the apple, then turning to the others. "A William Tell moment." But they didn't understand. Only the rabbi did. When Emil turned, the man was pleading for his life, with no words, of course, but human being to human being. And Emil remembered his outrage. Yes, outrage that he should be made a fool of and then reached for, tampered with, by such searching humanity, as though, if the apple were not in the rabbi's mouth, the man would say, like the kindest of fathers, *My boy, my boy, you are making a terrible mistake.*

She's right.

How can he live with himself? He can't.

Go. Go now, he tells himself.

He unfastens the box's catch and takes out the derringer, loads it quickly and then climbs the stairs to the bedroom. Petra sleeps in track pants and T-shirt on top of the seahorse-covered duvet. He places the gun to her temple.

I have often imagined that Petra woke.

I want her to rise and float above him like a Valkyrie. I want the woman who always had words to have a chance to speak them now. But the blood spatter showed that she was sleeping as he pulled the trigger, her face towards the wall.

Quickly now, Emil tells himself, before pity or right thinking or compassion, or any one of those emotions that she has told him he is "missing," can cool the clarity of this decision.

Go.

5

The Web of Life

Years have passed.

The earth—that blue-green ball of confusion and glory—has now gone twenty-five times around the sun without Petra on it.

The children have grown up. Rufus has become a civil engineer. Much of his firm's work has been developing buildings in the death strip of the former wall, some of the priciest real estate in Berlin. He inherited his maternal grandfather's male pattern baldness and almost always chooses to wear a cap. He's still not married, but (in answer to Katrina's gentle probing) he's not gay either. When he bikes to our place in Charlottenburg, where Katrina and I now live, he seems happy enough to visit us at first, but at a certain point he finds our politics tiring and begins to answer our questions with a clipped reserve neither of us can penetrate. Often he leaves early. Katrina tells me I should be pleased that he visits us at all.

"Lots of grown children don't."

"Did we stunt him?"

"Look." Sharply now. *"Be grateful."*

Her gratefulness has an edge to it, but she would hardly be Katrina without that customary bite.

———

Hannelore's issues are different. She is the director of an international environmental group, and her biggest fight at present is to stop rampant oil and gas extraction. She has huge hair, stands six feet tall in her stocking feet and inherited Katrina's startling cheekbones and hooded eyes. Hannelore was once stopped by a modelling agent, who gave her his card, which disgusted her. She'd rather spend her time linking arms, as she did recently, creating a human chain to protest Germany's slowness to respond to the climate crisis. She is so angry. Even I don't remember being so angry. But there is more for her generation to be angry about, not less. Despite our efforts, we have delivered them a world vastly more frightening than the one we inherited, a Europe once again in flames and a global crisis painful to face. I wake in the morning and think, first off, *Something is wrong, something is bad*, and then I remember: we are experiencing the death of species, a malaise that is altering the planet itself, a human-made sickness that is turning rainforests to deserts, causing birds to stop singing in the branches, frogs to wither, snakes to stand up and beg for water. I am appalled daily. It hurts to think about it. Despite all we did and tried to do as Greens, this is our generation's lasting legacy.

It grieves me to think of my daughter taking the pain of the world onto her back. Sometimes, when the climate change work becomes too much (the penguins, the walruses, the polar bears—all the animals dying in their polar melt), Hannelore breaks out in hives. She calls us at midnight from a bathtub full of calamine lotion, weeping into her iPhone. Even Ernst, our husky dog, gets worried, nudging us at the sound of her voice.

Then, last February, she couldn't go on. She took a leave of absence and moved back home, spending most of her time in her old bedroom, the desk and bed table strewn with half-eaten bowls of curry softened with scums of mould. Katrina and I were at our wit's end, talking *sotto voce* in the living room, as though in a house of mourning. But eventually, one Saturday in early March, Hannelore emerged from her stinking cocoon, her hair tied back with a triangle of multicoloured cotton. She gave us kisses and headed off to the demonstration I have mentioned in support of Syrian refugees. She strode out the door with the resilience of the young.

"I'll meet you down there," she called out to me as she ran down the stairs. "Text me."

After she left, I sat at my desk. I was, at this point, working on my Ph.D. thesis. Yes, I'd returned to it at long last, as a sort of retirement gift to myself. I was a very mature student indeed, but I wouldn't be the first sixty-eighter to return to the "long march through the institutions." I'd arranged with my advisor to pick up where I'd left off, writing a thesis about war guilt, but combining it now with insights into the political party I had helped to found. Yet every time I sat down, I found it hard to write even a single page.

On this particular Saturday, just the sight of my file cards covered in minute notes made me blanch. The truth was, I had nothing new to contribute, even though I had the information, the access, the knowledge, the past. I was at sea.

I was balling up paper and throwing it at the trash can, the parody of a frustrated writer, when Katrina came in carrying some laundry. She saw me in my mood and sat her stocky body down on the bed. Her short hair is permanently silver now, surrounding her face like a stark little helmet.

"Manfred," she said. "Nobody is making you write this thesis."

"I know it's not compulsory."

"Maybe you simply can't make sense of it all. Have you thought of that?"

"Useful. Thanks."

She was silent, then tried again: "I mean, maybe it—the past—doesn't take the form of a thesis." She straightened her back. I felt one of her "gratitudes" coming on and prepared myself. Instead, she said, "Can you look at me, please?"

I pushed back my chair to face her.

"What do you need to say that hasn't already been said?" This was what she asked. She reached for my hand, and with the touch of her fingers, my face grew hot.

"It's still Petra, isn't it?" She frowned. I thought she might get up and walk away, exhausted by these iterations, again and again, of guilt, love, silence, but instead she knelt by my chair and put her arms around me. "Tell me." She leaned back to look into my eyes. "Say it out loud."

I couldn't. But I felt the knot in my throat. It blocked my words and my breath. I thought of what I'd done, all the provocation, the faxes. How was I so different from the people who'd sent the anonymous letters, those stinking packages of hatred? I too had picked up the pheromone of hatred and let it carry me.

And what happened next?

Slowly, as Katrina held me and rocked me, in the thickness of my tears, I felt pity rise, first for myself, then for all of us. The pain in my throat was for Petra, and for myself, and for our youth and our mistakes, but it was also, unmistakably, for Emil, that lost man. With the weight of my own years, a scrim of incomprehension had fallen away. I saw him across time, and I pitied him, and I knew that this is what Petra would have wished for me—the Petra she became, the Petra I saw that final day in the market square—and that made me sob all the harder, while Katrina said, "It's all right, it's all right." But it wasn't. Of course it wasn't. How could it be?

———

Then I was out into the Saturday morning, that day in March that couldn't make up its mind. Tight fists of leaf buds in the trees. A cool breeze touching my cheeks as I walked from the U-Bahn towards Normannenstrasse, that building where I once spent hours of terror. The bout of crying had given me an unexpected lightness. I texted Hannelore, found her near the front of the protest, and to my delight her face lit up when she saw me. The right-wing contingent had been outnumbered by crowds of supporters for the refugees, she explained. It was a victory. Then she introduced me to her friends, Fouda and Josef, who lived in the temporary apartments for refugees in what had been the Stasi headquarters. Fouda pointed out the multicoloured streamers hanging from their window, which Hannelore had helped rig up.

At some point, still feeling the lightness in me, I made that comment about Petra. I think I said if she were alive she would have been fighting for refugee rights with all her energy. That was when that bearded boy, clearly besotted with my daughter, turned to me with his slice of inanity: "I know who Petra Kelly was—she was a figure skater!"

On the journey home by S-Bahn, my daughter beside me, I couldn't let it go. Maybe I wanted to keep Petra's name alive, now that I'd felt her so close. "I can't believe he said that," I said again.

Hannelore met my gaze. "Why not? It's not as though you or the Greens have honoured her, particularly. It's like this really fantastic person just vanished down a hole."

I was silent awhile as we bounced and swayed in our seats. Then I ventured, "All right, if I never talk about her, how do you know she was so fantastic?"

"Mother talks about her."

"What does she say?"

"She says that Petra was the best of all of you."

"Your mother says that?" A bolt of shock went through me, but Hannelore only shrugged. "I know she was your lover, Papa." She poked me with her elbow and then turned back to the window.

A flash of graffiti as we rattled over a bridge: a penis in red, pissing swastikas.

This was when I felt the bubble—something glowing, almost bright—a bubble of air tucked beneath my ribs.

It connected to Petra, and to Hannelore beside me on our narrow seat, the deep familiarity of her body, and to Katrina at home, returned from walking our dog. I felt Petra not in pain, not in guilt and silence, but as a kind of lightness, an inner possibility. She was urging me on, saying *Yes, yes, yes,* with the flash of the metal trusses, dark, light, dark, light, the rattle of the car on the tracks.

That night when I went to bed, I felt more excited than I had for weeks. Maybe for years. We turned out the bedside lights, and I pressed myself, for the ten thousandth time, up against Katrina's warmth.

I was thinking about where I might start, and about how any place could serve as an entry, because, after all these years, Petra in death seemed to exist in a different sort of time frame, where memories were connected not by chronology but by intensity, just as Freya had said to me. Petra's walk through the field with her father, him warning her of snakes, rested beside her scribbling that postcard to Emil Gerhardt. Her childhood self charging towards the sun existed beside her coming towards me that final time across the market square. It was all there, a web that seemed to connect all these strands together, and that reached beyond them into the green wonder of life itself, and into the darkness, too, into the invisible net of roots we cannot see.

I let my mind turn towards the pain I avoid, the source of my beloved daughter's hives. I stared at what I cannot bear to think of—the suffering earth. We were handed a garden and we couldn't tend it. We have set off a chain reaction of increasing temperature, and the beautiful things of the earth are dying.

It is anguish to stare this in the eye. Yet as I do so, another thought wells up in me. And I know this will sound crazy, but I feel Petra there beside me, telling me to *look*. Today my daughter got her strength back. Today she went to the demonstration, blowing us a kiss in the doorway. And later she sat on the train, challenging me to turn and face the past, to honour the memory of you, the woman I will always ache for, *because Katrina speaks about you all the time.* Yes, my wife holds your memory close, has tended to it for years. Love works like this.

I feel a shimmering on my skin as I catch a glimpse of its twists. I spring out of bed and find a pen—and this is what I write, the first of my notes, on the back of an envelope:

The missiles were dismantled.

Then: *The wall fell.*

Because this too must be part of your story.

And the Iron Curtain? Oh, wouldn't you laugh. Wouldn't you say, *Just look at that, Manfred. Didn't I say it could happen?*

Just this morning I read the latest article about what has been happening to the physical territory of the East–West border, the Iron Curtain: the symbol of oppression, barbed wire, hatred. Left alone for so long, nature has reclaimed it as a conduit for wildness, a slender slice of green that blooms with growth along the entire length of Europe, a home to butterflies, insects, ancient grasses— but also wolves. For the first time in two centuries, wolves have returned to Germany along the unused corridor of the Iron Curtain.

This, too, must be part of the pattern.

The darkness is there too—of course it is—but so is this other thing. It always was; it always will be.

It never stops.

6.

The Mountains of Tibet

She came towards me across the cobbles of the market square, pigeons scattering left and right. The clock in the city hall was chiming eleven, the time we had arranged to meet. Right away I could see that something was different about her, though it was hard to discern exactly what. I had expected her to be wearing her overwhelming puffy coat, but she had shed it in favour of a suede jacket with a knitted collar. She was thinner than ever, and as she got closer, I saw she had applied makeup to the discolouration beneath her eyes, managing to blend it to cover the circles. She wore red gloves and a matching wool scarf.

I am describing these details as though I had been able to focus on each one. In fact, they were the matter of a blurred moment. In a few steps she reached me. I stood, and we embraced. Her body beneath the coat vibrated with heat and energy, and I thought, *What has happened? She is back.*

We sat down together in the Stern Hotel's wicker-backed chairs, and she launched into conversation. Why had it been so long? And then: "Look at you! Fatherhood suits you to a T! How well you look—plump and prosperous. And Katrina? And do you have photographs? I want to see the baby, though she's much more than a baby now, isn't she?"

We were carried by her volleys of enthusiasm, her exclamations over the photographs of the children. When I returned them to my wallet, she was still beaming. The red in her scarf was contributing to the glow in her face.

"And the general?" I asked. "How is he?"

She frowned. "Ah—before I forget." She took off her gloves and brought a manila envelope from her purse and placed it on the table. "There are my papers for the Gauck Authority. Signed." Then, perhaps to cover her embarrassment for the absence of Emil's, she began a speech about how pleased she was that I was doing this, not just for us, but for history. It was important to know the truth, especially after the situation with Jürgen: it was time to shed light in the shadows. I really wondered how she could say this—that it might cause some break in her voice—but she was staring ahead with gravity, as though measuring something in the distance I could not see. Then she turned abruptly and gave me another huge smile.

"Even the air smells of fall! Can't you smell it?"

The sun was hitting a planter behind our bench, and yes, I could smell the scent of chrysanthemums in the warming earth. I could hear a man dragging a suitcase across the cobbles, and the babble of voices from the market. Yes, it felt like fall—crisp and blue-skied—the thirsty days of August set aside.

"And Emil? Where are his papers?"

She met my eyes gravely, shaking her head. "He says he needs a final night to look them over—which I understand, Manfred, and you must too. He has promised to courier them to you first thing tomorrow morning."

"I've waited a month, Petra."

"Then wait a day longer."

"The others are all waiting."

"Only until tomorrow."

"I won't wait a second past. Please tell him that."

"Yes." She tightened her lips almost primly. "I'll make sure to do that."

We were silent for a moment. I didn't know what to expect next. Twenty minutes before, I had been waiting for Petra with such trepidation. I had pictured her hobbling into view, a broken-winged bird, but she was altogether different. She was playful again. Not joyous, exactly, but a sort of mirth seemed to be flowing beneath the surface of her skin.

"Can we walk?" she asked suddenly.

"Don't you want coffee?"

"No, I've given it up; it's not good for my kidneys. You look surprised. Yes, I am taking care of myself now."

We started across the square. Petra had never liked to walk, but she clipped along, swinging her arms, getting air into her lungs, in much the way a child will parody an adult taking strides. *This is exercise,* she seemed to be saying. *This is how it's done.* We cut across the Hofgarten lawn, the smell of leaves, two dogs playing, one with a wrinkled black face, then descended to the pathway along the Rhine. I could hear the thud of a tour boat at the dock, diesel filling the air from its exhaust. Across the water was a steeple. It made me think of the postcard she'd sent to Emil, so long ago. The sparkling river view.

Petra was speaking about Tibet now, about the refugee Buddhist doctor who had assisted her by mail and telephone with her work. In the winter he had attended a conference in Frankfurt, and the two of them had spoken on a panel together, at last meeting face to face. I prepared to let my mind drift, as I usually did when she got into details of the Tibet issue, but all at once she stopped walking and began digging in her purse, producing a slender book with a blue cover. She handed it to me. *The Agony of Tibet,* by Jampa Pakshi. On the back was a smiling, handsome

Tibetan man, younger than either of us by a good ten years. I felt a sudden pressure in my heart.

"So this is your Buddhist doctor. I had pictured an old man."

"I'm going to Dharamshala. He has invited me to a retreat."

She couldn't contain herself any longer: "I'm in love, Manfred!" She fairly sang it out, to the wharf and the barge passing us, loaded with steel beams, and the pigeons taking crumbs from a nearby child and mother.

"And he?"

"Well, one can never say." Her face darkened, then brightened again, as though a cloud had passed over it. "But yes—I think it's mutual."

Then she told me about the work that had to be done immediately. A conference involving Tibetans still living in Tibet, as well as exiles living abroad. Farmers. Teachers. Students who had risked their lives printing and handing out illegal pamphlets. She and Jampa Pakshi were going to facilitate the conference together next month. This answered my question about the seriousness of the relationship: when Petra fell in love, it was always with a path full of shared work.

Others were promenading in the autumn sunshine too: suited men, and couples, and mothers with children in prams. We stopped at the old sundial, which we used to reach from the opposite direction, coming from Tulpenfeld. Like the World Clock at Alexanderplatz, it had major cities on every side. Copenhagen, Rome, Dublin. We touched the numbers at the top, her fingers finding the grooves, and she smiled at me.

"Emil must be suffering," I said, "if he knows about your new lover. Does he know?"

"Of course." She seemed astonished by the question. "You know I always tell the truth."

"He knows you're leaving him."

"For a conference. And yes, he knows I love Jampa. I have never hidden lovers from other lovers. You know that, Manfred."

"Indeed I do."

"Besides," she said with grim seriousness. "It was always his intention to return to Helena."

"But now she won't have him!"

"Ah—so you've heard. Nevertheless, that was his intention. And I lived with that for years."

He was under pressure, she said, and she felt genuinely concerned as a sister (those were her words) for the box he was now in. Yet even these words made it clear that it was *his* box. We walked on. The river was covered with scales of light. A rower passed along the surface, breaking a momentary path in the sparkles.

"A long time ago," I said, "a very long time ago—do you remember?—we talked about wanting to 'gentle the general.'"

"That was a terrible idea."

"You were going to fix the world one NATO general at a time."

"That was arrogant—and look at us: it certainly hasn't worked."

She was here again, as though she had passed through a fever that had burnt away everything insubstantial. And what of him? I pictured him sitting at home in the kitchen, the papers for his Stasi request spread out in front of him. And now Petra was dancing away from him, humming under her breath, or on the phone, day and night, long distance to Dharamshala. *Dear god, he must be frantic*, I thought. *Despondent, cornered, desperate.* I wondered all over again that Petra could be so calm. But she was on a journey towards the high and snowy mountains of Tibet, towards love— this younger man, with his dark skin and warm eyes.

I didn't think it would last long, and I suddenly felt a need to tell her that she should protect her heart. But she had never entered a love affair with caution; the thought of playing it safe was beneath her. In the heat of love, it must seem completely impossible that her younger lover might, in the near future, tire of her; that soon enough she would have only Emil to return to; that she, too, was in a box and that the sides were tightening. She stood before me, pleased with life, and she even laid a hand on my arm.

"Don't look so afraid, Manfred. It will all be all right. You and Katrina can come visit me, if I stay on in Dharamshala. And your children too. And Emil, if he decides that's what he wants to do. You see—" She took hold of the fabric of my coat with her red knitted glove and gave it a squeeze. "You must have some trust in life. Haven't I told you that?"

This is how I choose to see her, these many years later. The red-gloved fingers. The smile as she brushed a piece of hair from her face. How delighted she was to lecture me one last time. And the pleasure, too, at the work she faced. I haven't emphasized that enough. Woven into her conversation as we walked were images of the monastery itself, which needed repairing, and a hospital for refugee children nearby; a possible school. All of this growing out of the crooks of the mountains, in mysterious towers, her vision for a better world transplanted from Germany to the Himalayas—great kingdoms of clay and ideas rising up from the rocky soil, shining fiercely.

We walked as far as Tempelstrasse, then up the stairs and back through the city to the market. She gave me a parting hug, then she went quickly across the cobbles, almost running, the pigeons scattering up in arcs, fluttering and then landing again. Just as she reached the street, she turned and called to me, but I couldn't hear what she said. She was gesturing to the pigeons. I think she said, "Next time we must bring seeds to feed them." Then she was gone, around the corner.

—

Acknowledgments

This is a work of fiction inspired by real events. I have kept Petra Kelly's actual name, as I want to honour her memory (like many powerful women, she has been far too easily erased from history), but I have changed the names of those close to her to emphasize the fictional nature of my story, and because many of these characters are wholly invented or created from seeds scattered by the historical players. At times my story runs close to the historical record and at times is quite divergent. All leaps are my own.

My heartfelt thanks to the late Roland Vogt, and to Lukas Beckmann and Eva Quistorp—co-founders of the German Green Party—for deep assistance, meetings and sharing of precious memories and complicated truths about the woman who touched their lives.

My thanks to Klaus Trappmann—for opening his heart and his Berlin garden to me, and over a bottle of wine telling me his history in the sixty-eighter movement. Thanks to Robert Camp for assistance navigating the Petra Kelly archives. And to my Berlin family (now in South Korea), the Lambert-Teillets, whose life in that city first set me on this course.

I am extremely grateful to my first readers, who gave me crucial responses and advice: Barbara Lambert, Caroline Adderson, Eva Stachniak, Carrie Saxifrage and Claudia Casper. Also deep thanks to Wendy Wright, Madeline Hope and David Smith, for lasting friendship and creative insights that always seem to hit the mark. My agent, Martha Webb, of CookeMcDermid encouraged me through every phase of this book—I am so grateful for her support and involvement and for the timely and useful feedback of Anne McDermid.

Thanks to the entire team at Random House Canada. I'm particularly indebted to my editor, Anne Collins, for her lightning bursts of creative insight, for providing an acutely observant editorial eye, and for loving the complicated Petra as I do.

Thank you to the next generation, shining so brilliantly in the world and in my life—with special thanks to Lucy, Peter, Colette and Calla. A huge thank you to my brilliant parents, my brothers James and John, my aunt Lorna and my entire extended family for their love and support. I'd also like to thank my personal eco-warrior, Karen Mahon Carrington, whose passionate fight for the planet is endlessly creative—a bit like Petra herself.

Many books assisted me, but several got under my skin with their absorbing writing and compelling record of events, particularly Sara Parkin's *The Life and Death of Petra Kelly*, *Green Politics* by Fritjof Capra and Charlene Spretnak, and *What We Knew: Terror, Mass Murder and Everyday Life in Nazi Germany* by Eric A. Johnson and Karl-Heinz Reuband.

Most of all, thank you to Bob Penner—my fellow traveller in life and activism—whose deep knowledge of movement politics grounded me as I wrote this book. Thank you for keeping the adventure of politics in our life, through celebration and/or defeat. And for never giving up.

—

SHAENA LAMBERT is the author of the novel, *Radiance*, and two books of stories, *Oh, My Darling* and *The Falling Woman*—all of which were *Globe and Mail* top books of the year. Her fiction has been published to critical acclaim in Canada, the UK and Germany and been nominated for the Rogers Writers Trust Fiction Prize, the Ethel Wilson Fiction Prize, the Evergreen Award, the Danuta Gleed Award and the Frank O'Connor Award for the Short Story. Her stories have been chosen four times for *Best Canadian Stories*, and appeared in many publications, including *The Walrus, Zoetrope: All Story, Ploughshares* and *Toronto Life*. She lives in Vancouver.